THE NEXT BEST THING

His hand moved slowly upward again. This time he foiled her attempt to stop him and gently cupped his hand around her breast.

"Oh, my God . . ." April moaned.

"Don't think."

He was massaging the flesh, his thumb rolling back and forth over the nipple. There was an immediate response, surprising even April as sensation made it erect. She felt as if all the nerve endings in her body were going to explode.

The hard contact of his body only fueled the fire that burned beneath her skin. She heard her own voice, moaning in agitation, torment . . . longing. April's mind resisted, but her body responded of its own accord. She was grateful, and she was scared.

Fight Childhood Cancer.
Support St. Jude.

Dear Reader:

Several years ago I was introduced to the life-saving work of St. Jude Children's Research Hospital as a member of the National Ethnic Advisory Committee. Located in Memphis, Tenn., St. Jude is the world's leading pediatric cancer research center in the world. The doctors and researchers not only treat many forms of childhood cancer, they are finding new ways to treat sickle cell disease and pediatric AIDS, diseases dear to my heart.

St. Jude has treated children from all 50 states and more than 80 countries. St. Jude families never pay for treatments that are not covered by insurance, and families without insurance are never asked to pay.

Join me in supporting this great institution that has a rich tradition in finding cures and saving children. Log on to *www.stjude.org* to learn how you can donate to St. Jude and save a child's life.

Good health to you and yours.

Sandra Kitt
www.sandrakitt.com

St. Jude Children's Research Hospital
ALSAC · Danny Thomas, Founder
Finding cures. Saving children.

Sandra Kitt

THE NEXT BEST THING

ARABESQUE

BET BOOKS

BET Publications, LLC
http://www.bet.com
http://www.arabesquebooks.com

First Printing: June 2005
10 9 8 7 6 5 4 3 2 1

Printed in the United States of America

ACKNOWLEDGMENTS

I want to acknowledge the tremendous support and guidance provided by my agent, Lisa Erbach Vance of the Aaron Priest Literary Agency in New York. She's *the next best thing* to a guardian angel.

A heartfelt thank you to Laurie Clark and Gail Starkey for *being there*.

To Linda Gill, Vice-President and Publisher of BET/Arabesque, for giving me an excuse to travel to Venice. It was great fun reliving my experience in that fabulous city while writing *The Next Best Thing*.

Chapter 1

April Stockwood began smiling the moment she got off the plane.

"I can't believe it. I'm actually in Venice," she said.

"You're not in Venice. You're at Marco Polo airport," her friend Stephanie grumbled, adjusting her heavy shoulder bag, a tote, and a jacket.

"Close enough," April said, as she and Stephanie joined the hordes of travelers headed for immigration and passport control; one line for "naturals," another for foreign visitors. Most of the passengers were looking a little worse for wear after the nearly eight-hour trip across the Atlantic in the middle of the night. But despite the fact that it was barely dawn, passengers were chattering in half a dozen languages.

"Signora?" April heard the impatient voice of the airport guard directing her to an available line. With her freshly minted passport in hand, she stepped forward.

"*Buon giorno*," she said carefully to the young, uniformed customs officer.

Rather than responding, he efficiently leafed through the document and stamped one of the many blank pages. He slid the passport back to April without once raising his gaze, and with a careless wave of his hand, dismissed her. April stepped aside to wait for Stephanie.

"He wasn't very friendly," April commented as they continued through the rest of the newly built terminal toward baggage claims.

"April, you're the only person in the universe I know who wakes up and hits the ground running. What is your problem? It's way too early in the morning to be cheerful."

"I've never been to Europe before. I'm excited."

"Yeah, I got that part," Stephanie mumbled, stifling a yawn. "You should be glad the agent didn't find a reason to ask a lot of questions."

"He didn't even look to see if I was the person in the photograph."

Stephanie shook her head patiently, rolling her eyes. "You hardly look like you've come to overthrow the government. These agents must be bored as hell. They're not interested in your life story, girl."

Just then they both heard Stephanie's name announced over a PA system.

"Did you hear that?" April asked. "We just stepped off the plane and already someone is looking for you."

"I can't imagine who," Stephanie said. Without breaking her stride, she headed towards the information counter. She identified herself and was handed a phone.

While she waited patiently, April chalked up Stephanie's lack of sympathy and enthusiasm to cranky cynicism. Stephanie had often told her that business travel was not a paid-for vacation. No matter. April was eternally grateful that she'd been asked to tag along to keep her friend company. She had no intention of confessing that just heading out to Philadelphia International Airport the night before had made her giddy with anticipation.

She didn't pay much attention to Stephanie's conversation,

only guessing the call was not from Stephanie's former boyfriend, Harrison.

"Can't it wait a few days?" April heard Stephanie ask with some annoyance, continuing her conversation despite the distraction of all the noise around them. "I've already cleared customs. I was hoping to get the first meeting over with this afternoon . . ."

April glanced around at the other travelers. She felt a vague disappointment that everyone looked pretty much the same. Except for the occasional colorful attire of an African, or of someone from the Middle East, there was little to distinguish one nationality from another. She glanced down at her black stretch pants, boxy blue sweater, and denim jacket. On her feet were sturdy half boots. She'd left her sneakers home because she'd read that European women didn't wear sneakers or jeans. But were her shoulder-length dreadlocks, tinted blond, a dead giveaway that she was American?

". . . You are *not* serious. Right this minute?"

April followed Stephanie's restless movements with concern as Stephanie finished the call.

"What's up?" April asked. "I wasn't trying to listen, but it sounded like . . ."

"I have to fly to Milan," Stephanie informed her after she handed the phone back to the agent and started towards the exit. Another officer asked to see their passports again before directing them through a door that led to baggage claims.

"I know. You already told me you're going at the end of the . . ."

"No. I have to leave right now."

The conveyor belt began to churn into motion, signaling the arrival of luggage. Stephanie turned to watch for the bags belonging to her and April. Spotting the two suitcases, she yanked them from the moving carousel.

April stared at her. "You mean . . . right *now*?"

Stephanie pulled up the handle on her suitcase and began to wheel it behind her. "Yeah. Ain't this a bitch? I have to go book a flight to Milan and get there as soon as I can."

April started after her, her own suitcase in tow. "Wait . . . does this mean I'm not going with you?"

Stephanie stopped, and turned to face April. "No, you're not. But don't worry. I'm only going to be away today, I think. I'll catch up with you at the hotel some time tomorrow."

A swirl of apprehension roiled through April's stomach. This unexpected change of plans meant that she would be alone for twenty-four hours in a strange city where she didn't speak the language.

"What happened?" April asked, tamping down her initial urge to beg to go along.

"There was some sort of mix-up between my company's Italian handbag designer and an order meant for the Furla boutique in Philly. I was going to Milan after our trip to meet with him anyway. It's just that it has to happen today." Stephanie gave April a determined glance. "This is an important account and I can't afford to lose it."

"Of course not," April agreed.

"I'm really sorry about this. After I book my flight, I'll explain how to get to our hotel. You go ahead and check in. I probably won't get back to Venice until sometime to-morrow, but you'll be okay until then, right?"

What were the options? Stephanie was in Italy on business. She, on the other hand, was along for the ride—to hang out, enjoy the sights, and have some great pasta. She had blithely followed Stephanie, thinking that all she had to do was show up and bring lots of money, not realizing until now that she had expected Stephanie, an experienced traveler, to make her trip easy and comfortable.

"No problem," April replied dutifully, determined that she could do this.

***

After leaving the arrivals wing of the terminal, they headed to departures. Elegant shops lined the causeway. April was staring at the beautiful, luxury goods when, without warning, a man collided into her. Her shoulder bag slipped down her arm and turned over, spilling wallet, passport, birth-control pills, lipstick, and mints. Apologizing, the man helped her retrieve her things before quickly hurrying on.

"I thought the Italians were supposed to be laid-back and calm?" April asked.

"He wasn't Italian," Stephanie informed her. "Probably East European, from the accent."

She began talking nonstop as she weaved her way through the crowd to get to the ticket counter, explaining that there were no cars or motorbikes or buses in Venice and how April was to get to the hotel. People either walked the maze of narrow, winding streets, or made use of a system of waterbuses called *vaporetti* that traveled up and down the Grand Canal. April's sense of humor quickly returned. Stephanie had just given her her first lesson in Italian.

At the Alitalia counter, April waited as Stephanie negotiated a seat on the very next flight leaving Venice for Milan. She was impressed by Stephanie's savvy and self-confidence. When they'd first met, almost seven years earlier, it had been during Stephanie's struggles to balance a growing career as a buyer with being a single mother to her then–twelve-year-old son, Chazz. Stephanie's concerns had eventually become hers when the need finally arrived to make major changes in her own life, April reflected. That included everything from a career move to divorce to managing custodial arrangements for her daughter, Anesa, with her ex-husband, Sinclair.

"How long before boarding?" Stephanie asked the agent.

April, listening to the answer, realized that she and

Stephanie had fifteen minutes together before Stephanie had to clear security and head for her departure gate.

"I don't know where I'll be staying in Milan," Stephanie said. "But I'll call and let you know later. Let me show you where to get the *Alilaguna motoscafi* to the hotel stop. It's a smaller boat than a *vaporetti* and it makes fewer stops. These boats are just like using the bus or subway back home. Just read the signs and watch for your stop."

Stephanie waited while April exchanged some American dollars for euros. At the tourist booth April purchased both a seven-day *vaporetti* pass and an *Alilaguna* ticket. The agent gave her a map of the system, pointing out her stop. He spoke in halting but understandable English.

"Very easy," he said. "You go to San Marco Zaccaria. Then you walk."

"*Grazie*," April said gratefully when he had marked her map and handed it back to her.

"*Prego*." The agent nodded with a smile.

Stephanie chuckled as they turned away. "I can see you're not going to have any trouble. Just keep smiling and use *prego* a lot. It means both 'thank you' and 'please.' "

"By the time you come back tomorrow I'll be fluent," April said dryly.

"By the time I get back you'll probably have two or three Italian men trailing after you. I've heard that they find African-American women very attractive."

"Really? I guess that's nice to know, Steph, but I'm not here to get picked up. You come to Italy all the time. I never heard you talk about any guy falling all over you."

"Doesn't mean it never happened," Stephanie responded coyly.

At home that would have been a lead-in April wouldn't have let go, but it was time for Stephanie to make her flight. As they stood just outside security, April smiled reassuringly.

"Don't worry about me if I'm not in when you call later. I've got a map, a dictionary, and I'm good to go. I hope everything's okay in Milan. Hurry back so we can start having fun."

"I will. Be careful, April. I'll see you tomorrow."

April watched Stephanie disappear, her confidence moments ago replaced by focus and purpose. She glanced around at the hundreds of travelers, many of them apparently traveling alone. There was no sign that any one of them was nervous about their ability to get from point A to point B, and she wasn't going to be either. So she was in a new place and didn't know her way around. She knew how to read, how to ask questions, and how to yell loud and clear for help if it came to that.

April also recognized that a part of her was actually excited by the unexpected turn of events. She'd faced other challenges before, some with far more serious implications. With renewed confidence, she headed out of the terminal.

There was a line for the *Alilaguna* at the quayside outside the terminal. In a moment of confusion, not knowing if the boat already boarding was the one she needed or not, April hesitated. The boat crew spoke only Italian. It didn't immediately occur to her to just give the name of her stop. There was a final rush as passengers with luggage aggressively shoved onto the last available space and the small craft slowly motored away. April stood, alone on the wharf, feeling foolish and adrift.

The quay filled again with new passengers and more luggage as a second craft arrived. Everyone surged forward ready to board. April, holding tightly to her suitcase, approached the young man tossing suitcases and bags to a fellow crewman on deck.

"Zaccaria?" she yelled.

"San Marco?" the worker shouted right back, not breaking stride in his loading of luggage.

April thought quickly and said "*Si.*"

The man nodded and motioned her aboard. The boat rocked and bumped against the wharf as April gingerly stepped onto the deck and found her balance. The small boat was crowded, and she couldn't avoid being jostled or finding herself squeezed against partitions, piled luggage, and other passengers. Hoping she didn't look like a rank amateur, April found a small corner to stand in, copying the behavior of those around her who managed to find something to hold onto or lean against. She was able to look out over the bow to the shore. A flimsy nylon rope tied across the ramp entrance to the boat was the only barrier from the possibility of accidentally falling into the water.

After a quick covert glance, April realized that there were old men and women, children and toddlers, and young parents—carrying sleeping infants and wheeling their strollers—for whom this was a perfectly normal way to get around.

The boat rumbled to life, and the small craft, packed with sixty or seventy passengers and half as many pieces of luggage, slowly pulled away from the wharf and began to motor down the waterway. She turned her attention to the shore, unable to keep from smiling at the incredible realization that she was actually in Venice and that she was, not so nonchalantly, boating up the Grand Canal. For her it was history come to life before her very eyes, and she was there! Along both shorelines were magnificent palazzos and villas that had once belonged to Italian princes. She was thrilled at the prospects of walking the ancient streets.

"First time in Venice?"

April turned to find that the deep British accent belonged to a pleasant-looking man in his 50's. Like the actor Alan Rickman from *Die Hard*; with glasses, but heavier, she thought.

"I was hoping it didn't show," April confessed good-naturedly.

"My wife, Lilly, and I make a game of it," he said, putting an arm around the shoulders of a woman to identify her. She had a small knapsack on her back and was holding a camera. "We enjoy watching the expression on the faces of newcomers as the boat travels up the canal. You looked positively . . . awed."

"I guess it's fair to assume you've been here before," April commented.

"Andrew and I come every year," his wife said. "We eat our way from one end of the city to the other. We tell the kids they can join us if they want. Of course, we hope that they don't. Where are you staying?"

"Hotel Botticelli."

"Good choice," the man approved. "We rent an apartment for three weeks every year that's pretty close to your hotel. My name is Andrew St. Clair, and this is my wife, Lilly."

"I'm April Stockwood."

He glanced around. "Are you alone?"

"I'll be meeting a friend," April said.

"Venice is a very romantic city," Lilly added.

April didn't bother to correct Lilly's assumption. It wasn't necessary to clarify that she was traveling with a girlfriend. For a fleeting moment, April wistfully remembered that she had always hoped that she and Sinclair, her ex-husband, would make the trip together.

Amid the friendly chatter of the British couple April began to get a feel for the size of Venice, and the way the Grand Canal snaked through the city. She caught glimpses of ancient palaces, churches, and museums. April could see that the newer passengers were locals getting on as the waterbus headed into the city: men and women on the way to work, others out to do marketing or keeping appointments. All around her she heard the babble of voices, mostly in the musical language that was Italian. And there she was, on a mild June morning with the sun trying to break through

overcast skies, a stranger in a strange land that already was
starting to feel vaguely familiar.

The boat made short regular stops at quays along the canal,
passengers pushing their way off or on. The ride gave April a
firsthand look at the efficiency of the waterbus system. Her
gaze was drawn again and again to the elaborate—but in many
cases, crumbling—palaces marked by centuries of standing
along the canal. There were other public-transportation boats:
vaporetti, small private motor crafts, water taxis, and even
yachts on the canal, blending the old world with the new.

April knew she would always remember the exact moment
when she realized that what she had only read about in her
guidebook was suddenly, and amazingly, the real deal. The
Alilaguna made a slow curving turn to the left past the Academia and the Peggy Guggenheim Museum. The waterway
opened up into the Grand Canal and the Campanile of San
Marco Square . . . the watchtower . . . came into view. April
wasn't sure of her reaction, but an older woman standing in
front of her turned to smile as if she understood perfectly. There
were hundreds of people along the waterfront of the famous
square, dozens of souvenir wagons and kiosks vying for space
and customers. It was colorful and crowded and lively.

Nearly all of the passengers with luggage got off at the San
Marco stop. Others got on and jammed into the aisle. April
was glad to see that her stop, just beyond, was an easy walk
back to San Marco Square. The boat pulled into the quay and
she struggled off with her suitcase. On the dock, she stood
trying to get oriented as she was jolted and pushed. The St.
Clairs followed.

"We'll point you in the direction of your hotel," Andrew
offered.

"Thanks," April said, following them.

They had to cross over one small bridge and then turn into
a very narrow alley where a small branch of the canal flowed

through. The sidewalk, such as it was, was no more than six or seven feet across. The alley made a sudden sharp turn to the left and then right again. In the distance was yet another small bridge. April glanced behind her, wondering if she'd be able to find her way back if she had to. After another series of turns by the couple, she gave up trying to remember the steps they'd taken. At the corner, they stopped.

"All you have to do is go down that way," Andrew said, indicating the direction with his hand. "You'll pass three or four restaurants on your left, then some shops on your right. Just past the gelato stand, make a right turn, and the hotel is about halfway down the street. You can't miss it," he finished with a light laugh, a way of acknowledging that the streets were not exactly straight or easy to find.

"Thanks for your help," April said.

"We hope you enjoy your first visit to Venice. Feel free to call us if you need help with anything," Lilly offered, pointing out the name of their apartment on their confirmation letter.

"That's very kind of you. I hope you have a good time, too."

April watched a moment as they walked in the opposite direction from the directions they'd given her. She felt her spirits lift. She didn't want to waste one moment. She was going to check into the hotel, unpack, and immediately start out to explore the city.

The sun had made an appearance at last, throwing long shadows between the old buildings and reflecting off the surface of the waterway. In a matter of minutes April had located the hotel, inordinately proud of the way she'd managed on her own from the airport. Well almost all on her own, she thought, conceding a thank-you to the St. Clairs for their assistance.

A bell rang over the hotel entrance as she entered. The

lobby was miniscule, the front desk no bigger than her kitchen counter at home. Behind the desk was seated an older woman with no more than her bespectacled eyes and graying hair visible above the surface of the counter.

"*Buon giorno, buon giorno*," she said cheerfully.

April repeated the greeting and approached.

"I have been waiting for you. Miss Kingston, *si*?"

"No. I'm her traveling companion, April Stockwood. Miss Kingston will be arriving tomorrow."

"Oh, *si*," the woman shrugged, standing. Adjusting her glasses, she peered at April. "You sign in."

She repeated the terms of the reservation; seven days and six nights, double. Breakfast included.

"And we do have a private bath?" April confirmed.

"And a shower," the woman announced proudly.

It had never occurred to April that the two wouldn't come together.

"Please. I must see your passport. I write your number in here." She pointed to a ledger.

April set her things down and began searching through her purse. She was certain that she'd stuck the black case in her bag after getting it stamped at the airport. Or was it after she'd shown the passport a second time to an agent on the way out?

The woman was waiting patiently, watching with mild curiosity as April began pulling things from her purse and laying them on the counter. April smiled a little uneasily.

"It's in here somewhere."

"Take your time," the woman said.

April was down to just a cosmetic bag . . . but no passport. She kept herself calm, carefully sifting again through the things she'd already removed from her purse.

"Oh, I know where it is. I think I put it in my tote bag after I got my *vaporetti* ticket."

Abandoning the purse, April began digging through the

tote bag, her search a little more frantic. She could not stem the rising panic and fear, or the terrible realization that she couldn't find her passport because she didn't have it.

"Oh, my God . . ."

"Signorina, I help you, okay?"

April didn't respond. Trying to maintain some semblance of control, she took deep breaths to stop her heart from racing. She emptied everything from the tote and one by one replaced all the items. No passport case. She did the same with the contents of her purse, but even before she was halfway through, she knew she wouldn't find it. Her passport was gone, and she had no idea how or when she'd lost it.

"It's not here," she said helplessly. "I don't have it. It's gone."

"Are you sure? Maybe you look in a pocket, or your suitcase."

She shook her head to all the suggestions, her mind racing through a flashback of her movements since getting the passport stamped.

"Do you think I could use your phone to call the airport? I may have left it somewhere this morning. Maybe someone found it. Or . . ." Her voice trailed off on the worse of the possibilities that came to mind.

The proprietress placed the call for April, speaking rapidly in Italian. After a few minutes she passed the phone to April.

"They talk to you."

But the news was not encouraging. There was nothing airport security could do. No passport had been found and turned in. Passports were a highly desirable form of international ID that could be sold on the black market. Numb with disbelief, April's mind wandered to all the places and people she'd encountered between landing at the airport and saying goodbye to Stephanie. She reluctantly had to admit she was not sure what might have happened to her passport.

It was only after she disconnected that April fully realized the ramifications of her missing documents. Her passport case also included her return plane ticket, her credit card, and her bank card that would have allowed her to withdraw money from an ATM. All she had left was her driver's license and, at most, one hundred euros.

"Well, I've somehow lost my passport," April explained, her smile wry and bemused.

"This is terrible," the woman agreed sadly.

"At least I'm not homeless on the street. I'll check into my room and see if I can find some information in my guide book about what to do. I guess I should call the airline about my ticket . . ."

"I'm so sorry, signorina."

"So am I," April sighed.

"No, I'm sorry. You cannot stay. You cannot sign in."

"What?"

"It is the law. You must have a passport to register at a hotel."

There was at least one thing about Venice that April would have to say was just like back home. The police station. Dragging her luggage over uneven cobblestone streets, over two bridges, and down a number of steps, April arrived at the nearest station house in San Marco Square. It was small, plain, and functional. Even the officers seemed familiar; uniformed men with an air of authority and a watchful suspicion about everything and everyone who came into their domain—who, as April watched, were all tourists.

April stared blankly in front of her, no longer listening to conversations she couldn't understand, and having given up hope that her situation was going to move the officers into instant action on her behalf. Instead, she sat on a very hard wooden bench for the better part of two hours trying to decide what to do. Her options were few. She couldn't call Stephanie, and Stephanie couldn't call her. There was no point in calling home. Explaining to her family what had happened would only make them worry. April began to smile quietly to herself as she considered making up a sign and canvassing some of the local businesses WILL WORK FOR ROOM AND BOARD.

The four officers on duty occasionally glanced her way, but no progress report on her dilemma was forthcoming. They did, however, offer her a bottle of cold water, which she accepted gratefully. Mostly they answered phones, shuffled papers, and had low conversations among themselves which, as far as April could figure out, was the Italian version of cops asking each other, "What are you doing after work today?"

April glanced toward the door of the station and sighed in frustration. She could see beyond the columns of the arcade right out into the open square. It was busy with tourists, school groups, and vendors. She wanted to go out and look around the square, but didn't know how to ask if that would be okay. Here she was, in one of the most beautiful and historic cities in the world, and spending her visit in a grim police station.

Her reverie was shattered by the entrance of an attractive and elegantly attired woman speaking rapid-fire Italian. Trailing behind her were two men carrying several large packages that were crushed and sodden with water. The officers all came to attention, the one who was in charge greeting the woman by name. April thought she might have been in her fifties with a sophisticated coif of nearly black hair. She was curvaceous and very feminine, complete with subtle makeup, jewels, and expensive accessories. She was wearing a slender black skirt with a peach-colored light knit sweater, clearly designer, and burnt-orange high-heeled summer sandals the same color as her leather Ferragamo handbag.

There was a brief exchange between the woman and the officers. April watched as the officers' demeanor changed, becoming attentive and respectful. The woman launched into an animated monologue. Her story drew sympathy and some laughter from her male audience. After a few minutes, the two men who had come in with her left. She was offered a comfortable chair from one of the desks. Instead, she sat down on the bench a little distance from April, and they exchanged tentative smiles. The woman took out her cell phone, made a call and began a quiet conversation as if she were seated in the reception area of a salon or office instead of the police station.

April looked at the wall clock; it was almost one o'clock. Hungry, she opened her purse and rummaged around, looking for the roll of breath mints. It was better than nothing. She ate one and, on the spur of the moment, turned to her neighbor.

"*Prego*," April said, holding out the mints. The woman, who had finished her phone call, leaned forward, carefully removed one, and ate it.

"*Grazie*." She smiled and began speaking; pausing when she read April's confused expression. "*Parla italiano*?"

"No Italian. I'm sorry," April shook her head with regret.

"Ahhh . . . you are American," the woman nodded in understanding, her English slightly accented.

"That's right."

Surprising April, the woman reached out to finger one of the blond locks. "I love your hair . . . this thing with the twists. So clever."

"Thank you."

"My daughter, Andrea, is crazy for American styles. But her hair cannot do this, like yours," she said.

"It takes a lot of time," April said simply, not wanting to launch into a lengthy explanation of African-American hair.

The woman noticed her suitcase and tote bag. "You do not have a hotel room? This is not very good. Venice has so many visitors in summer."

"I have a reservation but I can't check in."

"But why?"

"I lost my passport. Well, I *think* I lost it. Or maybe it was—"

"No, no, no . . . Do not speak it," the woman lamented. "It is a problem all over the world. Have you called the American consulate?"

"No, I—"

The woman looked surprised. "But didn't they tell you that is where you get a new passport?"

"I filled out the forms. I think they're doing everything to help, but I don't think they speak English," April said quietly, not wanting to offend the officers, a few of whom were watching.

"Of course they do," the woman declared indignantly, coming to her feet and approaching the counter.

She immediately began interrogating the four men, first in Italian, but then switching to English. Much to April's surprise, the officer-in-charge answered her back in English. April was beckoned to the counter.

"How long has she been waiting?" the woman asked the officer, laying a soft hand on April's arm.

"A little time," he shrugged.

The woman looked at April. "Almost two hours," she corrected.

The woman was outraged. In a polite but admonishing tone she voiced her disapproval.

April waited for the officer to tell the woman to sit down and not interfere in police business, but that didn't happen. He turned to April.

"Signorina . . . I send your papers to Milan, but no answer. It is rest time. It is Sunday."

"I understand. I know you're doing what you can to help."

"But it is not enough," the woman declared. "*Per quanto*

tempo? Will you keep her here all day? Where will she stay tonight?"

"Signora, I do not know," the officer confessed.

"Here, if I have to," April said. "I put down this station address and phone number as my local contact."

The woman looked shocked. And then she started to laugh. "Impossible! You must do something at once," she instructed the officer, who looked like he was being dressed down by his mother.

"Signora Cesso, we do everything," the officer assured her.

The two men who'd first arrived with the woman returned. Everyone's attention shifted to them and after a few minutes of discussion some matter appeared resolved.

"I must go. My boat is not seriously damaged after all and is waiting," signora Cesso declared.

"Your boat? You had an accident?" April inquired.

"A speedboat with a driver . . . *stupido* . . . he ran into me. My new lamps fall into the water. See, they are ruined." She pointed to the mess on the end of the counter.

"At least you weren't hurt," April said.

"*Si*. I think this is good also. And you . . ."

"I have no choice except to wait. But," she couldn't prevent a note of longing from creeping into her voice, "I didn't want to spend my first night in Venice at a police station."

"No. This will never do. Let me think . . ." Signora Cesso narrowed her gaze at April for a moment and then suddenly brightened. "Come. I take you home with me."

"Excuse me?"

"Of course this is the answer. My son will know what to do. He will talk with his American friend who works for the consulate, in Milan."

Speechless, April looked at the officer for guidance. He didn't say anything but he also didn't seem to find signora Cesso's suggestion inappropriate.

"That's very nice of you but . . . I don't think it's necessary. Besides, you don't know who I am, or anything about me."

"You look like nice American lady. I know you are thoughtful. You offer me the candy. Don't worry; I am no crazy Italian lady. Please, you tell her," she instructed the officer.

"Signora Cesso is very fine lady. Her husband *es un medico*."

"Doctor," signora Cesso translated.

Still, April hesitated. All her life, growing up in Philadelphia, she'd been taught and had in turn taught her own daughter: *Never* go anywhere with a stranger. But that was back home, and the signora looked nothing like a deranged kidnapper.

Signora Cesso smiled again, touching her arm. "What is your name?"

"April Stockwood."

"April," she repeated. "Like the month of spring. This is a very good sign. I would very much like you to stay with my family, April. You call the police if we treat you badly."

April chuckled at the humor and irony of the signora's assurances. She glanced at the officer. He merely shrugged.

"It is okay for you to go."

"They know where I live," signora Cesso said.

April chuckled again, but doubted that the signora would understand the American joke.

"I will call signora Cesso when I hear from Milan," he said.

"I call you first," the signora challenged. "Now, we go. Giorgio will take your luggage."

One of the boatmen lifted April's suitcase effortlessly and she was swept along by the sheer force of the signora's personality. While she couldn't help but feel somewhat apprehensive about wandering off into the unknown without Stephanie or her family having a clue where she was, April also couldn't deny her instinctive sense that the gods were watching out for her, and that nothing terrible was going to happen. She'd leave a message for Stephanie at the hotel. She'd take a leap of faith and see where it landed her.

April followed signora Cesso through a series of tight little streets and passages toward the waterfront. Soon they approached a private pier where a small, sleek Chris-Craft cruiser was moored.

"We don't go very far. Across the water in Dorsoduro," signora Cesso informed April.

They were helped aboard the boat and April's luggage placed on the deck outside of the steering cubicle. They took seats under a canopy that protected them from the sun and elements, but they could still enjoy the gentle breeze off the canal.

The signora spoke glowingly of her son, Santiago, and kept referring to her son's American friend as her other son. She seemed confident that April's problem would be quickly resolved.

In less than fifteen minutes the small boat cut its engines and smoothly navigated from the Grand Canal into a narrow arm that took them inland. After several maze-like turns, the motorboat pulled into a private dock where it was tied to a mooring slip outside a small palazzo. Giorgio helped April and the signora to the tiny sidewalk. The signora approached the doors, a massive double panel of solid wood that was elaborately carved with cherubs and nymphs, and rang the bell before inserting a key into the lock and letting herself in.

"Here we are. Come in, come in."

April was surprised to see that they had not actually entered the house but were within a courtyard enclosure. There were dozens of large potted plants positioned all around the stone-paved yard to create a garden. Wooden benches and cushioned lounge chairs, along with several small makeshift tables, were placed here and there. A large oval table, for dining al fresco, sat in the shadow near the interior entrance to the house. A fat calico cat was stretched out in the shade of drooping fronds, its tail swishing lazily in blissful contentment.

She felt like she'd stepped into an enchanted world.

The signora burst into Italian. April realized that signora Cesso was speaking to two men who, April now saw as she peered across the courtyard, were seated at the large oval table. Casually dressed, they were enjoying drinks and quiet conversation. As they saw the women, the men immediately stood. Signora Cesso greeted one with an air kiss and an affectionate pat on his cheek. The other man smiled, and April's attention was instantly drawn to him.

He was tall, his skin a smooth, soft chocolate brown . . . African American . . . good-looking. Memory tickled at the edge of her consciousness. Her gaze bore into his face and although she realized that the signora was explaining to the young Italian man about her lost passport and finding her at the police station, her own focus did not veer from the silent man who watched her struggle with her memory. His face was older. His dark eyes sparkled at her, and April wondered if he knew who she was. Or was he merely amused by her predicament? But her memory began to clear. She realized she was trying to adjust a boy's face and eyes to the man he was now.

"Cutter . . ." April said triumphantly, able at last to put a name to the face she recognized from so long ago.

Chapter 2

He stared back at her. For a horrible moment she thought she'd made a mistake. Maybe he wasn't the person she thought he was. Then he spoke.

"April. April . . ." He searched for the rest.

"Stockwood," she supplied.

Her thoughts were a confused jumble of impressions from the past. There was no time to sort them out.

"I can't believe you remember me," she remarked, but then fell silent when he didn't offer the same observation.

She was aware that signora Cesso and the other man were watching. Her unexpected greeting had caused silence to fall upon the group. Then the slender young man stepped forward.

"*Buon pomeriggio,* good afternoon, Miss Stockwood. *Benvenuto alla palazzo Cesso.* I am Santiago." He took April's hand and bowed. For a brief instant, April found herself staring at a bent head with dark wavy hair. Then Santiago straightened up. His charming grin immediately put her at ease. He was just above average height and somewhat bookish looking behind rimless glasses.

"My son," signora Cesso confirmed with an airy wave of her hand. "You and Hayden, you have met before?"

Hayden, April repeated to herself, embarrassed that she had used his old nickname. "We went to high school together."

"A long time ago," Hayden said dryly.

"Ach!" the signora exclaimed. "So that is it. You and our Hayden are old friends!"

"Well . . ." April started, casting a covert glance in his direction. He made no attempt to help her and she felt it unnecessary to say that "friends" was an overstatement.

"But this is wonderful. I want to hear all about it," the signora said.

"I, also," added Santiago. "But first, I do not understand. My mother says something about the police and Miss Stockwood."

"Please, call me April," she said. "It seems I either lost or had my passport and credit cards stolen after arriving this morning. And then my friend Stephanie left me, and . . . well, it's complicated."

"Ahhh . . . you could not get a hotel room," Santiago concluded.

"Exactly."

"*Scusa,* signora?" the boatman queried, carrying April's luggage into the courtyard. "*Dove collocherò il bagaglio?*"

"Excuse me," signora Cesso said. "I'll show Giorgio where to put April's luggage."

Signora Cesso was off before April could utter a word and she was left alone with Santiago and . . . Hayden. April turned, only to find him regarding her with a thoughtful frown. Her smile faded, but she refused to fall prey to his air of disapproval.

"Please, let's sit down," Santiago said, touching April's elbow and directing her to a chair at the table where he and Hayden had been sitting. After seating her, he pulled out another chair and sat himself. There was an awkward silence. April shifted.

"I, er . . . I know this seems strange, signora Cesso inviting me, a stranger, to her home. I'm sorry . . ."

"Not at all," Santiago said easily. "I grow up with a mother who helps everyone. Ask Hayden. When he come here to work in Milan, he first stay with my family. This is where he learned to speak Italian. But very badly," he confided with a wink.

April laughed at his teasing humor. A maid approached carrying a tray on which sat a glass and a small soda bottle. She offered it to April.

"*Soda di limone*," Santiago said.

April accepted the glass and sipped. The lemon flavor was soothing, but the carbonation caused her stomach to make an unpleasant growling noise that she hoped neither man could hear. She put the glass down, her hands wet from the condensation. She felt Hayden's continued scrutiny, but she resolutely refused to look in his direction again.

"You called Hayden 'Cutter.' *Che questo significa . . .* ?" Santiago asked.

April caught Hayden's frown and said quickly, "It was a mistake. It doesn't mean anything."

It surprised her that Hayden remained silent. She thought for sure he'd have a quick comeback, something smart and funny. He'd always been the school cut-up.

Santiago turned to Hayden and quietly spoke in Italian. Hayden responded, his Italian seemingly flawless. Santiago grinned at April. "I tell Hayden I like your hair."

April touched her hair self-consciously. She hadn't looked at herself in a mirror to see what damage had been done since she'd gotten on the plane sixteen hours ago—in Philadelphia.

"The color is so good for you," Santiago continued. "The look . . ."—he used his hands as if they helped him conjure

up the right words—". . . *bellissimo*, eh? So different from
Italian women, you agree?" he asked Hayden.

Hayden nodded slowly. "It suits her."

It wasn't exactly a compliment, April thought.

"This is your first trip to Venice?" Santiago continued.

April nodded. "My first to Europe, period. I came with a
friend, but as soon as we landed she had to go on to Milan for
business. We're supposed to meet up again tomorrow, or
maybe the next day. One of my problems is that she won't
know what's happened to me, and—"

"Do not worry. Hayden works for the consulate in Milan.
He can help you with your passport."

Completely thrown off guard, April looked to Hayden. So
this was the American signora Cesso had mentioned. April
would never have thought that Cutter—no, she corrected herself, Hayden—would ever have grown up and gone to work
for the State Department.

She guessed that she shouldn't be surprised at how different he was from the boy she remembered. He seemed so
deadly serious. And sad. Maybe not so much sad as reserved,
April observed.

"I remember signora Cesso did say she knew someone at
the consulate," she said.

Santiago leaned forward. "My mother would like if you call
her Marina, yes? Signora Cesso is only for formal occasions."

"Hayden tells me I am like Tina Turner," Marina Cesso
added, joining them. "He says I have . . ." She looked to Hayden for assistance.

He smiled fondly. "Sassiness and energy."

"*Si*, just like her. I like this word, sassiness."

Passing Hayden to take a seat next to April, signora Cesso
patted his broad shoulders. April noticed that although Hayden didn't move an inch, his entire demeanor softened at the
gentle touch. As if that were the cue he was waiting for to

consent to participate in the discussion, Hayden leaned forward, commanding everyone's attention but addressing his remarks to April.

"I'm sure I can help you replace your documents. Do you have a photocopy of your passport with you?"

"No, I don't. I didn't know I should make one," April said.

"Most people don't," he responded.

"Hayden, the police make the report. April fill out a form," Marina Cesso informed him.

"Good."

Very methodically and professionally, Hayden continued to question April. If he had any sympathy for her plight he never let it show. She could have been any stranger in need of help.

"I'll call the consulate and see if they've received the fax from the police." He finished. "You'll have to get a passport photo in the morning, and we'll overnight it to Milan."

"How long do you think it will take to get a replacement?" April asked.

He shrugged. "Nothing is going to happen today. It's Sunday afternoon, and all the offices we need will be closed in . . . where do you live?" he asked April.

"I'm close to Philadelphia."

He seemed surprised. "You never left?"

"Did you expect me to?"

"Actually, yes."

She frowned. "Where to?"

"I don't know. The unknown. Out there. Some place interesting."

That surprised her. But April also had a vague feeling that he was somehow disappointed by her answer. "I always thought Philadelphia was interesting," she defended.

He sat back in his chair. "I didn't."

Santiago broke into the cocoon of their conversation

suggesting they should call the credit card company and see if she could get an immediate replacement. Surprised that she hadn't yet reported the card stolen, Hayden obtained the customer-service number and called them to report the theft. Luckily the main branch was in the States and was active twenty-four hours a day.

Then, before April could say "thank you" for his getting things started, he telephoned the airline. Since April had originally been issued an e-ticket, he was able to assure her that it would be easy to replace as soon as she received her new passport. If she'd had a paper ticket, it would have been much more complicated.

"You will stay with us until everything is done," Marina declared.

"I can't thank you enough for being so kind and for coming to my rescue," April said to the group at large, not singling out Hayden.

"My little sister will love that you are here. Andrea will ask you a million questions," Santiago said.

"She is fifteen and crazy for clothes," Marina lamented without rancor.

"And boys?" April asked. "It's universal at that age."

"Do you have kids?" Hayden asked.

April looked at him. It was the first personal question he'd directed to her, the first time he'd shown any personal interest in her at all since she'd arrived.

"My daughter, Anesa, is thirteen but thinks she's fifteen," she answered. "Her main concern these days is that her . . . er . . . her . . ."

"She wants . . ." Marina used her hands to pantomime the round projection of breasts.

"Yes. She's impatient. She wants everything right away."

"Like my Andrea. Why did you not bring her to Italy?"

"She's spending a month with her father in Washington. We're divorced," April said.

"You say you went to school with Hayden," Santiago asked, curiosity in his voice.

April was about to launch into an explanation when Hayden stood.

"Sorry to break this up, but I have to go."

"Go where?" Santiago asked in surprise.

"To take care of business," Hayden responded cryptically. "I assume we're still on for tonight?"

"*Si*," Santiago concurred. "Carlos will meet us later."

As their plans and arrangements were finalized, April studied Hayden covertly. The lanky, loose-limbed, irreverent teenager she knew had grown into a broad-shouldered man. Athletically fit, his firm jaw spoke of a man aware of his masculinity, the kind of brazen virility that drew women like a magnet. Absent was any sign of the cocky self-awareness of his younger days.

"Please. You come with us," Santiago said to April, interrupting her thoughts. "It will just be friends for a little espresso and lots of talk."

"Later, later," Marina stepped in. "I think April would like to go to her room. Maybe rest and change and have a little something to eat, yes?" she looked to April.

"Yes," April agreed.

April stood and held her hand out to Hayden. He looked at it before taking it rather gently in his own. April felt his long, strong fingers wrap around hers and engulf them with warmth, the kind that she hadn't known in a long time. She glanced at his face and found him watching her expectantly.

"Hayden, it was . . . nice seeing you again." He raised an eyebrow at her careful wording. "And thanks so much for your help."

"That's what I'm here for."

April didn't expect any special favors, but she thought he'd be a little more gracious. He didn't seem to realize how much it meant to her to see him, an African American—someone she knew and could relate to—in charge and able to reassure her in a way that maybe no one else could have.

He released her hand and stepped forward to kiss signora Cesso's cheek in the European fashion. Their exchange and good-bye was in Italian. She'd never have thought that the boy she'd known could have evolved into such a smooth, sophisticated diplomat. She was consumed with curiosity about his transformation and oddly disappointed when he didn't turn to look at her as he departed. April was left to wonder if she'd made so little an impression on him.

It was only after awakening from a ninety-minute nap that April realized how much she had needed the rest. She stretched languidly. The room, larger than her living room at home, was at the back of the Cesso palazzo, on the second floor. Like all the others in the palazzo, it had enormously high ceilings, which kept the interior of the house cool and comfortable. The walls were painted a pale, creamy yellow with touches of coral. The colors made the room seem even larger, open, and very bright.

The one window was wide and tall, opening out over a small tributary of the Grand Canal. A light breeze made the sheer batiste curtains curl away from the window. Sounds of people on the street below, or a melody being sung with gusto by a gondolier, gently wafted through the glass. While she might have wished for a firmer mattress, more lamps, and a potted plant or two, April concluded that this was heaven on earth. In Italy.

She didn't bother to unpack, merely digging through her clothing until she found a cool skirt and white top with a pair of sandals. She was happy to be out of the slacks and sweater she'd worn for nearly twenty-four hours. She used her hands to fluff and lift her locks, using a hair clip borrowed from her daughter to hold several errant locks from her forehead. The result, to April's satisfaction, showed off her best features: large dark eyes and beautifully curved lips that made it seem that she was always about to smile. Like a darker version of the Mona Lisa, she'd been told.

She finished by applying lip gloss. Years ago she'd gone for a free makeup application at a department store in downtown Philly and was told that if she wore the right lipstick for her skin color, she didn't need any other makeup, however much good that was. She had no expectations that anyone—that is to say, men—were paying any attention to a thirty-seven year old divorcée who needed to lose ten pounds.

Drawn to the sounds of community life, April leaned out her window to get a view of the surrounding neighborhood. Despite the obvious crowding and lack of open space, blooming flowers planted in boxes sat on many window ledges, apparently to make up for the lack of parks, trees or gardens in the city. Venice had been erected, essentially, not on solid ground but out of thin air, the foundation established on pilings driven into the water. Climate and age had taken its toll on the classic Greek and Roman architectural marvels. Peeling plaster and paint façades had survived centuries of war and destruction, rebuilding and restoration, to show an incredible beauty and splendor that made Venice unique. As much as she wished Anesa could be with her to experience the lively culture, April knew her very twenty-first-century daughter would have declared Venice . . . just old. And she would want to know where all the black folks were.

Leaving her room, April followed the sound of distant, muted voices coming from below. Something was being cooked in the kitchen. She inhaled deeply, reminded of how hungry she was.

As she neared the main salon, April heard a young girl's voice, plaintive and dramatic in tone, then the distinctive voice of signora Cesso. Something in the ebb and flow of the exchange told April that Marina Cesso was in a mother-daughter face-off. The young girl's plea was interrupted by a man's deep voice, quiet and less urgent.

"Hello," April said, stopping in the entrance to the salon.

"You are awake. I hope you are rested," Marina Cesso said. She nodded in approval at April's changed attire.

"Very. I guess I was a little tired."

A man got up from a club chair and came forward to greet her, cigarette in hand. Marina introduced her husband, Antonio Cesso. He welcomed her to Italy and, apparently having heard from Marina the full story of April's misfortunes, generously offered her the hospitality of their home for as long as she wished.

April liked him at once. Antonio was probably fifteen years older than his gregarious wife, and it was clear he adored and indulged her. Watching the tender interactions between Marina and her husband, April couldn't help but make a comparison to her failed relationship with her ex-husband, Sinclair.

"I'm April," she directed next to the teenage girl who was standing by a plush sofa. Marina beckoned and the young girl came forward to be introduced.

Andrea was taller than her mother, with a feline slenderness that was more than adolescent but not yet woman. Her hair was a wild mane of light brown that was styled off center to fall in loose curls. She had her father's hazel eyes, her mother's grace and mannerisms, and her own coquettish charm. April recognized the Dolce & Gabbana outfit: a short tight skirt that sat on Andrea's narrow hips in the current navel-baring fashion, with a spandex top.

"I'm Andrea. Nice to meet you," she said shyly, in flawless English, then turned to her mother and pointed at April's dreadlocks. "*Tua capelli, que bella! Mama, per favore . . .*"

April smiled. Even she could understand the gist of Andrea's plea that she would like to have dreads in her own hair. The ensuing argument reminded April of similar encounters with her daughter, Anesa, and she realized how much she missed her. Andrea reminded her of all the things that were both exasperating and so wonderful about daughters.

"Now we sit down for something to eat," Marina announced as they went out into the courtyard where the table had been set for four and a servant stood at the ready.

"Isn't your son going to join us for dinner?" April asked as she was directed to a seat next to Andrea.

"This is not dinner," Marina corrected. "It is a light meal for the afternoon. In Italy we do not have what you call dinner until later, nine or ten in the night."

"You eat so often?" April asked, spreading a napkin with a tropical floral print across her lap.

"Yes, but little food each time," she said. "Not so much like in America."

April couldn't refute the observation. She had yet to see any Italian who could even remotely be considered overweight. But she found the salad with shaved parmesan cheese and olive oil, served with warm slices of crusty bread, simple, delicious, and filling. The meal was accompanied by a fruity red wine. April drank cautiously and found herself changing her mind about wines, her past experience limited to inexpensive varieties either too bitter or tasteless.

The setting was so surreal and so magical that April thought again that she had to be dreaming. She could not possibly be in Italy, three thousand miles from home, having lunch al fresco in the sunny courtyard of a palazzo with one of the city's prominent families. It seemed a just and fitting conclusion to years of feeling that life was passing her by while she'd dutifully committed to the traditional routines of being a wife and mother in a black community.

She'd had the good man, the beautiful child, the accomplished career, the cul-de-sac home in the right kind of neighborhood. Praise for having gotten it right. And for years she'd been asking herself nervously, *is this all there is*? Even now, April could feel remnants of the frustration and anxiety from her so-called perfect life that had driven her into unhappiness and resentment.

As she settled into the roomy wicker chair, she felt more content than she had in a very long time. The sun was low on the western horizon, and the courtyard had a warm and quiet light, the air cooler than when she'd arrived. She was lulled by the conversation about signor Cesso's latest patients, and the signora's charity ball, which was to take place at the end of the week. She chatted with Andrea and discovered a sophistication and maturity that was surprising in a young teenager. She talked about her own home in Philadelphia, and about her daughter, Anesa.

"Do you have pictures of Anesa? May I see?" Andrea asked April.

"Yes, I do," April said with pleasure, digging through her purse. She pulled out a small leather folder. "Only two. You won't be forced to look through an entire album."

Marina and Antonio chuckled at April's disclaimer. Andrea looked at the pictures. One was of mother and daughter; the other of Anesa alone. "Oh, she is so pretty."

April grinned warmly. "That's very nice of you to say."

"Look, Mama," Andrea said excitedly, handing the leather folder to her mother so her parents could see.

"*Bella*," murmured Marina, passing it to her husband who also admired April's lovely daughter.

"Can I have a look?"

April turned sharply and saw Hayden Calloway approaching from the entrance of the palazzo. He had changed into light-weight summer slacks and a coordinated coral short-sleeved shirt that complimented his strong brown features. Remembering his cool attitude toward her earlier, she felt a bit awkward, and smiled politely but distantly. He said his greetings to the Cessos, kissing Marina's cheek, then stopped by the end of the table and looked at her, nodding at the photo folder. She slowly passed it to him though her attention was on methodically folding her used napkin as he studied the two images.

"Hayden, isn't she pretty?" Andrea asked.

He closed the folder and handed it back to April. "Like mother, like daughter."

"Thank you," she responded formally, although his compliment caught her off guard.

"Have you come to join us?" Antonio asked Hayden, gesturing that he should sit down.

"Actually, I came to get April."

"Really? Why?" she asked in surprise.

"Santiago and I are getting together with some friends, remember? You can see a little of Venetian nightlife."

"Can I come, too?" Andrea asked.

"Of course not," Marina said swiftly. "But I think it is very good for April to go."

"Yes, yes. Enjoy yourselves," Antonio added.

The problem was that April wasn't sure she wanted to go. While it was nice that he'd made the offer, she didn't believe that it was a genuine invitation. She would bet that Santiago had put him up to it, or even Marina Cesso.

"Unless you have something else planned for the evening," Hayden said, his tone indicating that he knew she had nothing else on her agenda.

"No. I don't," April admitted.

"It's up to you," Hayden said, as if it didn't matter to him one way or another.

She hesitated. "Unfortunately, I . . . I have only limited euros at the moment. And with my credit card gone . . ."

"You won't need any cash," Hayden assured her. "We're talking about espresso."

The evening stretched long and solitary in front of her. She looked at Marina, who nodded encouragingly. Despite their hospitality, April knew they had no more planned on having a guest than she had expected to be one. And there was no getting around April's longing to see some of the city. She took a deep breath.

"Thank you. I'd love to come along."

April excused herself to return to her room and get a shawl in case the evening became chilly, and her camera.

When she returned to the courtyard, Hayden was alone. She tried to ignore the way he scrutinized her, his expression deeply thoughtful, almost disapproving, she felt. But she smiled at him nonetheless and said, awkwardly, "Thank you for asking me to join you and your friends. I don't want to intrude."

Hayden shrugged as they left the building. "We're just getting together for drinks."

He led her to a small motorboat moored about twenty feet from the Chris-Craft belonging to the Cessos, then offered his hand to assist her onto the deck, following her on board. There was warm strength in his clasp, and despite her ambiguous response to him she felt protected, even if his attitude didn't exactly jibe with her fantasy.

She sat in a leather jump seat; Hayden, in the pilot's seat, started the engine. They glided out of the slip and into the estuary until they reached the Grand Canal. The approaching night glowed with the colors of the setting sun. April shot two photographs of the sun disappearing behind the ornate dome of a church in the distance. She reflected on her arrival in this unusual city just hours ago. Even the loss of her passport and credit cards seemed insignificant. She had finally fulfilled one of her long-held dreams. At that moment all was right in the world. Even Hayden's aloofness wasn't going to diminish that bright light.

"Are you settled in?" he asked.

"Yes, I am. I have a huge room that's as big as my whole first apartment," she quipped.

"They're great people. They've been very good to me."

She didn't miss the irony in his voice. "So what did you do to earn Marina Cesso's devotion? She thinks the world of you. I mean, that kind of faith is usually saved for those who walk on water."

Hayden chuckled dryly. "You mean you don't believe I can?"

She had to laugh at his conceit.

He glanced briefly at her as he navigated the small boat. "I left my cape at home tonight, but don't mess with me."

April stared. In that one little boastful remark she'd caught a glimpse of the teenager she'd once known. Cutter. The gregarious upperclassman, known for his irreverent humor, had had a tendency to cut class or to cut up when he did attend. Arguably the most popular boy in school, he'd been smart but bored in the classroom. He'd excelled at varsity sports and been constantly flocked by girls who flirted, and fought among themselves for position as his "main squeeze."

Cutter . . . Hayden . . . had personality, and then some. April had been on the outside looking in, when they attended high school, warned about the consequences of hanging around him. Cutter could charm a girl right out of her underpants, she once overheard a teacher say. Never mind that many would willingly have given them up.

"How did you meet Marina and Antonio?" she asked.

"Santiago was the first person I got to know when I came to Italy."

"How long ago was that?"

"About eighteen months. I hooked up with Santiago to improve my Italian. He's a cool guy. We hit it off. Then when my office was looking for another translator, I put in a good word for him. Marina has been thanking me ever since."

"Because you found her son a regular job?"

"No. Because it gave her access to wealthy American businessmen who she could then hit up for big-buck donations to her charities. Her main interest is the children's hospital where Antonio is chief of pediatrics."

"I think that's wonderful."

"Watch out," Hayden suddenly warned. A speedboat came out of nowhere, buzzing off the bow and sending a spray of water across the port side and onto the deck. April clung to her jump seat as the boat rocked back and forth from the force of the wake. Hayden reached out to grab her forearm for extra measure.

"Sorry about that. I didn't hear him coming. Hold on."

He made sure she was steady, then maneuvered the boat to less choppy waters.

"Did you get wet?" he asked as the motorboat stopped rocking.

April shook her head. "Only a little. I won't melt." Her shoes would dry out, as would her skirt.

"We're almost there."

In a matter of minutes, Hayden slowed the boat and docked at a tiny marina. After securing the lines to the mooring, he helped her out. Dusk had faded to evening. The city's narrow streets and alleyways took on deep and sinister shadows. Huge palazzos along the winding waterfront, so majestic during the day, were mostly dark and deserted at night.

They passed small eateries that were squeezed into

storefronts and tiny spaces. "Where is this place we're going?" April asked Hayden as he guided her through the maze of alleys.

"Right here," he said.

They were standing in front of an open-air café, its small bistro tables crowded with the young and chic. Santiago rose from where he was seated with several friends, shook hands with Hayden, and welcomed April. Two chairs were pulled forward, and she and Hayden quickly became part of the group. April was introduced to Carlos, from Spain, Anna, from Denmark, and Simone, who hailed from Tunisia. She was a fair-skinned and beautiful young woman, but who could have been a clone of Iman.

Everyone spoke English, but every now and then Simone and Anna would begin chatting in French, or Santiago would say something to Hayden in Italian. April was both impressed and envious. After all of her years studying French in school and earning straight A's, she could speak no more than a few phrases.

Quickly the table became covered with empty espresso cups and overflowing ashtrays. April noticed that she and Hayden were the only two at the table who did not smoke. She was perfectly content to just listen to the discussion, which was never about anything in particular. It was a rambling cross-conversation about other friends, an upcoming concert, whether they should fly to Lugano for a weekend . . . where to have dinner.

"Santiago told us you just arrived in Italy," Simone said to April.

Up to that moment April had been ignored by the North African beauty and was surprised that Simone even knew that much about her. "Yes, this morning. This is my first trip abroad."

"Oh. You are a tourist." Looking disinterested, Simone blew a thin veil of smoke from her cigarette.

"Only for a day or two," April responded, annoyed at the note of condescension in Simone's voice. "I adapt quickly."

"What are your plans while you are here?" Carlos asked, his tone much more friendly.

"Oh . . . boat down the Grand Canal. Every tourist must do that," April said lightly. Anna glanced at Simone in amusement. April continued, this time more seriously. "But I also want to master making a Venetian mask, and I want to learn how to cook risotto."

Anna, Carlos, and Santiago laughed. Hayden's hand covered his mouth, which hid his reaction. Only Simone didn't smile.

"You are going to make masks?" she asked, as if she thought April was insane. Without waiting for an answer, she shrugged, then turned to Hayden and said something in Italian, effectively excluding April from the conversation.

Anna and Carlos talked about the mask shops, and then suggested other Venetian attractions that April had to see.

"I've already marked them in my guidebook," April said.

"You must not miss the Lagoon Islands. And Burano, of course," Santiago added. "They make beautiful lace there, very traditional." He threw a glance at Hayden and Simone, and then said, his eyes gleaming, "I think Hayden should take you there tomorrow."

"I'm sure I can get there on my own," April quickly countered, not wanting Hayden to feel he was being pressured to take her sightseeing.

"I think I first need to see about getting her a new photo and passport," Hayden responded, turning away from Simone to Santiago.

All business, she thought. While she couldn't disagree with his priorities, this was still her vacation, her trip of a lifetime. Annoyed, April wasn't sure she wanted to share her memory-making moments with Hayden Calloway, even if he had agreed to go with her. Though she was wildly curious to find out more about what he'd been doing since high school and how he'd ended up in Europe.

"We're going to leave soon to get something to eat," he said. "If you're bored I can take you back to . . ."

"Oh, no. I'm not bored at all." She glanced at her watch. "It's only nine o'clock. It's early, isn't it?"

"By Italian standards, it is. But you're not Italian."

"Neither are you. I don't mind the late hour. I'm worried, actually."

"What about?"

"My friend Stephanie is in Milan on business. She was going to call me sometime tonight at our hotel. I know she's going to be concerned when she finds I never checked in."

Pulling his cell phone from the clip on his belt, Hayden handed it to her. "Why don't you try to call the hotel? Find out if she's left a message."

"Thanks," April said, gratefully accepting the unit.

"I'll add it to your bill," he said dryly.

April was pleased that he was being so helpful with her problems, but she was fully convinced that Hayden would call in his marker, sooner or later.

She located the hotel's business card and punched in the Botticelli's phone number. The manager remembered her and said that there had been a call from Ms. Kingston, who left her number in Milan. April scribbled it down on the edge of one of the restaurant coasters, disconnected, and then called Stephanie who went into a tirade of relief, disbelief, anger, and sympathy.

"I'm fine, Steph," April reassured her friend over and over again. "I'm not being held prisoner . . ."

"Well who are these people who've taken you in?"

"Signor Cesso is a doctor, and his wife seems to be in the habit of rescuing people. They couldn't be nicer. I'm perfectly safe, don't worry."

Although Hayden had turned his attention back to Simone, April had a suspicion that he was eavesdropping.

"Girl, I was ready to call in the local authorities when I couldn't find you. The manager at the hotel told me what happened."

"I'm so sorry. So much has been going on. It's been incredible. I didn't know how to reach you."

"So what happens now? The consulate is in Milan, and they're the only ones who can issue a new passport."

"One of the duty officers is a friend of the Cessos'," April assured Stephanie. "He's here in Venice and is going to help me."

Hayden glanced at her. He *was* listening.

"Really? Who?"

"I'll tell you all about it when you get here. When do you think you'll arrive? Tomorrow?"

"That's one of the reasons I was trying to reach you. The airport mechanics are on strike in Milan. By the time I realized what was going on it was too late to reserve a seat on the train and they've all sold out. I've booked a seat the day after tomorrow."

"You're kidding."

"The Italians go on strike at the drop of a hat."

"Stephanie . . ."

"It'll work out. I'm just glad you're safe and someone is on the case with your papers. Can I reach you on his phone if I run into another snafu?"

"I don't know. Hang on," she said. She turned to Hayden and asked him if he would mind if she gave Stephanie his cell number. She repeated both his number and the Cessos', which he gave her as well, to Stephanie.

"Sexy voice. Is he cute?"

The question surprised April, and then made her laugh. Hayden looked at her again. Afraid that he might guess that he was being talked about she turned away slightly before saying, "Yes, as a matter of fact."

"Has he hit on you yet?"

"Of course not."

"He will. Girl, you are something else. I leave you alone for a few hours and look what happens. I'm sorry your first day in Venice turned out to be a bust."

April looked back at Hayden. He raised his brows, silently asking if everything was working out.

"On the contrary. Stephanie, my first day was fabulous."

Chapter 3

By the time Hayden located April the next morning, he was ready to cut her loose. He'd told her the night before that he'd see her in the morning. But when he'd arrived at the Cesso home, he was told that 'the signorina is out.'

"Out? Out where?" Hayden questioned, exasperated. It's not like she had friends or family in Venice.

"Out," Marina clarified with a shrug. "She wake up early and go out to see the neighborhood. You go look for her. You will find her."

It hadn't taken him long. Seeing her safe, Hayden wondered why he'd been angry. She was seated at a bistro table outside a local bar, the kind where Italians would typically stop each morning to get breakfast: a sandwich or pastry and a cappuccino. Hayden stopped across the piazza, taking a moment to simply look.

She was wearing a simple, pale-yellow sundress that showed quite a bit of her shapely legs, which were crossed at the knee, one stylish sandal hanging from her toes as she flexed her foot back and forth. Her ears were double-pierced, and she wore both small gold hoops and studs. Her hair was tied away from her face with a printed scarf folded down to headband width. And her face . . .

She was slowly munching on a half-eaten *panini* and sipping from a cup of frothy cappuccino, the milk leaving a faint hint of white on her upper lip in stark contrast to her rich, milk-chocolate complexion. Her eyes, protected from the early morning sun by a pair of dark glasses, were hidden, but he knew their almost-black depths would reflect intense interest and humor.

She was studiously poring over the pages of a book. She seemed not only very much at home, but also content. So why had he imagined that she'd gotten herself lost and needed to be rescued?

Hayden remembered April as a pretty girl, not like a model, but way above average. She didn't have that thang that some black girls got too early: a full-developed body where the booty and boobs were the only identifying attributes. In school she'd been tall and skinny, her chest nearly flat—but, he thought in appreciation, she'd certainly outgrown that. She was great-looking with a grown-up attractiveness that appealed to him; slender but not thin, breasts perfectly rounded, and a smile that brightened her face and everything around her.

But it was more than her looks that caught his attention. Hayden recalled that April was really smart, an honor-roll student on the President's List of Young American Scholars. She was admired by all the teachers for it, and shunned by all the popular students, most of whom had accused her of being snooty. It couldn't have been easy for her to deal. It wasn't that she was a snob; she just didn't run with his crowd. She was classy, too good for most of the guys at school . . . including himself. He was never sure if she was shy or just didn't like him, but every time their paths would cross, she'd only acknowledge him if no one else was around. And then it was a quick "Hi" before she rushed off. He assumed she just didn't want anything to do with someone who didn't take school seriously. Back then, April had also reminded him too much of his older brother, Reese. Only two years Hayden's senior, Reese, like April, was a top student, a really hard act to follow. Hayden knew he could never live up to his brother's legend, so he hadn't bothered to try.

Hayden took several deep breaths and shook off his memories. From the moment he'd seen her in Marina and Antonio's courtyard and April had blurted out a name he hadn't heard in more than fifteen years, he'd felt like he had come face-to-face with his past. It had unnerved him that she'd recognized him instantly. Remembering her had taken a few seconds longer, if only because the images in his memory were stuck in time.

He'd thought about it the whole night and tried to make the necessary adjustment from what he remembered about her to the woman she'd become. Still achingly beautiful, she now had a woman's confidence that made her more appealing to him than she'd been when they were younger. He'd have to watch out, or she could, unknowingly, affect him again. More than he wanted to deal with.

A waiter sauntered from inside the restaurant to where April was reading. She beamed at him and pointed to her book. He leaned—too closely, Hayden observed—over her shoulders to read the text she indicated.

Feeling foolish standing just twenty feet away, Hayden started toward her table. She was laughing, the waiter speaking to her slowly, carefully pronouncing his words.

"Good morning." Hayden smoothly announced his arrival, his gaze boring into the waiter, who took the subtle hint and quickly moved several steps back. "I'll have one," Hayden said, pointing to her cup. He sat in the vacated chair. The waiter hurried away to fill his order.

"*Buon giorno.*" April smiled at him. Her glasses were so

dark he had no hint of the expression in her eyes. "You found me. Were you looking for very long?"

"It's a small district. I had an idea where to go."

"It feels so strange having cappuccino for breakfast. I'm used to having it after dinner back home."

"Well, there you go," Hayden said. "You're not in Kansas anymore, Dorothy."

She grinned and shook her head at his comeback. "Don't you work or something? You seem to have a lot of free time."

"I guess Marina didn't tell you I don't actually live in Venice. Like you, I'm on a break this week. Even though I'm with the American consulate in Milan, most of the people I know and hang with are here in Venice."

"Couldn't you have flown back home to the States to see your family?"

"I decided not to, and it's a good thing for you that I didn't."

Her smile became wry and apologetic. "You're right. I'm very grateful for your help, Hayden. Sorry if I haven't already said so."

"Not enough," Hayden said, taking the sting away with a subtle grin.

He could see April was stunned by his reply. Then she started laughing.

"Are you going to force me to give up my firstborn male child, or something like that?"

Hayden leaned back in his chair, the upper part of his body easing into the shadow of the building. He pressed his lips to keep from breaking out in a grin and said, solemnly, "Do you have a firstborn male child? What would your ex say about a deal like that?"

April shifted uncomfortably in her chair. Her smile didn't completely disappear, but Hayden could tell he'd struck a sensitive nerve.

"I've been divorced for almost six years. There's only Anesa. Sorry."

"You don't owe me an apology."

April averted her gaze momentarily, but she was calm and open. "I'm not. These things happen. It was for the best as far as I'm concerned."

He shifted, uncomfortable with where the conversation had moved. He asked, instead, "What are you reading?"

"The section on the Jewish Ghetto," April said, as eager as he to change the subject. "I think the waiter was asking me if I'd ever been to Italy before. In Italian, of course," she said, bemused. "What does *affasinare* mean? He kept saying that word to me."

Hayden let his gaze wander over her face. "It means 'charming.' He was scoping you out, flirting with you."

"Please," she said skeptically.

"It's true. Italian men are big flirts. They love women." Hayden watched her adjust her glasses nervously, but he could tell the idea pleased her.

"I'm here to sightsee, not flirt."

"Just go about your business and be yourself. You'll get more attention than you know what to do with."

The waiter reappeared with his cappuccino. Hayden settled back to sip it.

"I think that was a compliment," she murmured, peering at him through her sunglasses.

"Just an observation," he murmured innocently.

She sat back, letting it go. But Hayden felt a little peeved for perhaps saying too much.

"Here's the plan. We'll get a passport picture taken and express it to Milan. I'll call and tell them to expedite your new passport. Then we can stop by the American Express office to see if your new credit card has been issued. How does that sound?"

"Not a whole lot of fun," she said, wrinkling her nose. "I was hoping to just walk around a bit and explore. Maybe browse some of the shops. Have some Italian ice cream——"

"Gelato."

"Right. And I was told that the secret tour of the Doge's Palace is a lot of fun."

"Business first, then we can play," Hayden stated firmly.

"You're mean."

He chuckled. "I've been called worse," he said, finishing the cappuccino.

April stuffed her guidebook into her large tote. "How do you like living in Italy? I have to tell you I think you're very lucky."

"Do you? How come?"

"Because this is great! You're actually living and working in another country. Don't you find that exciting?"

"I guess I don't see it that way," Hayden said honestly. "My job just happens to be overseas. It's still work."

"You don't make it sound very romantic," April sighed.

"It isn't romantic, at least not to me."

"Too bad," April said, accepting her bill from the waiter and opening her purse to get her wallet. "I think you're missing half the adventure. I know when you were in high school you probably never thought of leaving Philly."

"You're wrong. I definitely wanted to get out. I just didn't know where I wanted to go." Hayden glanced around. "Nothing I planned worked out the way I thought it would."

"Isn't that the truth," April murmured, her smile rueful. "I always wanted to live in Europe. I thought it would make me seem sophisticated and worldly. I thought maybe France, or Spain."

"Italy is great, but it took me a while to get used to being here. People are pretty friendly, and I like them. Like Santiago and his family. Marina Cesso treats me like another son.

I admit that's nice. But sometimes . . ." Hayden paused and shrugged. "I think I could kill for some black music. I miss fried chicken, macaroni and cheese, my grandmother's pecan pie. Things like that."

April nodded in understanding, but Hayden suddenly wished he hadn't revealed so much.

"Are you and Simone dating?"

He was stunned by the question, but then laughed. "Man. You just put it out there, don't you?"

Hayden understood April's curiosity, but to explain what he was to Simone Renault would have meant confessing to his own naiveté when he'd first come to Europe. His libido had received a swift kick in the ass with his first few forays in dating European women.

He'd met Simone on his first getaway to Venice. Santiago had invited him for the weekend. Simone had been at the club they'd gone to and he'd been immediately drawn to her because she was black, the only thing they had in common, as it turned out. She'd put the move on him first, a relief after the coy games of the sistahs back home. He got really turned on by her cool sophistication. He'd enjoyed the way she stalked him with her sultry eyes and body language. Her invitation had been up front and *very* personal.

It wasn't that they'd tired of one another, exactly. She was more sexually adventuresome than any woman he'd ever known. And that may have been the problem. Her accusation that he was too provincial and too American was true. Casual sex just wasn't his thing. They became an on-again, off-again couple, with nonexclusive rights and the freedom to see whom they pleased. But they'd remained friends. That had been an important breakthrough—that he could actually be friends with a woman. He wished suddenly that he'd been able to have that kind of friendship with April. Maybe if he'd had that with her in high school, it might have made the difference now, seeing her again after so many years. Or, maybe not.

"I don't mean to get into your business," April said, bringing his attention back to the present, "but . . . I take it you're not married. I'm curious about how dating works over here. What I mean is, Simone's black. I haven't seen any other black people since leaving the airport. I just thought . . ."

He narrowed his gaze at her. "I don't remember you being this nosy."

April looked only slightly shamefaced. "Well, unless I ask, I'll never know. And I'm surprised you remember anything about me at all. I wasn't exactly one of the "in" crowd. No one paid much attention to me."

Hayden took advantage of the shift in conversation and snatched the check from her hand, putting it together with his. He gave them both to the waiter, with euros. "You're the one who reminded me you're on vacation. No thinking allowed. No third degree." Hayden handed her the tote. "Let's go." He steered her out into the street. She half ran to keep up, and tripped over one of the cobblestones. He grabbed her arm, steadying her, and was rewarded with a grateful smile.

Hayden made no attempt at conversation as they walked. April silently followed his lead but didn't really try to keep pace with him. He glanced at her and then at the time. They were behind schedule. It took a moment for Hayden to remember he wasn't on any deadline. And while there was a lot to get done, April seemed to be operating on her own time, and she wasn't about to be hurried. Hayden took a deep breath and patiently tried to settle down to her speed.

April was looking all around, her attention captured by the small details of everyday life in Venice. She stopped to glance in shops, to watch an older woman argue with a vendor over the quality of his onions, to listen to people at Mass as their voices drifted out from the open doors of a small church.

Every now and then she stopped to take a photograph. Hayden couldn't believe the things that interested her, things he'd never paid any attention to before.

April fell behind, and Hayden turned to see what held her curiosity this time. She was staring through the window of a bar at an array of pastries and cakes. Inside, a young waiter beckoned, encouraging her to step into the shop. April shook her head but mouthed a "thank you" for the offer. The man disappeared only to reappear seconds later at the doorway with a small plate of what looked like cream puffs. He said, in rapid Italian, that it would be the greatest pleasure for such a beautiful lady to sample his pastries. April stood listening as if she understood, Hayden thought in amusement. Then she thanked him and turned away. Even as she walked to where Hayden stood and waited, he could hear the waiter's persuasive entreaty.

"He's persistent," April remarked, a hint of laughter in her voice.

"I told you. Italian men like women. All shapes, ages, and colors. Would you like a pastry?"

"Absolutely not. Otherwise I'm in serious trouble. That piece of pastry will end up right on my hips."

"I don't think you have anything to worry about."

She raised her brows. "Another compliment? In high school I was called "Stickwood" instead of Stockwood because I was so skinny."

"I didn't know that," Hayden said.

"Stuff like that got around," she said easily. "I knew you were called 'Cutter,' and I knew why."

"It never bothered me. Yeah, I cut classes and school a lot, but the only subject I got a D in was Chemistry. A D is not an F. And I did graduate."

"Well, I *did* care what I was called. Maybe it's a girl thing," April admitted quietly as they had to sidestep the increasing numbers of people on the narrow streets. "I was too thin, and I know I didn't wear cool clothes. And I know the boys didn't pay any attention to me. 'Miss Goody Two-shoes' was another name I was called by."

Hayden looked sharply at her but wisely said nothing.

She grinned wistfully. "I knew about that one, too."

"What difference does it make?" he asked. "You were smart. You were going places. All you had to do was survive."

"You're right. You can survive anything when you have to."

Hayden saw her expression change and wondered, but when she remained silent, he didn't pursue it. Could it be as bad as what he'd gone through?

"We'll take the *vaporetto* over to San Marco," he said. "And go to the American Express office. You can get your passport picture at a photo studio there as well. While we're near the square we might—"

Hayden had to stop again when he realized April was nowhere in sight. Frowning, he muttered an oath. What was it with her?

He slowly retraced his steps, glancing into the open shops on either side of the street, checking the other pedestrians that passed him. His puzzled expression was close to being thunderous when he saw her amble out of a store, her wallet and a small bag in her hands. She glanced up and, seeing him, managed to look only innocently contrite.

"I'm walking and talking to myself. I look around and you're gone from sight." He knew there was an edge to his voice.

"I'm sorry. That store had really pretty postcards and I had to buy one to send home to Anesa."

He thought better of saying anything, and turned toward the waterfront and the *vaporetti* stop about twenty yards away. He'd been in Italy for going on two years, and he couldn't recall sending postcards to a single person in all that time.

"I promise not to do that again. If I want to stop I'll say so, okay?" April said.

He clenched his jaw and forced himself to remain calm. "It's easy to get turned around and lost in Venice. You don't want to have another bad day like yesterday."

April shook her head, puzzled. "Yesterday wasn't a bad day at all. I lost my passport but I had a wonderful first day."

He sighed, defeated. "Fine. Let's have some sort of signal between us, okay? If you want to stop to check something out—"

"I'll say, 'Hayden, can we stop for a minute?'"

"That works for me. And if I think we're running really late I'll say, 'T minus ten minutes and counting.'"

"Fine with me. One more thing . . . please, don't get impatient with me," April added, her voice soft, but firm.

"I'm not impatient. I . . ." Hayden wanted to defend himself, but reconsidered when he felt his voice hardening, and saw her eyebrows rising. "Okay. You're right. I didn't mean to sound off like that."

"My ex-husband was always impatient with me, always lecturing me, always pointing out my shortcomings. I hated it."

April's unexpected confession had a strange affect on him. Hayden didn't know squat about her ex, but he knew he didn't want to be compared to him.

"I'm used to just getting things done fast," Hayden offered by way of explanation and apology.

"I don't want to rush. Look, I know this is really awkward for both of us, all right? I know you resent getting involved in my little crisis. Just because we went to the same high school doesn't mean we know each other. So, I'll understand if you want to go your own way. I'll manage. I'm an adult. I'm not afraid of being alone, or getting lost."

Hayden listened to her earnest little disclaimer, taken aback by her declaration of independence. She didn't need him. Maybe he had been mixing up the past with the present. If there was one thing that Hayden was sure of, it was that April had grown up into a surprisingly strong woman. His smart but reserved classmate was full of life—and fearless.

"I guess you're forming a really bad impression of me," Hayden said.

She watched his face carefully, and Hayden could see the warmth returning to soften her features. As a matter of fact, April now had a wide range of emotions displayed in her eyes and in her smile.

"That's not true. Back in high school, you didn't seem to take anything seriously. Always making people laugh. But I am impressed with how you've changed. I know when you look at me you also see someone different. So why don't we begin there, okay? We're not teenagers anymore. A lot of years have passed, but we're both still standing. I'd say it's a good thing we grew up." She looked him up and down. "You've reinvented yourself, and from what I see you've done a good job. Mostly."

"Mostly?"

She ignored his query. "But I'm still a work in progress. I make mistakes, I like trying new things, and I keep going."

He pursed his mouth rather than grin at her quick sound bites. He found her expression and mannerisms animated, her personality frighteningly honest. That alone was a novelty.

"So you're really saying I'm full of myself," Hayden ventured.

"Your words, not mine," she grinned.

April found that Hayden was true to his word about all the stops they had to make in order to complete the process of applying for her new documents. And even though it was all on her behalf, she felt surprisingly indifferent. If not for her daughter and a job back home, she would have made an adventure out of it; maybe tried to arrange to stay longer in Italy, find a job, a place to live, or simply hang loose. The idea of being unattached and not responsible for anyone but herself was appealing, even if just for a while.

She felt her precious time in Venice slipping away. Eight days boiled down to five after taking into consideration two days lost to travel and yesterday's adventure. April stuck the replacement airline e-ticket in her purse. She now had a way to get home, although it was ironic to learn that without a valid passport she would not be allowed back into the U.S. And she still didn't have a credit card, which meant she didn't have access to any money.

"I'm sure the card will get here tomorrow," Hayden said as they left the American Express office. He looked at his watch. "It's getting late. Do you still want to—"

"Yes," April jumped in.

"You don't even know what I'm going to say."

"Hayden, it doesn't matter. I'm in Venice for the first time in my life. I want to do everything. I know I can't, but I want to try."

"Let's stick with the 'try' version," he said dryly. "We'll keep plans small for now. If we hustle a bit we can still boat over to Burano and Murano."

"Okay. Which island is which? I remember reading that one has to do with making glass. How big are they?"

"I don't know," Hayden shrugged, guiding her through the congested alleyway leading to San Marco Square. She tripped again and he quickly took hold of her hand. "I've never been to either of them."

April glanced up at his handsome, strong profile. His hand, wrapped around hers, was large and firm. She didn't object to the support he offered.

"I thought you said you've been in Italy for almost two years."

"That's right."

"Well, what have you been doing? What do you think I should see while I'm here?"

Hayden tugged gently on her hand to direct her past the Campanile and the Doge's Palace toward the waterfront. "I don't know. I haven't seen all that much."

"Why?" April asked, astonished.

"I just haven't. I don't know anything about art, and I don't remember much from history except stuff about Napoleon, the Civil War, and Hitler."

"Those are all about wars and killing people."

Hayden suddenly stopped. "Look, I've made a suggestion but what do you want to do?"

It was on the tip of April's tongue to tell Hayden that what she wanted was a companion who'd be as excited as she was to explore every last inch of Venice: to poke into the alleys and small streets filled with color and people from everywhere; to turn a corner and be awestruck by a building that had stood in the same spot for centuries; to listen to the beauty of an operatic aria as she leaned over a bridge railing to watch a gondola pass. What she didn't want was to share those experiences with someone who couldn't see the wonder and beauty all around him. But curiosity held her back. What had happened to the Hayden Calloway from high school? The lanky teen who was funny, who thought nothing of challenging the teachers, whose natural leadership ability and mesmerizing personality kept him out of trouble. How did *that* Hayden come to be replaced with this wonky bureaucrat?

"Let's do the two islands. Maybe they'll be fun," April responded to end the what-do-you-want-to-do, no-what-do-*you*-want-to-do discussion.

And they were, interesting and small and charming although she thought that Burano, the island known for its traditional lace-making, was prettier. Many of the small houses and buildings were painted in eye-catching, bright crayon colors. The shops, all catering to the tourists, sold bed linens, clothing, table accessories, and souvenirs, all made of or with lace, the same products repeated store after store.

April was both surprised and pleased when Hayden, rather than becoming bored as she thought he would be, willingly . . . or at least silently, for the most part . . . followed her around as she wandered in and out of the charming shops. She learned that authentic Italian handmade lace was expensive because crafting it was tedious and time-consuming work. In Italy, it was legal to claim that consumer goods were Italian-made if the assembly was done in Italy. But much of the lace-making was actually done by machine in China. With the help of an older Italian woman willing to point out the genuine thing, April quickly learned to tell the difference.

"What are you going to buy?" Hayden asked. "I know we're not leaving here until you have something to take back home."

"I can't afford—"

"I'll pay for everything. You can owe me."

"Hayden, no. I can't accept any money from you. I'll wait until I get—"

"You won't have time to come back. You can't go home without a present for your daughter. Besides, I expect you to repay me. This is a loan."

Seeing her conflicted expression, Hayden winked at her. "Want to write me an IOU? Will that make you feel better?"

"No. But I will pay you back. I don't want you to think that . . . like I'm trying to . . ."

"I know you're not. You're not that kind of woman. Do you think charging an interest rate of twenty-five percent is too high?"

It was a minute before she realized he was joking, and she shook her head and laughed. "I can see my daughter in this lace skirt and top." She carefully examined both the design and craftsmanship. "Isn't this beautiful?"

When he remained silent, she glanced up. He was considering her, an unreadable expression on his face. He reached behind her and removed an exquisitely detailed dress from the rack. She stood still while he held it up in front of her and scrutinized the effect. The bodice outlined her breasts, the skirt hem brushing against her knees. She was suddenly too aware of Hayden's innocent touch.

"You should get this for yourself," he said abruptly. "You'd look really good in it."

"Really?" April asked. "Isn't it a little revealing? There's not much to the top."

"You've got the figure for it. I like this one. What do you call this color?" His voice was warm and friendly.

April realized he wasn't trying to be fresh or funny, and she was gratified to have her instincts confirmed that he wasn't manipulative or slick. She suspected it would have been understandable if Hayden were a player. After all, he was good-looking and smart and probably would not be classified, in the words of Stephanie, a dog. In April's mind, Hayden was anything but.

"Oh . . . eh . . . I think you would call this a pale peach. Or apricot," she said.

Hayden chuckled and handed her the garment. "I would have said pink."

"You would have been wrong."

"Yeah, well . . . peach and apricot were not colors in my crayon box when I was a kid."

April laughed. She looked longingly at the dress Hayden had selected for her then firmly returned it to the rack. She held up the skirt and top. "I think I'll take this for my daughter. I hope she likes it. Do you mind if I look around for something for my mother and sister."

"But nothing for yourself?"

"Hayden, this trip is my gift to me. I'm satisfied."

"And easy to please," he observed quietly.

After he'd paid for her daughter's outfit, Hayden suggested that they catch the boat to Murano. On the short ride over, Hayden asked her about her life since high school. She deliberately avoided talking about her marriage and divorce, concentrating instead on her work.

"I became an English teacher."

"A teacher?" he said in some surprise, "I can see that but I kind of thought you'd become something bigger. How do you like teaching?"

"I quit. About seven or eight years ago."

"Why?"

She thought about her answer before speaking and he was aware that she was editing the content.

"It began to feel like a dead-end job. Students in, students out. They're not really interested in good grammar or literature. I decided to do something that might be more useful to them."

Hayden lounged back against the railing. "Something useful? How to balance a checkbook? How to nail a job interview?"

"Hmmm. That's close," April responded. "I wanted to teach them how to be explorers."

Hayden had to admit it sounded unusual, and innovative. She proceeded to explain seeing his quizzical expression.

"I found that students never see beyond their own neighborhood. They never think about traveling or trying new foods or even learning a new language. Not because they have to, but because it's different and fun."

"And educational on the side?" he asked. She grinned. "Sneaky. So where is this place where you work?"

April, leaning next to him, turned to face him. "I started an organization called Step Up, Step Out. The big thing I'm working on now is encouraging them to seek internships, not in their local community, but in other parts of the world. What do you think?"

He was impressed. "It sounds ambitious. Having any success?"

"It's a new concept. The jury's still out."

The boat docked in Murano, and they prepared to disembark. April stepped from the *vaporetto* onto the landing. The dock was uneven, and she caught her heel. She felt herself tripping and grabbed blindly for his hand, trying to keep her balance. Steadied, she glanced down at the wispy sandals on her feet.

"This is what I get for trying to be so cute," she said, half-amused and half-annoyed, wondering if wearing such stylish sandals had been a good idea.

"You are cute," Hayden said agreeing. "But do yourself a favor and wear something more practical tomorrow."

It was the first mention that he expected to be with her the next day. The idea was fast becoming appealing. He tugged at her hand—firm, protective and caring, and said, "Would you also like me to carry you?"

April made a face at him and pulled her hand free.

Murano had a more industrial, modern look than its sister island. They watched a demonstration of glass blowing with interest, even Hayden was fascinated by the process and technique. April diligently searched for gifts for special friends and for her family. She found a pair of glass earrings and a matching pendant for her sister, June, and a handblown red glass bowl for her mother.

"This bowl will do my mom's potato salad justice," April said.

"It's heavy. I hope you're not planning to carry it home with you," Hayden commented.

"How else will it get back to Philly?"

"Ship it," he said.

And it was a done deal. April stood by while he instructed the shopkeeper how to package the glass bowl, requesting that it be insured. April provided her address to Hayden as he completed the shipping forms.

"You're so efficient," April observed when they left the shop.

"Just lazy," he shrugged. "I don't like carrying a lot of stuff myself. But you women . . . man, you become pack mules."

She giggled at his comment and realized that, despite her initial reaction, she was enjoying his company. While it was true that he was much more serious than he had been in high school, in the moments when he seemed to lighten up, he could be funny and good company.

"Where to now, oh great leader?"

He chuckled silently. "It's up to you. I'm only here to obey and serve."

April shook her head. "I don't think so. Besides, I don't need you to serve me. This is your time as well. I'm willing to bow to your opinion."

"Okay," he said, leading her back to the pier to wait for a waterbus. "Then let's head back to San Marco Square."

"For?" she prompted.

"You'll find out when we get there."

"I don't like the sound of that."

"What happened to bowing to my opinion?" he asked dryly.

"Maybe I spoke too hastily."

"Relax. You're going to like it," Hayden assured her as they boarded the *vaporetto* and found seats.

Contented, April sighed, settling onto the hard wooden bench. She glanced around at the other passengers, the majority tourists, then looked out at the wide expanse of the water and the skyline of domed churches and pillared palazzos on the far shore. Every scene was a postcard image.

"What are you thinking? Is Venice living up to the hype?"

"You have no idea," she said quietly, her eyes still riveted to the vista.

"What is it about Venice?" Hayden asked.

"It's not just Venice," April said, swiveling to face him. "It's anything and everything outside of Philadelphia. I mean . . . Philly is home, and you grow up knowing everyone in the neighborhood and all the kids in school, and after a while it's the same people all the time. And everybody knows everybody else's business. I wanted to get out and see more."

"Why?" Hayden asked.

"Why?" April repeated, as if the answer should have been obvious to him. "Because I knew the world had to be bigger. I didn't want to treat Spain and Africa and China like they were just places on a map, or something I was force-fed in history class. I wanted to see them. I wanted to experience other cultures."

"So, all your life you've been trying to get out of town," Hayden surmised.

April grinned ruefully and shook her head. "No, not really. I just wanted to know I *could* try new things. Go places and see the world."

Hayden sat back, casually laying an arm along the top of the seat behind April's head. He nodded. "*I* always knew you would."

"You did?"

"In school I figured you were going to do something big, like become a senator, or a lawyer, or CEO somewhere. I think what you're doing is more important."

"Thank you. That's nice to hear."

The *vaporetto* began to fill with more passengers. Hayden moved her packages from the seat to his lap, and then slid close to her, making room for an older Italian woman. He kept his arm on the seat back, her shoulder scant inches from his chest. She took a furtive glance into his face and realized she could see how closely he'd shaved that morning, realized she could smell the faint odor of sandalwood soap clinging to his skin. She turned her head to gaze at his strong profile.

"What were your dreams? What did you want to do when you were in high school?"

"To get out as fast as I could."

"I'm serious, Hayden."

He sighed, his eyes reflecting a sudden pain. He squinted off into the distance. "To do anything that would make my mother proud of me."

"Is she? Of course she must be."

Slowly, Hayden removed his arm. She watched his shoulders tense and his mouth become stiff. He clasped and rotated his hands together until the knuckles cracked.

"I don't know," Hayden responded finally. "She's never said so." Forestalling any more questions, he said, "This is our stop."

Hayden gathered her packages as the boat slowly glided to a stop against the wharf at San Marco, and they got off.

April recognized the stop, San Marco Zaccaria, where she'd first disembarked from the *Alilaguna* the day before. They crossed a bridge, dodging and maneuvering around a large Japanese tour group and hundreds of bored-looking teenagers on school trips.

"We're here," Hayden said.

April looked around, confused as to what "here" meant. Then he smiled and steered her to a small stand. She saw the open air shop and what it was selling. It was the same stand that Andrew and Lilly St. Clair had used as a landmark when they directed her to her hotel.

"Real Italian ice cream," she said, her voice containing

delight. All the colors of the rainbow were represented in the gelato the man was selling.

"What would you like?" Hayden asked.

"I don't suppose he'll let me sample all the flavors?"

"I doubt it. But if you have gelato twice a day until you have to go home you'll probably make a dent."

April settled on a gigantic waffle cone filled with scoops of amaretto, pistachio, and banana.

"Aren't you getting one?" April asked as she savored the cool feeling, letting her tongue roll a gob of it into her mouth.

"I'd rather watch you," Hayden said. "You better hurry up. It's starting to melt." They walked past the church and found a seat for themselves on a stone step.

"I'm . . . licking . . . as fast as I . . . can," April said.

But the already-soft, creamy-textured ice cream was quickly melting in the afternoon sun. Hayden laughed. The ice cream drips were winning the race against time.

"Here, let me help," he said.

April held out the cone. Instead of taking it from her, Hayden wrapped his hand around hers and bent forward. April watched the deliberate motion of Hayden's tongue and lips gaining control of the dripping cone with long precise licks. Then he sat back and let her hand go. He wiped his mouth with a paper napkin.

"Can you finish the rest?" he asked.

"Yes," she responded, staring at the depleted mound of ice cream. Not because there was less, but because it was marked by him in a way that felt far too personal.

She had a moment of déjà vu: being in high school and hoping that Hayden would miraculously notice her and ask her out. It seemed absurd to April that she would be revisited with that thought now. She'd outgrown the past, outgrown childish daydreams, had withstood the disappointment of half a dozen unfulfilled desires in her adult life, and had survived far worse.

Quietly and thoughtfully, she finished the cone, feeling embarrassed and very conscious of the tracks left by Hayden. She had no explanation for the surge of her wishful thinking now, that was decidedly grown-up in nature.

Chapter 4

Hayden rose and balanced her packages with ease.

"We'd better head back to the Cessos."

It *was* getting late, April realized. He'd given up an entire day to spend with her. He'd been very gracious, not complaining or appearing bored or impatient. She stood as well and together they headed to the nearest *vaporetto*.

"Let's take this shortcut," Hayden said, guiding her through a small alley to another street where, much to April's surprise, several black men were lined along the street selling handbags and totes, their wares displayed on a piece of canvas spread out on the promenade. She turned to Hayden for an explanation.

"They're West African. They sell knockoffs."

April slowed to take a look. Each of the West Africans was vying for the same customers. Four of the men, seeing she was black, rushed to get her attention.

"Sistah, you buy. I give you good deal," one said to April, holding up an armful of bags.

"Is that a Fendi?" April asked Hayden in awe, discreetly pointing to a shoulder bag.

"I don't know," Hayden shrugged. "I don't use handbags myself."

April rolled her eyes at him.

"Sistah, over here. See what I can sell you," another called. "Fendi. Laurent. Beautiful, yes?"

"Hayden, I think these are the real thing," she said sotto voce.

"Could be. But it's illegal in Italy to sell or buy designer merchandise off the street. And it's illegal to bring them back to the United States if they're not real."

She gnawed her lip. "But if they are real . . ." She looked through a small Louis Vuitton bag, examining the lining and the leather. "How much?"

"Ninety euros," one eager vendor told her.

April thrust the bag back into his hands and scoffed. "Ridiculous." She turned to Hayden. "How do you say ridiculous in Italian?"

Hayden grinned. "Don't worry. He understood."

"Fifty euros. Just for you, sistah. Good deal."

April shook her head and tried to walk around the persistent salesman who attempted to block her path. "Too expensive," she said.

"What you pay? Tell me. I give it to you for good price. You like me, sistah," he insisted.

April knew he was making reference to both of them being black. But she wasn't sure that skin color was going to cut it as a real bargaining point.

She indicated the small Vuitton bag. "Twenty euros."

"You trying to beggar me good," he protested, turning away in disappointment.

April picked a tote with the Fendi logo. She looked over her shoulder at Hayden. He was watching with an expression that was a cross between skepticism, amazement, and humor. "What do you think?"

"I think you're going to end up in jail," Hayden said caustically, looking around the street in case there were actually any police patrolling.

"This for thirty," she told the vendor. "I'll take them both for fifty euros."

"I think I should remind you that you're broke," Hayden whispered dryly.

"No, no! Seventy for everything. Seventy euros. You take. Good price," the vendor complained.

"No," April said firmly, prepared to walk away.

"Okay, okay sistah. I give you. Fifty for two."

April waved off Hayden's attempt to pay for the two bags. She dug through her purse and wallet and triumphantly managed to come up with the money. When the exchange was completed, April and Hayden walked away. She gloated, putting all of her packages into the larger tote.

"I'm impressed," Hayden said. "I didn't know you had a black belt in shopping."

April giggled, pleased with herself and her purchases. "Is it really illegal to buy from the African vendors or were you just trying to discourage me from spending any more of your money?" April asked.

"No, what I told you was the truth."

"Now I feel guilty. But it was a good deal. And the vendors didn't act like they were afraid of being arrested."

"I noticed my warning didn't make a bit of difference. You're not out of the woods, yet. Customs could take them from you at the airport when you leave the country. And the same could happen when you go through customs in Philly."

"Do you think it will help my case if I smile and say it was a gift for my daughter?" April asked.

Hayden reached for his cell phone and flipped it open. "You have a great smile . . . but I'm not sure it will keep you from being detained. Hello? Yeah, hi. You want to speak with

April." He suddenly laughed. "I'm an old friend. Sure, she's right here . . . Stephanie," he said, giving April his phone.

"Hi, Stephanie. Where are you?"

"I'm at the Milan airport. The strike is over and I think I'll make the last flight this afternoon to Venice. And as *soon* as we get together I want to know about your 'old friend.' How in the world did you manage to meet up with someone you know from home? Is this the same guy who's helping you with your passport?"

April wasn't sure if Hayden was listening or not, so she ignored Stephanie's question. "That's great that you're finally leaving Milan. So what time do you think you'll get here?"

"It'll be late this evening. Where are you now . . . with your 'old friend'?"

"I was out all day seeing some sights and shopping. I can meet you later at the hotel."

"Don't bother. That's too much of a hassle. Just come in the morning. I called the hotel to make sure we could still get a room."

"I didn't even think of that," April said.

"I've stayed there before, so they were good about it. So everything is okay with you?"

"Yes, I'm doing great. I got a replacement airline ticket for my flight home. I'm still waiting for a new credit card and my passport," April said.

"What about meals and things?"

"It, er . . . that's being taken care of," April said carefully.

"That sounds like your 'old friend' again. I want details and up-to-the-minute news when I see you."

"Okay. See you tomorrow, Steph." April closed the unit and handed it back to Hayden. "She'll be here tonight. I told her I'd rejoin her tomorrow at the hotel, assuming my passport arrives by then."

"I could speak with Antonio and Marina. I don't think they

would mind your staying with them for the rest of your trip," Hayden suggested as they stood waiting for a *vaporetto*.

"I couldn't. They've been incredibly kind to me, but I don't want to wear out my welcome. Also, it wouldn't be fair to Stephanie. We were supposed to be making this trip together." April looked at Hayden. "And it wouldn't be fair to you. You said this week was supposed to be a break for you, and you've already lost two days because of me."

He shrugged, his expression unreadable. "I wouldn't say the time was wasted or a hardship. I'm starting to enjoy myself. And I'm still curious to know what happened to the April Stockwood whom I heard was valedictorian of her class."

April averted her gaze, shaking her head somewhat shyly. "Things change. She woke up one day and realized that her life was not what she'd hoped it would be."

April checked her room to make sure she'd left something out to wear the next morning. She'd packed, assuming that her paperwork would be in order and that she'd meet up with Stephanie at the hotel. She was astonished to realize that her purchases in the last twenty-four hours made closing her suitcase a challenge. Pensively, she wandered to the large window and stood gazing out. It was dusk, and the setting sun spread a veil of warm colors over the sky. April's eyes quickly adjusted to the subtle remaining light that cast a magical and mysterious aura over the city. She could hear the quiet sounds of conversation and faint music from local bars and restaurants. Robust laughter carried on the air. She closed her eyes, the better to hear, and felt like she was assimilating Italy, absorbing the life here into her body.

So far, Italy was proving to be every bit as wonderful as she'd hoped. April inhaled the sweet air. If she had any regrets, it was that she hadn't been able to persuade Anesa to come along with her.

On the other hand, had Anesa come, or had April not lost her passport, or had Stephanie not gone on to Milan, April might not have met Hayden, might not have ever known the man he'd become.

Sinclair, her ex-husband, had not only looked great on paper, he had talked a great line, treating her with the respect and reverence she'd been taught were desired behaviors in a good black man. But she'd grown up and learned that what was supposed to be good for her was not always what was best for her. Always doing the right thing didn't get you any more Brownie points. She'd spent just enough time with Hayden to realize how true it was that you shouldn't judge a person by appearances. No one would have bet on him to achieve anything in life, yet he'd gone on to move mountains and become a man worth admiring.

April heard a quiet giggle below her window. She leaned out. She could just detect a couple standing under the light of a doorway, making no attempts to hide their affection or intentions. She openly watched as they hugged and kissed and whispered to one another. Envious, April turned away from the window. Across the room was a full-length mirror. She moved to it and critically looked at her image, pleased with what she saw.

She ticked off her attributes: warm, healthy-looking brown skin; dark eyes; thick, shining hair. As it had grown out, the texture had changed, lending itself to dreads. She absently touched a lock, but remembered vividly when there was nothing there to touch.

She added her new look to her list of second chances.

More than a change of hairdos, April had seen the style as a reinvention of herself, of reaffirming hope and life. Her gaze roamed down her body. Did she still look like a woman? Did she still have what it took to attract a man? Unconsciously, her hand rose to her chest, checking again in the mirror to make sure the image was balanced. When she was sure, she sighed deeply in relief.

It was odd that feeling like a woman caused April's thoughts to return to Hayden's earlier "good night." She had stood with him outside the Cessos' door—much like the couple below stood—and realized that she was sorry the day was over.

"Well . . . here we are," she had said unnecessarily.

"Home again," Hayden murmured.

"It's funny, but I almost feel that way."

"You got into Italy right away. I didn't feel like this was where I live for almost six months."

"Oh. How sad. All that time wasted," she lamented, shaking her head at him with a rueful smile.

"Yeah, I guess so. Anyway, I more than made up for it today. What's the saying, better late than never, right?"

She groaned. "I hope I didn't act like some parent trying to stuff culture down your throat."

"No," Hayden protested. "I would say your enthusiasm was catching. I enjoyed myself."

"I had a great time, too," April said simply. "My feet are so sore I know we must have walked about fifty miles. I bet I'll have nightmares about all the gelato I had this afternoon . . ."

"*We* had this afternoon," Hayden reminded her.

She smiled. "Thank you. I can't say it enough. I can never repay you for all you've done for me."

He put his hands in his pants pockets and stepped closer. "I think I better tell you that I'm keeping a running tab. By my last count you owe me seventy-five euros, a gelato cone, and your firstborn male child. Have I forgotten anything?"

"Of course I'll pay back all the money I owe you."

"Fine. But I'm not sure yet if I'll forgive the other debts.

You know, I could have your new passport revoked if you don't come through."

"I can't believe you'd blackmail me."

"It depends." Hayden's voice softened.

"I'm not going to ask on what," April responded dryly.

There was no mention again of their getting together tomorrow, no suggestions from Hayden of other things she should do and see . . . with or without him . . . and no invitations to join him and his friends. An unexpected wave of disappointment swept through her. Had Hayden just been acting as a diplomat, performing his duties as a Foreign Service officer to an American in distress?

April thrust out her hand toward him. "It was great to see you again, Hayden. I wish you all the best during your time in Italy, and wherever the State Department sends you next."

Hayden never took his eyes from her face, never responded to her little farewell and, in fact, gave no sign of having listened to a word she'd said.

He reached, not to shake, but to hold her hand in an old-fashioned, courtly manner. He let her fingers rest against his palm, then bent over and pressed his lips to the back of it. The gesture, the touch of his mouth, was so unexpected that she felt disoriented. He hadn't learned *this* in Philadelphia.

When Hayden straightened, he kept hold of her hand, squeezing her fingers gently and massaging the soft skin.

"I used to think there wasn't much about my past I wanted to remember. You've just changed my mind . . ."

He'd said all the right things to make April feel like a desirable woman. It had been so long since she'd felt that way. She liked this older Hayden, his features strongly defined with planes and edges, his voice a little deeper . . . and when he laughed, it was a loud guffaw that sent shivers through her body.

April left her bedroom and made her way downstairs to the

large open salon that served as the living room in the Cesso home.

She found Marina, along with several well-dressed women, standing around a table upon which was laid out a floor plan of the Ca'Rezzonico. Marina explained that the women were members of the hospital fund-raising committee and that they were reviewing plans for the masquerade to benefit the pediatric division. She introduced April, who apologized for interrupting and moved toward the door to discretely exit. Marina asked her to please stay, as their meeting was about to conclude. Agreeing, April walked to a distant part of the room and sat down on a sofa. Andrea entered soon after. April smiled as Andrea plunked herself, in universal teenage fashion, into an opposite chair. The family cat immediately jumped into Andrea's lap and settled down to be petted. Andrea obliged. She looked up after a moment and asked, "Did you have a good time today?"

"Yes, I did."

"Hayden called. He asked if you are okay."

"That was nice of him to check. I had a lovely day, thanks to him. What did you do today?" April asked, quickly redirecting the conversation.

"I go with my mother to the Ca'Rezzonico," Andrea answered, sounding bored. "She had to make sure everything is fine for her party. Every year mother makes everybody give lots of money to the children's wing at the hospital."

"It's for a good cause, don't you think?"

"Oh, yes. But there is no one my own age. I wish your daughter could be here with you. Then she would come to the ball with me."

"I'm sure Anesa would have loved that."

"The next time you come to Venice, you bring her?"

April smiled at the possibility of a future trip to Italy with her daughter. She would like nothing better, but knew it would be a long time before she could afford that. "I definitely will think about it."

Andrea uncurled herself from the chair, shaking her mane of hair over her shoulders. The cat protested, but then decided to lie on the top of a credenza.

"I show you what I am going to wear, okay?"

"Yes, please. I'd like to see it."

She ran from the room, returning a few minutes later carrying a long, gauzy garment of a pale pink material that glittered with sequins.

"I'm going to be a wood nymph," Andrea said, holding it up. "I have a pair of gossamer wings and a tiara for my hair. But I don't know how I will . . . you know, with the tiara," she tried to explain, gesturing with her hand.

"Attach it," April said.

"Yes, attach."

"Andrea, darling, do not worry. We will make it work and you will look lovely. Oh, but I cannot wait. So many details . . ." Marina Cesso moaned, joining her daughter and April after seeing the committee out.

"You always say that," Andrea reminded her mother.

"I think it's really incredible that you do this every year," April said.

"It is such a little thing to do for children, yes? You have a daughter, you understand."

"Actually I have many children."

Marina looked astonished and April laughed at the expression on her face.

"I run a program for students, encouraging them to do new things, see new places, and meet people different from themselves. I find places for them to work, or volunteer. I want them to be prepared for a global world."

"We must find a way to bring them to Italy," Marina said.

"That's what I'm beginning to think. It would be so wonderful for these young men and women to experience your culture and way of life. Maybe they can do some sort of internship. I'd have to find a way to fund Italian-language immersion classes."

"Ahh . . . did you tell Hayden about this?"

"Well . . . no, I haven't. It's just an idea right now," April said. The thought of asking any more favors of Hayden made her uncomfortable.

"But this is good. My Andrea, she asks all the time to go to America. Can she be one of your kids?"

"I want to see Hollywood and Brad Pitt," Andrea said.

April laughed. "I'm afraid I don't know Brad Pitt, and I haven't been to Hollywood, either."

"Many American cinema stars come to Venice in the season," Marina commented. "But none will be at my ball this year. I hope Hayden will come. Last year, he did not. It was a very bad time for him." She changed gears, her energy strong. "April, you must attend. I will have a costume for you. I have a friend who owns a shop. I will ask him to send several for us to choose from."

"That's very generous of you," April said carefully. "But I don't think I should. My friend Stephanie is arriving from Milan, and—"

"She must come too, of course," Marina declared with an imperial wave of her hand. "There. It is settled."

"If you're sure we won't just be in the way."

"You will enjoy yourself. There will be music and food, and everybody dances."

Andrea quietly interrupted her mother, speaking rapidly in Italian. It was clear she was pleading to be allowed to do something of which Marina was reluctant to approve. After several minutes of harangue, Marina apparently gave in. Her long limbs and hair flying, Andrea ran from the room.

Marina shook her head indulgently and shrugged. "What can I do? She is spoiled and impossible."

"And you love her and want to see her happy."

Marina made a little moue with her lips. "You know how it is, I'm sure."

"Oh yes, I do," April said reflectively.

"So, tell me all about your day with Hayden. What did you see?"

April gave Marina a recap of how she and Hayden had spent their day together. She stuck to the facts and was surprised when, at the end, Marina raised her brows and spread her arms.

"Is that all? You did not talk? I thought you are friends."

"Not exactly," April said. "He and I went to the same school in Philadelphia, but we really didn't know one another. I mean, I knew who he was. He was very popular, but we had different friends. We never even talked . . ." her voice trailed off.

"So then, it is good that you find each other, no? Now you can become good friends. He is a wonderful man, but very sad. I think it is because of that other woman."

Marina suddenly burst into a rush of Italian to more adequately express her feelings about "that other woman," leaving April to wonder who that might be and what had happened. She took a deep breath and shifted slightly in her chair. Although Hayden was not married, that didn't mean he hadn't been at one time or another, or that he might not have a commitment to someone now. Simone came to mind, but Hayden had not, so far, confided anything about his personal life.

Maybe she shouldn't misconstrue a little thing like Hayden holding her hand as they picked their way across the cobblestone streets of Venice, or her reaction to the sight of him slurping at her ice cream cone with a certain salacious gusto that had inappropriately driven her imagination. Her short reverie was broken by a commotion in the corridor, and then Santiago appeared in the entranceway.

He was accompanied by a rail-thin young woman who was

fashionably dressed in a clinging silk dress and narrow-strapped, high-heeled sandals. Her dark hair, thick and wavy, framed her delicate face. There were, as usual, warm greetings between mother and son. April noticed that the young lady was also greeted affectionately by Marina.

"*Ciao*, April," Santiago said. "This is Julianna, my fiancée."

"How do you do?" April said. Julianna looked toward Santiago, her gaze questioning. April realized at once that she most likely did not speak English. "*Come lei fa?*" she repeated. "*Buono sera.*"

The young woman smiled shyly.

"Excellent, April," Marina approved. "You will be speaking Italian in no time."

"Julianna and I are going to meet friends for dinner," Santiago told them. "Then we go to a club for music and dancing. April, please, you come with us?"

"Thank you so much for asking, but I don't think I will tonight."

"Hayden take her all over Venice today. Perhaps April would like to be quiet and rest," Marina informed her son.

It was more than that, April knew. There was a better than even chance that Hayden would be among the people Santiago was meeting. And after the way he'd said good-bye and where her thoughts had led her, she wasn't ready to face him again so soon.

"I thought it would be nice to spend some time with your mother," April explained as they all moved to the garden.

They sat together having wine and a light meal for more than an hour, and then it was decided that Santiago and Julianna would escort his sister to her friend's house on their way. Before they could leave, signor Cesso returned home and the greetings and conversation took another hour. It was almost ten o'clock when Santiago and Julianna left with

Andrea. Antonio went to bed, pleading an early surgery the next morning, and Marina and April set out.

"We just go and see some of my friends," Marina said.

While April was beyond tired, there was no way she was going to pass up an invitation to spend time with Marina.

They walked through the narrow streets and alleys until they came to an open *campi*, a square. They stopped at a small café overflowing with people inside and out. All the tables were full, and April was sure they'd be turned away until signora Cesso was greeted effusively by the manager and a table was miraculously found. Even as they were seated, Marina was hailed by nearly half a dozen of the patrons. April was introduced and welcomed like a long-lost friend, and she loved feeling a part of the well-established circle. Marina ordered a *café corretto* that April "must try." It contained some alcohol that April couldn't identify. But no matter: *When in Rome* . . .

Their chairs faced outward toward the street, and they could people-watch as they sat. Content to just listen to the beautiful cadence of the Italian language, April was somewhat surprised when, after a while, she realized she could actually understand some of the words. Gathering at a café seemed to be a regular evening activity. And, she realized, she didn't feel like a tourist. The thought was liberating in its own way.

As the conversation rose and fell like a symphony around her, she played a game, watching the other diners and trying to decide who was a tourist and who was not. It was amazing to be sitting in a little café somewhere in Venice close to midnight and finding that the streets were crowded and busy. April smiled, reveling in the joy of being exactly where she'd always dreamed of visiting. Closing her eyes, April heard not just Italian, but the melody of French, the thin cultured tone of the Queen's English, the harsh guttural cadence of German and the familiar ring of American slang. She opened her eyes to see a group of young college students, their knapsacks slung across their backs, walking by.

Beyond them, people casually strolled along the street as if it were morning. It seemed like life was so much more relaxed here than at home. Not that her life was so hard, but there was no question in April's mind that until recently her stress level had maxed out at a ten. She understood that illness sometimes did that to a person. It felt good to be alive.

Out of her peripheral vision she noticed a man who drew her full attention. With a sense of disbelief and shock, she realized that it was Hayden. She wondered if her imagination was playing a trick on her. Had she actually conjured him up out of the air? She felt her stomach flutter and her heart skip a beat.

Impulse led her to call out his name, but before she could, she saw that Hayden was not alone. Her gaze following him closely, she watched him tilt his head to the side, the better to hear the woman accompanying him. She walked with an assurance and allure that showed she'd staked a claim. Simone, April thought, recognizing her.

She watched the couple until they were well past where she and Marina were seated, and then they were lost in the crowd. She glanced at Marina, who, busy with her own conversation, had not seen Hayden walk by.

Her momentary excitement dying, April slowly settled back into her chair. She sipped at her coffee and let her gaze wander again to the parade of late-night strollers. She'd been thinking of Hayden all afternoon, ever since they'd separated to go their own ways, a day that had ended with parting words that may have held a promise. Perhaps she'd misunderstood, April considered. Maybe she'd left no lasting impression after all. Obviously, for Hayden, it was out of sight, out of mind.

***

Hayden focused his attention on the music of the small three-piece band, and on the several couples attempting to dance on the tiny floor at the back of the club. This club and his friends were a nightly ritual he took part in when he was in Venice.

To his left at the table were Santiago and Julianna. They'd arrived just a little while ago after having had dinner alone. But, given the intimate way in which they were whispering and cuddling, Hayden believed they were oblivious to their surroundings. Such was the power of love. Or so he imagined.

Santiago informed him that he'd seen April earlier in the evening at his mother's home. Although he had invited her to join them for the evening, April had declined. Hayden speculated. Would April have said yes to him? Or had she only seen him as a convenient and glorified escort?

Being with her had reminded him of his other life in the States and the things he missed: familiar people, places, and traditions; humor, language, and attitude. She had reminded him that he'd forgotten how to laugh and he was surprised at how much he'd enjoyed being with her. Saying good-bye had come too fast; he hadn't been ready.

Hayden stood as his friends, Carlos and Anna, prepared to leave. He shook Carlos' hand and, in European fashion, kissed both cheeks of Carlos' wife, Anna, a striking Nordic blonde. Wishing them both good-night, he took his seat again.

"You never kiss me like that," Simone's sultry voice complained softly in his ear.

"I thought that kind of thing wasn't your style, Simone," Hayden responded smoothly. "Too gentle, too polite, too . . ."

"Ladylike," she finished, and shrugged. "I sometimes have little patience for it, but I think it is a good sign of something. And it depends on the man. In my country, there is no need for shows of affection."

She leaned forward until her cheek was almost against the

edge of his shoulder. She slid her cool hand down his forearm to thread her fingers with his. "Are you going to make me ask?"

"If you have to ask I might not mean it."

Simone impatiently withdrew her hand and sat back. She reached for her pack of cigarettes and slowly lit one. She exhaled the smoke in a thin stream as she regarded Hayden. "You didn't call me today."

"I was busy. I hope you didn't wait around."

"Not very long."

"Good." Hayden regarded her briefly as he reached for his drink. "You once told me not to expect you to always be available. I took that advice seriously."

"So you are getting even? Hayden, that is so childish. So . . ."

"American? That's what I am and always will be."

"That can be very attractive, and also very distracting. I find it difficult at times."

"Maybe if you stop expecting me to change . . . I am who I am. I learned that much from you." He frowned at her. "How do you think I'm getting even?"

"By ignoring me. I only speak the truth. Why should I lie about how I feel? I have never tried to pretend to be something I am not."

"So I made a fool of myself expecting something real to happen between us?"

"It was surprising and sweet, I suppose. But unnecessary. I'm glad I was able to persuade you that we should just have a good time. Enjoy one another when we're together."

"Then why do you care if I don't call?"

"You are not very nice to repeat that to me," she said in a quiet, annoyed voice.

"I thought we were being honest?" Hayden looked at her. He knew that Simone knew exactly the effect she had on men. Sexuality seemed to exude from her pores like some kind of exotic perfume, intoxicating and seductive. His nostrils flared involuntarily at the promise in her eyes, at the memory of her lithe body in the privacy of a darkened room.

"You are still angry with me," she pouted.

Hayden chuckled softly. "You're wrong. I'm not angry. I'm grateful."

"I don't understand."

"When I came to Italy, I was running away from a bad situation at home. Another woman. I turned to you on the rebound, but it wasn't a good idea."

"I do not understand 'rebound.'"

He shrugged. "You wouldn't like it even if you did. I expected more from you than I should have. My mistake. You don't want a relationship."

"But I do want you, Hayden. Have I not shown you, many times? Isn't that better? So uncomplicated."

Simone trailed the back of her fingers delicately across his cheek to his ear where the skin was much more sensitive to her touch. "I think perhaps you find someone else."

Hayden chuckled. "Don't tell me you're jealous?"

"I am not," Simone denied, reaching for another cigarette. "I too can find another lover. I expect you to be honest, as I am with you. This is always best."

"I couldn't agree with you more."

"Good. Now we go to my place," Simone said, unfurling from the chair. "Enough talk."

Hayden signaled Santiago that he and Simone were leaving. They didn't bother with the slow late-night service of the water-bus but walked through the dark and nearly deserted streets, arriving at Simone's flat—an unpretentious building that had once served as headquarters of a private export company—in short order. The four-storied structure had been divided into spacious studio and one-bedroom units. Simone's one-bedroom flat was on the third floor. It was comfortable and modern, and uncluttered with possessions. Hayden had always found it impersonal and sterile. Simone didn't attach herself to things any more than she seemed to be able to make long-term connections to people. Her life had a temporary, constantly on-the-go feel about it. She lived entirely in the moment. Hayden accepted that she was willing to share some of the moment with him.

Simone poured two glasses of wine. Hayden sat on a sofa that he had always found too soft, too deep, too big. Simone joined him, drawing her feet up and under her. Her dress rode above her thigh, leaving her legs provocatively bare. Her knees pressed against him. She touched his face, sliding her fingers down to his throat and chest, beginning a seduction that left little to Hayden's imagination.

Hayden knew the routine. Simone's foreplay was a subtle tease that was all the more effective because she moved so slowly. She leaned forward to nuzzle the side of his neck, sending electric signals to his nerve endings until the ensuing heat started to flow through his body. Simone's body, conveniently placed, made it easy for him to stroke her leg, to let his hand glide up her smooth skin to her hip. She had never been shy about expecting more. At first, her boldness had shocked him, but Hayden had eventually seen Simone's experience as a way of tracking his own. What bothered him was that she'd actually helped him improve his lovemaking.

Simone gently pulled away. Gracefully, she came to her feet and stepped out of her heels. She headed to her bedroom, stripping off her clothing on the way. She was completely naked before she'd reached the bed. Totally comfortable with her body, nudity was merely a way to express freedom and show off her assets.

Hayden pulled his polo shirt over his head and tossed it aside. His slacks and shorts followed. She lay in a pose of blatant invitation. For a moment, Hayden stood still, looking down at her, wondering why he hesitated.

And then he knew, as April's face, with her bright smile, filled his mind.

He couldn't imagine what had prompted him to go off on such a tangent. The shock of it created a muscle spasm in his stomach. He brought his mind back to the present, the moment, and Simone.

He closed his eyes to obliterate April's image as Simone reached out and pulled him down. He sank to the bed. They began to kiss and he pushed all thoughts but those of Simone and this moment from his consciousness.

Hayden automatically applied protection and climbed onto the bed. Simone undulated beneath him in an erotic thrusting of her hips, encouraging him with guttural sighs and breathy moans. She stroked. He reciprocated. By the time his body joined with hers there was a part of Hayden's psyche, part of his soul that felt like he was not in control.

Disoriented, dizzy, Hayden craved and searched for his physical release as if it would purge him and set him straight again. Release came at last with a shattering intensity that was both cathartic and cleansing, far beyond anything he had ever shared with Simone before.

It was great sex. But that's *all* it was.

And suddenly, *he wanted more*.

Chapter 5

"*Grazie*! *Grazie* . . ." April waved.

She didn't know how to say "very much" in Italian, but the Cessos' boatmen seemed to understand her appreciation. They waved and smiled in return as the small boat reversed from the quay where April stood, and began to motor away.

"*Arrivederci*," she added for good measure, and gathering her luggage, she headed in the direction of the Botticelli Hotel. She remembered walking this same path the first day of her arrival in Venice, a time that was now a surreal memory.

With confidence she maneuvered the narrow corridor of streets to the hotel as if she'd lived in Venice forever. When she entered the lobby, the very same woman who'd been there when April had first arrived greeted her as if she were a long-lost relative.

"Signorina! *Buon giorno*. You come back."

"Yes, I finally made it," April said, standing in front of the desk. "Is my friend here? Stephanie Kingston?"

"*Si, si*. Signorina Kingston comes last night," the proprietress nodded, giving a registration form to April to fill out.

"Good. So much has happened since I last saw her," April said, presenting her new passport. She'd been disappointed this morning when it had arrived by courier. She had hoped Hayden would bring it by himself. But no matter. She certainly wasn't going to let it ruin her day.

The signora gave her a key. "I am sorry you lost so much time."

April took the key and smiled. "That's the thing. I didn't lose any time at all." With a jaunty wave, she picked up her luggage and climbed the stairs.

She found the room, on the third floor, and inserted the key in the lock. Before she could get the door open, she heard her name being called. A second later, it was pulled open, and there stood Stephanie. She was still in a nightdress and wrapper, hair rollers attached over her ears and at the nape. She gave a little squeal of greeting and fell into April's arms. They both began talking at once, laughing and exclaiming, their conversation a jumble of excitement.

"I'm so glad to see you," April said, once she'd gotten her luggage inside the room and the door had been closed behind them.

"Me too," Stephanie said, eyeing her friend up and down. "Well, you certainly don't look like anything terrible happened since I last saw you."

"That's because nothing really terrible happened. I think you had a worse time than I did."

"It's a toss-up. We'll have to compare notes," Stephanie said, sitting on one of the twin beds.

April sat on the other. She glanced around the small but attractively appointed room. There was only one window high on the wall, open wide to the morning sunlight and those now distinctive city sounds. The room seemed very comfortable, and although she knew that she and Stephanie would manage very well, April couldn't help but think that a hotel room, even one as nice as this, couldn't hold up against the charm, size or coziness of the private one she'd had at Marina and Antonio Cesso's palazzo.

"So what time did you finally get in last night?" April asked Stephanie, curling her legs beneath her as she settled comfortably on the other bed.

"Oh, around eight or so. I was tired and hungry and just glad to finally get here. I was going to call you, but I went out to a local place I know to get something to eat. By the time I got back to the room, it was too late. I went to bed and that was it."

"I don't think I got to bed myself until after midnight. I was out late, too."

"You were?" Stephanie asked, sounding both interested and surprised. "Doing what?"

"I went to a café with Marina Cesso. We had espresso, socialized with some of her friends, and watched all the people passing by."

Stephanie looked amazed, and then she started to laugh, shaking her head in wonder. "Girl, you are something. Anybody else would have been having a hissy-fit 'cause things had gone wrong. You go out and have a good time."

April smiled peacefully. "That was the whole idea of this trip, right? Everything turned out okay. Thank goodness for Marina Cesso. Thank goodness for . . . everyone."

"I can't believe you actually went off with a strange woman in a city you don't know to a house you have no address for and you not knowing more than five words of the language. You must have been out of your mind."

"Stephanie, I never felt in any danger. If you knew Marina, you'd have understood. Besides, I'm taller than she is, and if things had gotten ugly, I could have taken her easily."

Stephanie laughed merrily at the thought. "I would pay to see the proper Miss April Stockwood throw down with some woman who tried to get over on her."

"Marina Cesso couldn't have been nicer. She treated me like a member of the family. Her husband, Antonio, is a doctor. They have a son, Santiago, and a daughter, Andrea. It was great. And on top of that, Marina has invited both of us to attend her charity masquerade ball the day after tomorrow."

"You've breached the inner circle. Makes you wonder though if you would have gotten the same kind of treatment from some white family in the States."

"I don't know, Steph. I think people can surprise you, if you give them a chance." April was aware that Stephanie was regarding her not only with a look of amazement, but also concern. She laughed lightly. "Now don't go getting all mother-y on me. I thought you'd be proud of the way I managed all by myself."

"I am, but after everything you've been through in the last few years, I really wanted this trip to be stress-free. I know coming to Italy was always at the top of your wish list. And if that skank ex-husband of yours hadn't been so controlling, you could have come here a long time ago, when you were . . ."

"The point is, I made it. I'm here now. And that skank ex-husband of mine, as you call him, isn't a horrible man. We just couldn't relate after a while."

"You're right, you're right," Stephanie said, throwing up her hands in surrender and getting up from the bed. She opened a small armoire and began looking for something to wear. "Defend him if you want. I always thought you deserved better."

April sighed. "Yeah, well . . . you can't always get what you want. I've been blessed, Stephanie. I have a beautiful daughter, I love my work, I got through chemo and only lost my hair, and I'm doing really well on maintenance. *And* I'm in Italy. As far as I'm concerned, all's right with the world. Life is good."

"Amen," Stephanie murmured.

"Now, I didn't come all this way to curse Sinclair, bemoan my fate because of the Big C, and complain because I lost my passport. What are we doing today?" April caught the pained expression on Stephanie's face. "What is it?"

"April, I don't think I'm going to be able to do much with you today. The meeting I was supposed to have when we first arrived in Venice is rescheduled for this afternoon."

"Oh. Well . . . that's okay. I keep forgetting you're here on business."

"But we can hang out until then," Stephanie offered, slipping into a pair of beige linen slacks and pulling a teal sleeveless sweater over her head.

"Good. I'm up for anything. What time is your appointment?"

"Around two. Right after the siesta break, businesses open up again."

"I can entertain myself. I want to go to the Rialto Bridge. My guidebook says there are lots of markets and stalls in that area."

"It's also very crowded with tourists," Stephanie warned.

"I hate to remind you, but I am a tourist. And it's not like I have a lot of time left. I have a short list of one hundred things to do and see in Venice in five days. I'm only up to number seven."

Stephanie laughed. "Girl, you're crazy."

"Thank you. I prefer being called crazy to 'Miss Goody Two-shoes.' "

"What?"

"It's a long story. I ran into this guy I used to know in high school. He was cute and kind of a bad boy back then. Fact is I used to have a crush on him, big time."

Stephanie stood in front of a bureau mirror combing her hair and applying lipstick and blusher. "The one whose phone you used?"

"Yes. His name is Hayden Calloway. He works for the consulate in Milan but he's on a break in Venice. He's a really good friend of Marina Cesso and her son, Santiago."

"This sounds complicated," Stephanie said. She grabbed her purse from a chair and beckoned to April. "Let's go get something to eat. Then I want to hear all about this Hayden person and what he's got to do with anything."

"A *lot*," April said mysteriously.

She allowed Stephanie to lead as they left the hotel and snaked their way through alleys and over small footbridges. Every now and then, a black-framed gondola would glide beneath a bridge, the gondolier explaining some history or anecdote to the passengers. April quickly came to appreciate that she and Stephanie's hotel was located on an interior street, away from the busier and more popular areas. It was so quiet she felt like they'd stepped back in time to the fifteenth century.

They didn't actually go very far. Stephanie finally stopped in front of a café that had—typical of any Italian eatery with more than five feet of sidewalk space—several tables outside.

"We're here," Stephanie said, deciding on a table and sitting in one of the chairs.

April looked around. "I love dining outdoors like this," she said, taking the chair opposite Stephanie. "I wish we had restaurants like this in Philly, especially during the summer."

"No you don't," Stephanie said, trying to peer into the open door of the café. "There would be traffic and fume-filled air. It wouldn't be the same."

"This is nice," April said, glancing around. "Do you come here when you're in Venice on business?"

"It's one of the places I go. It's close to the hotel, and the food is always good."

"*Buon giorno,* signorina," a quiet voice said.

April looked up from settling herself in her seat to see a

man of average height greeting Stephanie. He was dressed in dark slacks and a sparkling white shirt with the cuffs rolled back over his wrists. His dark, thick, wavy hair was peppered with gray and grew down to the top of the shirt collar.

"*Buon giorno*," Stephanie returned with a vague smile as she accepted a large laminated menu and immediately became busy reading the entries.

"*Come sta?*" he said quietly to Stephanie.

April was sure he was asking "How are you."

"*Sto bene*," Stephanie responded just as quietly, although she didn't look at him.

"It is nice to have you back."

"Thank you," Stephanie murmured, finally sparing him only a brief look.

The man bowed his head briefly before turning to April and giving her the second menu.

April rested the menu under her chin and looked at him over the top of it. He raised his dark brows, his strong and pleasant face registering surprise. He seemed mildly amused.

"Already you have decided?" he asked.

"I love your country," April said warmly.

It was clear that this was not what he was expecting to hear. For a moment he looked taken aback and not sure what to say. Finally, he pressed a hand to his heart and bowed again slightly.

"*Molte grazie*." He sounded pleased. "This is your first time in my country?"

"Yes. My friend invited me to come along with her. She travels a lot to Europe on business."

April realized that the waiter was looking, with a quiet intensity, at Stephanie, who was studiously ignoring him, buried behind her menu.

He said, "How fortunate you are to have such a good friend. It is my pleasure to serve two lovely ladies."

"Thank you," April said, pleased.

Stephanie raised her gaze almost to his face. Her hands fumbled with the menu and she abruptly placed it on the table.

"I know what I want," she said.

"*Prego*." He listened intently to her selection, then to April's, not writing anything down. He gathered the two menus and left.

"He speaks English very well, don't you think?" April commented.

"I suppose. Most of the service people learn."

"And he remembers that you've been here before. Isn't that nice?"

Stephanie shrugged. "He's just being a smart businessman. Flatter the customers so they return or recommend him to their friends."

April squinted into the dim interior of the restaurant. The waiter who had just left them was talking to several busboys, who at once gathered silverware and napkins.

"I really think he was being friendly and sincere," April countered, still watching. A balding waiter was standing behind the counter near an intricately designed copper espresso machine. The headwaiter spoke to him. He nodded and proceeded to prepare two cups of cappuccino. April could hear the shrill ring of a phone; the charming waiter went to answer it. Turning to Stephanie, April frowned. "Why do you keep coming here if you're uncomfortable around him?"

"Like I said, this place is easy to get to from the hotel," Stephanie said dismissively.

"I like it here."

"I guess years of traveling has made me suspicious," Stephanie said.

"I guess so, but years of traveling should also tell you that he seems like a nice man."

Stephanie peered earnestly at April. "You think so?"

The bald waiter came from the restaurant carrying two

cups of cappuccino. He placed one in front of Stephanie, the other in front of April.

"Wait a minute." Stephanie protested. "I didn't order these."

This waiter, however, spoke no English. Or at least, not enough to be understood. He kept pointing inside before he shrugged and left.

"I think he's trying to say that the other man instructed him to bring these," April said, understanding the pantomime.

"Well, I didn't ask for cappuccino and I'm not going to pay for them," Stephanie announced firmly.

"Maybe they come with the meal," April suggested.

"*Nothing* comes with the meals. You pay for everything."

April took a sip of hers, licking the foam from her top lip. "Hmmmm. Good. Look, it doesn't matter. I'll pay for them. What's one more cappuccino? You'd better drink yours before it gets cold and the foam flattens."

Smelling the aroma, Stephanie gave in and took a careful swallow. The first waiter returned.

"How is the cappuccino?" he asked, placing silverware on the table. "In America you drink at night. In Italy, we only drink in the morning."

April said, "For the rest of my life now, I'll only be able to drink these in the morning."

"Good. You become Italian," he smiled at her. Then he held out his hand. "I am Marcello. I am the owner," he said, waving a hand to indicate the café.

"I'm April."

"April?" he repeated carefully, frowning.

"*Aprile*," Stephanie suddenly said in Italian.

"Ahhh," Marcello said. "Like the month. Very pretty." He turned to Stephanie and held out his hand again. "And *la* signorina?"

For a moment April thought Stephanie would refuse to give

either her hand or her name. April was surprised. It was unlike her to be so reticent. There was a moment of silence before Stephanie lifted a soft, manicured hand. "Stephanie," she said flatly.

Marcello took her hand, holding rather than shaking it and looked closely into her face. "Stephanie," he slowly repeated. "*Benvenuto. Casa mia es casa tua.*"

He left them then and Stephanie visibly relaxed.

"See, that wasn't so bad," April teased. "You're supposed to be this super world traveler and you act like Marcello's a vampire after your blood."

Stephanie gave her a wry look. "So now you're on a first-name basis? You don't think he's a vampire?"

"I think he's cute. He seems very polite. And he owns this place."

"I'm not interested," Stephanie said haughtily.

April frowned. "I'm not suggesting that you are. But you were pretty cold to the man."

"Let's not talk about it. And don't think I've forgotten about this guy you said you ran into from high school. Who is he?"

April's attention was easily diverted. She kept the story simple, explaining what an incredible coincidence it was running into Hayden in Venice, and to learn that he was also a friend of the Cessos'. During the telling, their food was delivered, not by Marcello this time, but by the balding waiter who spoke no English. They bit into the simple sandwiches—called panini and made with thin slices of ham and cheese—with gusto.

"Well, if you had to meet up with someone you knew years ago, at least it was the right person, in the right place, and the right time. Thank God he was able to help get your papers replaced."

"Except for my credit card. I have to stop by the American Express office today and sign for it."

"And he actually lent you money to help you out? That was nice of him. And unusual. What did you have to do in return?" There was a wicked gleam in Stephanie's eyes.

"It wasn't like that. Hayden was actually understanding and patient," April said.

"What was he like in high school?"

April grimaced wistfully. "He was very good looking. Still is, only grown up. He goofed off a lot and had a reputation for not going to classes, but he wasn't dumb. All the girls in high school wanted to go with him."

"How about you?"

April chewed thoughtfully for a moment and then shook her head. "I didn't stand a chance. But . . . like I said, I did have a terrible crush on him. Even when he was seventeen, Hayden was larger than life. *Everybody* knew who he was."

"Don't you think it's interesting that you just happened to meet up with him now? How did he get into government work?"

"I don't know. It's one of the things I'm curious about, too. I don't know if he was ever married. I can't imagine that he wouldn't have been."

"How do you know he's not now?" Stephanie asked, shredding a piece of the focaccia bread from the *panini*.

"Because I think he would have said something. And I've seen the woman he's been dating."

Stephanie chortled cynically. "Do you know how naïve you sound? What makes you think he doesn't have both a wife *and* something on the side?"

April felt chastised but didn't take offense. "I think I can tell if someone isn't being truthful. He doesn't seem to have that kind of attitude. He's actually changed a lot from what he used to be like. As a matter of fact, when we first saw each other at the Cesso's house the day I lost my passport, my first impression was he'd become way too serious and lost his sense of humor. Anyway, what difference does it make? Men don't want women like me."

"Well, those aren't the kind of men you'd want, anyway. Are you going to see him again?"

"I don't know. Probably not. I mean, I have three days left, and he didn't make any mention of getting together again. He didn't call me before I left this morning to meet you."

"You can always call him."

April considered it, but, "No. I don't think so. I don't do things like that."

"Maybe the old April wouldn't have, but don't forget what you told me after your diagnosis. Life's too short to hold back. You don't want to have any regrets later about what you should have done."

"Yeah . . . but this is different. Someone like Hayden Calloway would go for a woman who's sexy and gorgeous. That leaves me out. There's no reason for me to believe he likes me anymore now than when I was Skinny Minnie in school."

"Oh. He's a player."

"I don't think so," April said, reflecting.

"Well, so much for Hayden," Stephanie shrugged, considering the subject closed. "What are you doing this afternoon while I'm at this meeting?"

April wiped her lips with her napkin and set it on her empty plate. "I don't have any definite plans. I want to walk in the direction of the Rialto bridge, to see the markets."

"Be careful there. It gets crowded and you have to watch out for pickpockets. Remember what happened to your passport."

Marcello reappeared, asking how they enjoyed their meal.

"It was perfect," April smiled. Marcello turned expectantly to Stephanie.

She put on her sunglasses and became busy looking in her purse for her wallet. "It was good."

"Only good?" Marcello questioned. "*Scusa*. I do better next time."

"*Quanto*?" Stephanie asked him, pulling euros from her wallet.

"No, no. My pleasure, signorina," Marcello said, refusing payment for the food.

"No, I want to pay," Stephanie persisted.

"I insist. I do not take your money," Marcello held fast. "You come again. I cook special meal just for you."

April, seeing that Stephanie was ready to go to the mat on principle, leaned forward and grabbed her wrist.

"Stephanie, say thank you to the nice man. I will definitely come back again."

Marcello smiled appreciatively at her. "*Grazie*." He reached into a shirt pocket and pulled out two cards, passing one to April, the other to Stephanie. "Here is my card. You let me know when you come. I cook for you."

They gathered their things to leave under the watchful, smiling eyes of Marcello. It was only as they were about to walk away that Stephanie turned to Marcello and with a brief nod of her head said, "Thank you very much."

Hayden sat, along with ten other people, crowded into the small conference room of the British embassy in Dorsoduro. Like him, they were attending from all over Italy to learn of plans for various international festivals, concerts, and performances to be brought into Italy by sponsoring foreign governments. It was Hayden's responsibility to make a recommendation, when he returned to his consulate, of which events he thought would be appropriate to host.

The problem, Hayden realized, was that his attention

tended to wander at critical points of information delivery. This was due not only to speakers whose varying degrees of accented English were a challenge to understand, but also to the room, which, only minimally air-conditioned, was stifling. Rounding off his list of complaints was his tendency to drift toward thoughts and images of April Stockwood.

"Perhaps the Milan office can provide the visiting groups with not only translators but local families to act as hosts. This will help with hotel expenses for the lesser-known performers," the Australian agent suggested.

Hayden nodded and made a note. "I'll speak with the hospitality coordinator about it. There is a list of approved households used for hosting visitors."

"Excellent. Now we need to . . ."

Hayden restlessly rocked his pencil between the index and middle fingers of his right hand. He shifted in his chair, and swiveled it so that he might gaze toward the windows, even if he couldn't look directly out because the shades were drawn. It was the only way he could escape into his own thoughts.

His relationship with Simone was not working. Hayden acknowledged that although this had nagged at him before, it had never been with enough force for him to do something about it; like end their affair. Things had changed after last night. He knew, suddenly, that he didn't have to settle for what was offered. He could seek out what he really wanted: a real give-and-take with someone he cared about and respected; a relationship, not an affair of convenience.

The meeting ended, and everyone prepared to leave. Santiago, who had been asked to attend as both translator and representative of the Cesso family, squeezed past the chairs to stand next to Hayden.

"Where are you going now?" Santiago asked.

"I don't know. Want to stop for something to eat?"

"That is a plan," Santiago said.

Hayden chuckled at Santiago's adoption of the common American phrase.

"Have you rented your cape and mask for my mother's ball?"

"To be honest, I'm not sure I'll attend."

"My mother will be disappointed," Santiago said as they left the Palazzo Querini where the British embassy was housed. "She was hoping that you will agree to stay by your American friend, April. She will not know anyone there."

Hayden tried not to show his surprise. "April is coming to the ball?"

"My mother invited her. And her friend. I go now to find a costume. You can change your mind and come with me."

Hayden nodded as they walked to the nearest *vaporetti* landing stage. "Maybe I will."

They ended up at the shop Balo Coloc to look for a costume, and Hayden found himself getting into the spirit. Santiago decided on a mask that named him a Romeo. Hayden had to laugh at his lovesick friend's obvious choice, since it was clear that Santiago's fiancée, Julianna, would come as Juliet.

Hayden chose a simple, deep-purple cape and a full face mask that was gilded in shiny gold. It had a fancy head wrap attached at the top with mauve and red plumes that curved down and under the chin.

Santiago suggested having both costumes delivered to the palazzo because it would be easier for them to dress and leave for the ball from there. They left the shop, Hayden amused that he'd been so easily talked into attending.

He listened as Santiago recited Marina's glowing opinion of April. He learned that even Andrea had fallen under her spell and found April "*tutto* fun." He felt foolish, like maybe he was trying to impress April. He doubted she'd even notice.

He found that he was concerned about what April thought and wasn't even sure why.

After twenty minutes or so of walking, Hayden and Santiago found themselves near the markets on the Grand Canal. The streets were brimming with shoppers and open-air food stalls. The Rialto Bridge, which spanned the canal, looked like it was crawling with insects it was so crowded with tourists taking photographs. They found a table that allowed them to sit apart from the frenzy and enjoy their drinks.

Talk turned to a yachting trip Marina and Antonio were planning for the month of August. Andrea didn't want to go on holiday with her parents, and no decision had been made about what to do with her. Santiago reported that he and Julianna might not go to Lake Como with their friends after all.

"We want someplace alone," he said with a sly smile. "You understand, no? But you go with Simone."

"I don't think so."

"Everything closes in August. Will you stay in Milan with the tourists? You can stay at the palazzo, but you will be alone."

"Thanks for the offer," Hayden said. "I'll think about it. I don't know what I want to do yet."

They were about to pay for their drinks and leave when Santiago became distracted by something in the crowd.

"Ahhh, look. There is April." Hayden followed Santiago's pointing hand. "Yes. She is with someone," Santiago said. "A man. She looks a little upset."

Hayden scanned the crowd again. Santiago was correct. It was April. Despite the dark glasses he recognized her animated features under the cap of blonde locks. He could see the chartreuse of her tank top and the splashy tropical print of her skirt. Her style of dress was so distinctive that she stood out like a bright light in the pedestrian crowd.

Hayden said nothing to Santiago, but rather quickly got to

his feet and, maneuvering through the tight cluster of chairs and legs, hurried to the street. He tried to keep April in sight, but she kept bobbing in and out of the crowd, heading across the bridge to the opposite side. Hayden began an easy jog up the incline of the bridge in pursuit. He called her name, hoping she would hear him and wait, but by the time he'd reached the zenith of the Rialto, April and her questionable companion were out of sight.

He stopped to scan the waterfront, stunned that she'd disappeared so quickly. He looked up and down the street, decided on the most likely direction she would have taken, and started off again. Almost immediately, Hayden heard a flurry of Italian, and then a female voice responding—in English— "No, thank you. *Grazie*, no."

He turned and saw April about twenty or thirty feet away, weaving in and out of people and stalls.

"April!"

She stopped and turned at once in the direction of his voice. She didn't call out for help, call his name, or even appear scared. If anything, she appeared frustrated and bemused.

"April . . ." Hayden reached her side and placed a protective arm around her, without actually holding her.

"I'm fine."

April glanced up into his face, and whether she knew it or not, sidled closer to him.

"What's up?" Hayden asked. He was looking at the man, who was still talking rapidly. He could only make out the repeated, "*Scusi . . . scusi . . .*"

She was grinning. "I think he said he wanted to come home with me. Or he wanted me to go home with him."

"What?"

"I'm not sure but he kept saying *amore amore*, and holding

his hand over his heart." She shrugged helplessly. "I didn't know what to do."

Hayden could only stare at April and her erstwhile suitor as if she had lost her mind. A small but curious group of on-lookers had stopped to watch the unfolding drama. Hayden wasn't sure what to do because he still wasn't sure there was a problem.

"What's he saying?" April whispered.

Hayden motioned for her to be quiet. He listened, and then replied. His answer seemed to satisfy the man who shrugged in defeat. He stuck out his hand to Hayden, who readily shook it. More conversation took place. The man turned to April and bowed formally, blew her a kiss, and wandered away into the crowd. Some onlookers laughed appreciatively. And then it was over.

Hayden was aware that April was still standing close enough for him to feel her arm pressing lightly into his side. Close enough for him to detect not perfume, but baby pow-der on her skin. Close enough for him to wonder if she would know that he'd been with another woman the night before.

"You get into more trouble . . ." He used his hand on her back to steer her in the direction of where he'd left Santiago.

"How was I in trouble? I was minding my own business when suddenly this man came out of nowhere . . ."

"Careful." Hayden grabbed her hand as she stumbled on the descent from the bridge. She never stopped speaking.

". . . and started following me. I tried to explain that I don't speak Italian but that didn't seem to matter. It was as if he thought that if he kept talking, he would make me understand. Where are you taking me?"

"I left Santiago sitting alone at a café. When I saw you, you looked like you needed some help. He's probably still wait-ing, wondering what's going on."

"What was that all about? Was I right?"

"About what?" Hayden spotted Santiago who was waving an arm to attract his attention.

"I think that man was propositioning me."

"I told you. Italian men love women," Hayden responded smoothly.

Santiago held a seat for April and eagerly asked her what had happened. She explained, briefly, amusing him with her dilemma.

"At first I thought I was being set up, to have my purse snatched or something. My friend Stephanie told me I had to be careful."

"You are very good," Santiago complimented April. "Like Italian lady. Fearless. Other tourist would call the police, scream. Not necessary. Italian men make love, not war."

"I'll try to remember that," April grinned, taking off her sunglasses and dropping them into her bag.

Santiago, remembering that he was to meet Julianna, soon excused himself. Hayden continued listening as April recounted her morning adventures.

"Stephanie arrived last night and I got to the hotel this morning. We had breakfast together, but she has business to attend to this afternoon."

"What kind of business?" Hayden asked.

"She's a buyer for an expensive store in Philadelphia. Stephanie was a model for a hot minute, as she puts it, but didn't like it very much. And then things changed for her, so she got out of it."

Hayden leaned forward, resting his elbows on the table. Unlike many of the travelers he knew or had met in Europe, April apparently did not believe in sleeping in, even on vacation, but got up and out early. He found her enthusiasm and energy captivating.

"What do you mean, things changed for her?"

"Oh . . ." April hesitated, shrugging and struggling for

words. "It got hard to stay at 120 pounds. She got tired of trying. She suffers from a black woman's ailment called spreading hip."

He chuckled softly. "How did you two meet and become friends?"

He was surprised when she stopped, stared blankly at him, then averted her gaze as if the question was not only unexpected but unwelcome. "At a doctor's office. In the waiting room," she said quietly and then, "Oh, I almost forgot. I have something for you." She opened her purse and rummaged inside. "I didn't know when I'd see you."

"I was going to call you, but—"

"Why didn't you?"

Hayden thought he heard genuine interest and even a bit of disappointment in April's voice. "I assumed you had plans."

"No hard and fast ones. I wouldn't have minded at all if you'd wanted to join me."

"You seem to enjoy getting lost in the city."

"That's because I know I'm not really lost. I like being surprised. You know that commercial a few years ago, 'Just do it'? That's what I'm like now."

Intrigued, Hayden asked, "What were you before?"

"Always doing what I was supposed to. Never causing any trouble. Never complaining."

"But no more?"

"I hope not. Things changed." She pulled a folded white envelope from her purse. "Things happened that weren't planned. Here."

Hayden took the envelope cautiously. "What is it?"

"Don't *you* like being surprised?"

"Not particularly." He unfolded it and peered inside. "Euros?"

"I got my credit card this morning and immediately went to find an ATM machine."

Oddly, it seemed like April was rejecting all of his assistance, as if she didn't want to be beholden to him. He put the bills into his wallet. "This could have waited." He felt awkward. "I trust you."

She zipped her purse and looked up. "That's nice to hear, but I didn't want you to think . . ."

"I don't. Anyway, I know where you live."

"You didn't even count it. What if I shorted you?"

"I'll send you a bill." She grinned. He was glad to see her smile again. "With interest. Now, I have something for you."

Leaving her at the table, he walked to the café's gelato stand, made a selection, paid for it, and returned to the table.

"I think these are the flavors you like."

April looked at him, then at the waffle cone in his hand. "Oh, Hayden. This is wonderful. I was thinking of treating myself." She began licking the nearest flavor. "Hmmmm. Raspberry."

Hayden took his seat again, settling back and deriving pleasure out of watching her attack the ice cream.

"You're sneaky." April observed him over the top of the cone.

"Moi?" he asked with feigned bewilderment.

"Don't think I don't know what you're up to."

"I don't know what you're talking about."

"I notice you didn't bother getting one for yourself. I suppose you're expecting to share mine again."

Hayden grinned. It wasn't a question, but a statement of fact. He waited. Like the first time, April held out the ice cream. As before, he held her hand and brought the cone to his mouth.

"I thought you were never going to ask."

Chapter 6

April followed behind the small cluster of tourists as they were led by the guide from one huge council room to another in the Doge's Palace. The former seat of Venetian government had been turned into a visitor attraction that was one of the most popular in San Marco Square. But it had started raining midway through the day, and the historical building was overrun with people.

The teacher in April was genuinely fascinated by the history of the palace, as well as the colorful anecdotes of one of its most famous prisoners, Casanova. Despite all of that, she found her attention constantly drifting back to her unexpected encounter with Hayden near the Rialto Bridge.

Seeing him emerge from the crowd as she fended off the advances of a stubborn stranger, she'd experienced a wave of relief. He'd handled the problem with ease, a credit to the State Department. But it was after, when they'd sat and talked, that April saw a side of him that was more down to earth, more playful, more like she remembered.

And there was that ice cream thing.

The guide indicated that they were nearing the end of the tour. April followed her group, passing a number of oppressively small prison cells, before emptying into a courtyard just off the square near the Basilica. The overcast skies made the late afternoon look even darker.

She opened her small travel umbrella against the light but steady downfall. Now familiar with the layout of the district, April began walking across the square toward the jewelry shop where she'd arranged to meet up with Stephanie.

The rain was not heavy enough to stop people from angling for good photo ops, or children from buying bags of nuts to feed the San Marco Square pigeons. Nor, apparently, was the rain a deterrent to couples huddled together under one umbrella, oblivious of anything but one another. The air was warm but humid. Nonetheless, April felt a slight chill pass over her skin that had an odd effect of making her feel isolated. It seemed to her that Venice had more people in love per square block than any city she'd ever visited. For the first time since arriving in the city, April felt a wave of loneliness. Not because she was alone, but because she felt like something was missing in her life.

In that moment she missed Anesa terribly, wishing she could see her daughter and know the calming, blessed reassurance of her existence. April only rarely missed being in a classroom filled with skeptical but smart and engaging students. The work she was doing now in her organization for teens was, in many ways, more satisfying. Even marriage to Sinclair had been, at the beginning, a wonderful, affirming bond, giving her a perspective on love, sharing, and family that she might never have known. But none of these spoke to the sensations that swept through April since meeting Hayden, that left her feeling just a little bit . . . suspended.

"*Scuzi* . . ." Someone muttered, suddenly rushing past and tromping through a puddle that splashed on April's bare legs. She grimaced, but her feet were already wet in her open-toed sandals. Her "silly shoes" as Hayden called them. Cute, but impractical. Only a man would think her Ferragamos were useless. On the other hand, her shoes had led to Hayden offering his hand against the possibility that she might accidentally trip and fall.

The memory brought a small smile to her lips. Thinking of him confused her more. Feelings of dread and anticipation, excitement and fear coursed through her body like a tug-of-war. She had faced the ultimate battle between life and death and, so far, she'd won. Was she ungrateful to wonder if there was room and time for something more?

April took a deep breath and tried to pull herself away from such confusing and reflective thoughts. She gazed around her, grateful that she was alive and in Venice, living out a dream.

She found the shop where she was to meet Stephanie, but when she approached the door and could see inside the tiny store, she realized that Stephanie was not there. April stepped back to double-check the building number. Then she realized that the proprietor was signaling to her through the window and she walked inside.

"You are signorina April, *si*?"

"Yes, I am."

"Ahhh, good."

"How did you know?"

"Signorina Kingston. She says you come here to meet her. She says, 'You must buy these earrings.'"

"Where is Miss Kingston?" April left her wet umbrella on the floor by the door as she joined the jeweler at the counter.

"At another shop but . . ." he shrugged in resignation. ". . . she purchased a beautiful necklace here. In Italy, we only make jewelry with 18-carat gold. Signorina Kingston is very good customer. She always comes back to Carlo.

"She tell me, 'Show these earrings to my friend. Tell her to buy them for her daughter.'"

April shook her head at Stephanie's directive. But when

she was shown the small gold loops, slightly wide bands that seemed little more than ear cuffs, she could immediately visualize them on Anesa.

"Oh, these are nice."

"For pierced ears," the shop owner explained.

"Yes. My daughter will love these. Of course she loves any kind of jewelry but . . . I've already spent so much money on her. I'm afraid I'm spoiling her."

"But these are special. They are from Venice. *Prego*. Do not take her only, how do you say, a T-shirt." He made a face. "I have seen this joke."

April laughed. " 'My mother went to Venice and all she brought me was this lousy T-shirt?' "

"*Di preciso!*"

"Oh, all right. They will look great on her. It's only money, right?"

"Money is not important. Do it for love. This is the most important thing in life, no?"

"Yes," April said, her voice wistful and soft.

The shop owner charged the earrings, wrapped them, and handed them to April. As she left the shop, she headed into the plaza. Then she heard her name. She looked around from beneath her umbrella and saw Stephanie who was waving from under one of the colonnade bordering the western side of the square.

"Did you buy the earrings for Anesa?" Stephanie asked as they fell into step together and began walking.

"Yes, I did. But that's the last thing I'm getting her."

"Did you buy anything for yourself?"

"No. I don't need any jewelry," April said, dismissing the idea.

"That's not the point. You should have something to re-member this trip."

"I will. All the memories I'm stockpiling in my head, and my photographs."

Stephanie shook her head. "You talk like you're never coming to Italy again."

"I probably won't, you know. I'm trying to live in the moment, and enjoy what I have now."

"Nobody understands better than I do why you feel that way. But it's like saying you only deserve 'this much' happiness and good fortune. You're going to get back home and regret that you didn't buy something."

April didn't argue. She looked at the bags and packages that Stephanie carried. "Looks like you made up for what I didn't buy. What did you get?"

"Not all of this is from shopping," Stephanie said. "Most are leather accessory samples from a designer who's trying to break into the U.S. market. I'll show them around at some of the stores I represent."

"You know, you haven't done anything fun since we got here."

"Business travel is *not* fun. It's work. There are many trips where I never see anything more than the airport, my hotel, a restaurant or two, and client showrooms."

"I always thought it was more glamorous than that," April confessed.

"Most of the time it's not glamorous at all. I travel to Europe so much for business that I'm past the point of buying things every time I come. But I did see this really adorable dress in a shop window after I left my meeting that had my name written on it."

The rain soon turned to a soft mist as they headed back in the direction of their hotel. They stopped several times to window shop, meandering in and out of streets. They purchased a bottle of *pinot grigio* and a bag of biscotti. The day ended around them, fading into a quiet evening of glistening wet streets and deserted outdoor café tables.

"I'm tired," Stephanie said. "Let's eat someplace close to the hotel before we go back to the room."

"Do you have someplace in mind?"

"No. Not specifically."

"Let's go to that place where we had breakfast. I'm a little tired myself."

Stephanie studied her briefly. "Are you okay?"

"Yes, I'm fine. I'm probably not eating exactly the way I should, and I'm doing a lot more walking than I'm used to. Which is good. Maybe I'll lose a little weight."

"Girl, you don't need to lose any weight. You're looking healthy and beautiful. I see the way men have been paying attention to you."

April looked at Stephanie and frowned. "What men are you talking about?"

"At the restaurant this morning."

"Please. If you're talking about the owner, Marcello, he was being very nice, but I thought he seemed interested in you."

"He's probably married with half a dozen kids."

"I don't know. He didn't look the type. He seemed very respectful."

Stephanie laughed. "Oh, so now you're an expert on men and their lying ways, with your vast experience of one ex-husband?"

"It's not the numbers, it's the quality," April said with a righteous grin.

"Touché. How did things go today?" Stephanie asked as they slowed their pace crossing over a small bridge. "I guess you managed okay on your own."

April hesitated. "Actually, I wasn't alone."

Stephanie looked sharply at her. "Oh."

"After we went our separate ways this morning I started toward the Rialto. This man suddenly appeared out of nowhere and started talking to me. I didn't understand a word he was saying—"

"Did he touch you? Did he try to lure you away or take your purse?" Stephanie asked.

April smiled at Stephanie's protective demeanor. "No, he didn't. He was just . . . persistent, and I wasn't sure what he wanted. I kept saying 'No, no, I'm not interested.' I know he understood 'no,' but that didn't stop him."

"He wouldn't leave you alone?"

"No," April grinned, reliving the encounter and, in hindsight, finding it funny.

"Well, what happened?"

"Hayden Calloway showed up and came to the rescue. He sort of took care of it."

"Hayden who?"

"Remember? I told you about him this morning. I went to high school with him. He knows the Cessos . . ."

"Oh, right."

"Anyway, Hayden talked to the man who finally apologized and went away. That's it."

"That's it?" Stephanie asked, incredulous.

"Well . . . he and I did sit somewhere for a while and talked. I gave him back the money he'd loaned me. We had ice cream, and then walked around the market. Then I had to come and meet you."

"Sounds like you had a pretty good day."

"I enjoyed it," April said, more to herself than in response to Stephanie.

Hayden had asked her if she wanted to see anything special. But they'd simply walked along the quayside, observing and commenting on all the sights. He'd made her laugh when he said if she wanted to visit the fish market she'd have to go alone. But Hayden had found it funny to watch her pantomime—with a stray Italian word from her dictionary thrown in—when she tried to question a vendor about his array of cheese.

She and Stephanie reached the restaurant. Despite the

discouraging weather, there was one couple seated outside. An awning had been rolled out which gave sufficient coverage from what was now just a drizzle. A young waiter, different from the one who'd saved them that morning, came out to wipe down two chairs and a table so they could sit, even providing an extra chair so that April and Stephanie wouldn't have to set their packages on the wet ground.

They were poring over the menu when Marcello spoke. "Ladies. I am honored that you have returned."

"Hi," April said smiling, not surprised to see him at their table.

Marcello greeted both of them with a smiling nod. Stephanie was hidden behind her menu again. Marcello gently pulled it out of her hands and slipped it under his arm. April looked to see what Stephanie's reaction was to this, and found her uncharacteristically flustered.

"You do not need the menu. I will make something special for you tonight. You trust Marcello?"

"Absolutely. Doesn't that sound great?" April asked Stephanie.

Stephanie silently shrugged.

"Unless signorina Stephanie has something else in mind?" Marcello questioned.

"Stephanie, let Marcello surprise us," April quickly said.

"Fine," she gave in.

"Would you care for a glass of wine?" Marcello directed his question to Stephanie. "Or would you prefer a Bellini?"

"I'd like to try a Bellini," April spoke up.

She noticed that as Marcello left them to fill their order, he lightly touched Stephanie's shoulder in passing.

"Stephanie," April whispered, leaning across the table. "I think Marcello likes you."

Stephanie fiddled with her hair, played with her onyx earring. "I know."

"For how long? Did he say something to you? Does it bother you? Are you interested, too? What's going on?"

"Well, there's nothing going on," Stephanie said, peevishly. "To be honest, Marcello has been a perfect gentleman. Would you believe I didn't even know his name until he introduced himself this morning? I guess I have you to thank for that. You were so friendly, and I was trying to be strictly a customer."

"But if you don't care, why do you keep coming back to his restaurant?"

"The food is good; it's convenient to the hotel where I always stay—"

"And you're curious about him," April supplied, excited.

"That's probably all it is. Marcello is always nice to me."

"So then, I don't get it. Why do you freeze up and try to freeze him out when there's enough sparks between the two of you to incinerate a forest?"

"Like I said, he's probably married with kids, and I'm an easy target. Lonely traveler. Exotic African American."

"None of which explains your attraction to him."

"I never said I was attracted to him," Stephanie said haughtily. "He's Italian. He runs a restaurant. He's shorter than I am."

"Only because you wear two-inch heels. So what if he's Italian? He speaks English. And he owns a business. He's probably more solvent than a lot of men you've known in the past—including *your* skanky ex-husband who put you in credit-card debt, fooled around with your next-door neighbor, and left you to raise a son alone. All I hear are excuses. What do you *feel*?"

"Nervous."

April was about to say something else when Marcello returned with the two Bellinis, a slice of peach floating in each. He sat a glass in front of each of them.

"Thank you for coming to my place," Marcello said, almost as though he were giving a toast. He turned to April. "I hope you are enjoying your visit and will come again." He turned to Stephanie. "And it is always a great pleasure to see the signorina Stephanie."

And then Marcello returned to the restaurant. April and Stephanie exchanged glances. April silently raised her brows, as if to say *Well? What are you going to do about this?*

Stephanie raised her glass.

"To life," she said significantly.

"To love and the pursuit of happiness. You left that out," April said, sipping from her drink.

"What do you think I should do?" Stephanie asked.

April grinned. "You're asking me for advice? Give the poor man a chance. Maybe you'll become nothing more than friends, but you never know."

"Like you and this Hayden person?"

"That's different."

"No, it's not," Stephanie countered. "I *do* remember you telling me you used to like him a lot. You've been with him every single day since you arrived. What's up with that?"

"Nothing."

"See, when I turn the heat on, you don't want to be honest. Do you think he's interested in you?"

"No. I don't fall into the category of what men want," April said, as if the idea were laughable.

"You're smart and honest and a very nice person."

April chortled. "Men don't want nice women."

"Has he changed since high school?"

"Definitely."

"For better or worse?"

"At first I thought for the worse. Now I see he's really matured. He's smarter and he's still very funny."

"Does he seem like he likes you?"

"Well . . . he's been good company, and he's really watched out for me."

"Okay. So here's the big question. Do you think you two will get something going?"

"I doubt it."

"Why?"

April looked at her friend with an expression that was vulnerable and uncertain.

"I'm like you. Nervous."

"Then you understand how I feel. The difference is, you haven't seen anyone since you divorced Sinclair. How many years ago was that?"

"I had more important things on my mind, Stephanie. Like staying alive."

"You don't have that excuse anymore."

Just then the waiter appeared with their dinner.

"Oh, it looks delicious," April said as a plate was set before her.

It was an *antipasto di mare*, an assortment of fresh seafood on a layer of mixed greens. There was also a smaller plate of mushroom *risotto* for the two of them to share. Conversation was momentarily suspended as they began to eat. Marcello appeared after a while to see how they were enjoying the meal.

"My compliments to the chef," April said.

"The *risotto* is perfect. I'd like to know your secret," Stephanie added.

"Perhaps I will tell you sometime," Marcello said quietly to her and bowed away.

"Oh, my God. What am I doing?" Stephanie moaned in agitation. "Now I'm flirting with the man."

"Relax and enjoy the experience," April advised.

"I could tell you the same thing. Relax and have fun. That's what this trip was supposed to be about. If it happens to include an old boyfriend—"

"Hayden was never my boyfriend."

"That's even better. Are you going to see him again?"

"He asked me to go to the Lido with him."

"Well, that's different. The beach is actually nice. Not too sandy and very clean."

"It means wearing a bathing suit. I don't think I'm ready for that."

"Did you bring one?"

"Yes, because I thought you and I might go."

"You should go, April, if you have the chance. The island is lovely."

"It's a moot point. I don't think it's ever going to stop raining."

"*Molto grazie*." Marina Cesso thanked the housekeeper who'd placed the tray on the coffee table. She passed an espresso to Hayden and took one herself before settling back in her plush sofa and crossing her legs.

"It is nice that you keep me company. Everyone else has deserted me tonight. I need to rest as much as possible. The ball is one day away. Thank you for making sure the Ca'Rezzonico will have enough security, especially with so many bringing their boats."

"Glad I could help you."

"Andrea is just a child. Antonio returns in the morning from a conference in Prague. Santiago is useless these days. You know how it is when you are in love. Everything is *Julianna, Julianna*."

"Are you happy that he's finally engaged?"

"Of course. It is time for him to settle down and have children."

Hayden sat forward, resting his forearms on his thighs. "Somehow, I can't really see you as a grandmother."

"I will be the most glamorous grandmamma in Venice, *si*?"

He laughed. "*Si*."

"Are you enjoying your stay in Venice?"

Hayden slowly nodded and sat back again. He put his cup on the tray. "I think I'm having a most excellent time."

"I am happy to hear this. Simone is a beautiful woman but, how do you say? High-maintenance."

Hayden looked thoughtful. "This has nothing to do with Simone. I've already decided to end it with her."

"So you are not sad about this?"

"Not at all."

"Ahhhh . . . there is someone new."

"I don't know if I'd say someone new." He had no real idea how he felt about April, except that he enjoyed being with her. She was more than just good company; she was comfortable to be with. No drama or histrionics. No manipulation or mood swings. It was in such stark contrast not only to Simone, but to every other woman with whom he'd ever been involved. Of course, Hayden corrected quickly, he wasn't involved with April. He realized after a moment that Marina was looking at him expectantly.

He answered, "I thought, perhaps, April Stockwood."

"You like her?"

"Yeah. I think I do."

"I like her, too. She is a lady. She is strong, and she is kind. And I love this thing she does with her hair. Not for me, of course . . ." Hayden chuckled and she continued ". . . but interesting."

They were interrupted by the housekeeper, who informed Marina that she was wanted on the telephone. Marina looked apologetically at Hayden, excused herself and left.

Hayden rose and began idly wandering around the large room, his thoughts leading him. He was amazed and apprehensive about his admission to Marina. In a way, he realized he should be grateful for having met April again, for had they not met in Venice, it might have taken Hayden longer to recognize what he wanted.

"You will not believe. That was April," Marina said, rejoining Hayden. "I left a message that she is to meet me tomorrow to pick out a costume for the ball. After, she will come here with her friend for something to eat. I tell her that you are here, and she says that she is grateful to you for helping her."

Hayden felt a little let down. But what did he expect?

"I tell her that you will be at the ball, and she says that she will be glad to see you again."

Glad, Hayden repeated to himself. That was much better. "She's changed a lot since high school."

"Of course, this is a good thing. You know nothing in high school. Then you grow up. When I first meet you, you were very sad. Slowly, you are happier. Do you think you have forgiven the past? Your mama and brother?"

"I could say I have, but I don't know. I *want* to. I'm tired of feeling sorry for myself. I've gotten more respect and affection from you and your family than I ever got from my own. Even April, whom I haven't seen in twenty years," Hayden murmured introspectively, "treats me with respect and kindness."

"You will see her again?" Marina asked.

"We'll see."

"What about Simone?"

"It's over. I should have ended it sooner between us."

"Why didn't you?"

"I don't have a good excuse, I'm afraid. Maybe I continued because of the way I used to feel about her. But that seemed such a long time ago." Hayden shrugged. "She never felt the same."

"I tell you before. Simone is not the right woman for a man like you," Marina said sagely.

He grinned affectionately at her. "I didn't realize you were watching out for my best interests."

"I am watching out for your heart." She pressed her hand to her chest.

"Thanks, Marina. I appreciate that. I know I didn't make it last year to your ball, but now I'm looking forward to it."

"Yes, and then . . . *Que será, será*," Marina said philosophically.

Chapter 7

The day was gorgeous, without any sign that the one before had been rainy and gray. As much as April loved the way the early morning sunlight created diamond-like sparkles on the surface of the Grand Canal, there was a part of her that wished the weather had remained inclement. Rain would have put an end to Hayden's plan to boat over to the *Lido* for a day on the beach where she would have to wear a bathing suit that would expose more than just her shape.

From beneath the canopy of the *vaporetto* April glanced up at the sky, hoping for signs of an impending storm, but there wasn't a cloud to be seen. The sky was so unbelievably blue it looked like a painting; the weather couldn't have been more perfect.

When Hayden had called her at the hotel the night before, she had been foolishly pleased to hear from him. Then he'd reminded her about his plan to spend the day on the *Lido*, a skinny sandbank beach resort. He then suggested that it made more sense for the two of them to meet up in one place. So here she was, at the start of a day that had all the signs of being sunny and hot, motoring toward the *Lido*. But during

An Important Message From The ARABESQUE Publisher

Dear Arabesque Reader,

I invite you to join the club! The Arabesque book club delivers four novels each month right to your front door! It's easy, and you will never miss a romance by one of our award-winning authors!

With upcoming novels featuring strong, sexy women, and African-American heroes that are charming, loving and true… you won't want to miss a single release. Our authors fill each page with exceptional dialogue, exciting plot twists, and enough sizzling romance to keep you riveted until the satisfying end! To receive novels by bestselling authors such as Gwynne Forster, Janice Sims, Angela Winters and others, I encourage you to join now!

Read about the men we love… in the pages of Arabesque!

Linda Gill
PUBLISHER, ARABESQUE ROMANCE NOVELS

*P.S. Watch out for the next Summer Series **"Ports Of Call"** that will take you to the exotic locales of Venice, Fiji, the Caribbean and Ghana! You won't need a passport to travel, just collect all four novels to enjoy romance around the world! For more details, visit us at www.BET.com.*

SPECIAL OFFER! 4 BOOKS FREE!

BET★ BOOKS

www.BET.com

A SPECIAL "THANK YOU" FROM ARABESQUE JUST FOR YOU!

Send this card back and you'll receive 4 FREE Arabesque Novels—a $25.96 value—absolutely FREE!

The introductory 4 Arabesque Romance books are yours FREE (plus $1.99 shipping & handling). If you wish to continue to receive 4 books every month, do nothing. Each month, we will send you 4 New Arabesque Romance Novels for your free examination. If you wish to keep them, pay just $18* (plus, $1.99 shipping & handling). If you decide not to continue, you owe nothing!

- Send no money now.
- Never an obligation.
- Books delivered to your door!

We hope that after receiving your FREE books you'll want to remain an Arabesque subscriber, but the choice is yours! So why not take advantage of this Arabesque offer, with no risk of any kind. You'll be glad you did!

In fact, we're so sure you will love your Arabesque novels, that we will send you an Arabesque Tote Bag FREE with your first paid shipment.

* PRICES SUBJECT TO CHANGE.

YOU'LL GET 4 SELECT ROMANCES PLUS THIS FABULOUS TOTE BAG!

THE "THANK YOU" GIFT INCLUDES:

- 4 books absolutely FREE (plus $1.99 for shipping and handling).
- A FREE newsletter, *Arabesque Romance News*, filled with author interviews, book previews, special offers, and more!
- No risks or obligations. You're free to cancel whenever you wish with no questions asked.

FREE TOTE BAG CERTIFICATE

Yes! Please send me 4 FREE Arabesque novels (plus $1.99 for shipping & handling). I am under no obligation to purchase any books, as explained on the back of this card. Send my free tote bag after my first regular paid shipment.

NAME _____

ADDRESS _____ APT. _____

CITY _____ STATE _____ ZIP _____

TELEPHONE ( ) _____

E-MAIL _____

SIGNATURE _____

Offer limited to one per household and not valid to current subscribers. All orders subject to approval. Terms, offer, & price subject to change. Tote bags available while supplies last.

Thank You!

AN055A

ARABESQUE

Accepting the four introductory books for FREE (plus $1.99 to offset the cost of shipping & handling) places you under no obligation to buy anything. You may keep the books and return the shipping statement marked "cancelled". If you do not cancel, about a month later we will send 4 additional Arabesque novels, and you will be billed the preferred subscriber's price of just $4.50 per title. That's $18.00* for all 4 books for a savings of almost 30% off the cover price (Plus $1.99 for shipping and handling). You may cancel at any time, but if you choose to continue, every month we'll send you 4 more books, which you may either purchase at the preferred discount price. . . or return to us and cancel your subscription.

THE ARABESQUE ROMANCE BOOK CLUB
P.O. BOX 5214
CLIFTON NJ 07015-5214

THE ARABESQUE ROMANCE CLUB. HERE'S HOW IT WORKS

PLACE
STAMP
HERE

the entire boat ride, April's anxiety was so great that she felt almost nauseated.

As the *vaporetto* cut its engines and slowly slid to a stop along the wharf, her apprehension grew, her heartbeat began to accelerate, and adrenaline pumped through her system. She recognized the symptoms at once as a fight-or-flight reaction. She tried deep, meditative breathing, but her anxiety only increased. The passengers began to crowd off the boat and disperse on the shore. She froze. *What was she doing here?*

Moved along by the other passengers, April stepped off the boat, keeping her gaze down until she'd reached the landing platform.

"April . . ."

She looked up and saw Hayden waiting for her. It would have helped if he'd smiled or stepped forward, but instead he stared at her through the dark of his sunglasses. He looked healthy and clean, and handsome dressed in casual white linen slacks and a teal-blue Henley shirt. A canvas bag hung over his shoulder and across his chest, the contents resting against his hip.

"Hi," she said as an opener, trying to ignore the churning in her stomach. Her voice sounded faint and thin to her own ears. Her smile felt forced.

Hayden stepped forward, pushing his sunglasses to the top of his head. He reached out to take hold of her arm, frowning. "Are you okay?"

She nodded. "I'm fine." But she could see concern darken his eyes.

He released her arm and carefully removed her own sunglasses, closely studying her face. "You don't look fine."

"Thanks a lot," April said, keeping her voice light. "Just because I didn't wear any makeup."

"I mean it," Hayden said. "You look upset. Did anything happen on the boat on the way over?"

April took her sunglasses out of his hand and put them back on. "No, nothing. I'm just feeling a little . . . I don't know . . . queasy."

"Seasick?"

"No, I don't think so."

"Did you eat anything this morning?"

"I . . . didn't really feel like it. And there was no time."

"Then that's it. You probably have the urry-ups."

"The what?" She let Hayden steer her through the wharf terminal and out into the sunshine.

"You know what I'm talking about. That growling sound your stomach makes when you're hungry." He then proceeded to demonstrate, emitting a strange noise from the back of his throat, working his mouth and lips like someone in agonizing pain. April burst out laughing.

Hayden smiled warmly. "That's better."

April was surprised at how quickly and smoothly he'd taken some of the edge off her tension. What was also pleasing to her was recognizing that Hayden was still capable of creative humor. He seemed so much more relaxed now than when she'd arrived in Venice. What a difference a few days could make.

He pointed to the small plastic shopping bag she carried in addition to her tote. "What's that?"

April held it up. "Lunch. A couple of sandwiches, something to drink. Marcello recommended Crodino."

Hayden took the bag from her. He shifted his tote and opened it, stuffing the lunch inside. "Who's Marcello?"

"He owns this café-bar near the hotel. Stephanie goes there a lot when she's in Venice on business . . ." Her voice trailed off when Hayden stopped in front of two bicycles leaning against the outside wall of a newspaper stand. She pointed to them. "What are those for?"

"Us," Hayden said, rolling the first one to her, and then retrieving the second.

April stared at him. "You're kidding, right?"

"I kid you not." He climbed onto his bike and positioned it. "I thought we'd ride around the island first, than head over to the beach to relax. Don't tell me you don't know how to ride a bike?"

"I know how to ride, but . . . I haven't been on a bicycle in years, Hayden. At least not since college."

"So you'll brush up on your skills. Are you game?"

He certainly wasn't giving her any time to think about it, much less say no. She put her tote into the front "girly" basket. She was wearing a denim skirt that buttoned down the front, and a short-sleeved yellow top with a boat neckline. Not the best outfit for biking. Gingerly, she climbed onto the seat and gripped the handlebars, silently praying that she wouldn't disgrace herself and fall off.

"Ready?" he asked.

"Ready," she said, which wasn't exactly true.

"Call out if you need help."

Don't hold your breath, April thought, gritting her teeth with determination.

"I'll lead," Hayden said, pushing off slowly.

For the first hundred feet April wobbled precariously, the front wheel of her bike swinging wildly left to right as she struggled for balance and control. She knew that Hayden glanced over his shoulder several times to check on her progress, but he never said a word . . . and he didn't stop.

With a great deal of satisfaction, she began to settle into a uniform movement. The bicycle stayed more or less steady and she started to relax. They hadn't made much progress when April noticed that Hayden was stopping along the Grande Viale, the main street of the *Lido* district.

"Why are we stopping? I was just beginning to get the hang of this," she complained.

"Before we go on I want to get you something to eat."

"Hayden I'm fine. I don't need . . ."

"Cappuccino and maybe a *zaleti*." He leaned the bike against a lamppost and did the same with hers.

"What's a *zaleti*?"

"A biscuit thing with vanilla, lemon, and raisin filling. It's pretty good."

"Sounds sweet and fattening."

"Probably."

"Okay," she quickly acquiesced.

He laughed, that wonderful barking sound that was short and so distinctly masculine.

They took a seat at a small, round table along the sidewalk. It occurred to April, as a waiter placed a menu in front of them, that she really enjoyed eating al fresco. She let Hayden order for her, simply enjoying the sound of his voice as he spoke to the waiter.

"How long did it take you to become fluent?" April asked once the waiter left.

"I can't say that I actually speak Italian." Hayden leaned forward, his elbows on the table. "I manage to make myself understood. I took a basic conversation course for a few months before I was assigned to the Milan consulate. I learned more just being here. Santiago was a great help."

"I'm impressed," April said sincerely, with a smile.

"Thanks." Hayden averted his gaze shyly.

"I've been dying to ask. How in the world did you get into the Foreign Service?"

"The truth is, I had no idea what I was going to do with my life when I was in high school. I liked sports, but I knew my chances of going pro were slim to none. I liked organizing things. I liked solving problems. But how do you turn all of that into a career?"

"Wasn't there just one thing you always wanted to do with your life? Like become a doctor, or a scientist?" April asked, eager for him to continue.

Hayden slowly shook his head. "Not really. I mean I did want to succeed and make a lot of money and have respect. I just didn't know how that was going to happen."

"But your family must have encouraged you, no matter what it was you wanted."

Hayden merely shrugged. Not much of an answer, April thought. And somewhat confusing.

"When I was in college I deejayed at parties. I'd find the up-and-coming bands, look for a place to showcase their talent, and arrange for them to do gigs at local clubs. I was good at talking club owners into giving them a shot and great at getting press coverage. I have to admit," Hayden added wryly, "that back then I didn't know what Foreign Service was. It always sounded like something to do with the CIA."

April grinned broadly. "What was your major?"

"Business. I thought it would be the most useful subject I could study. I needed an elective one semester, so I took something called International Relationships."

She was served her breakfast. April noticed that Hayden had only ordered a cappuccino. She took a bite out of the *zaleti*, which she knew, instantly, was worth every calorie. She held a piece out. He didn't seem at all surprised by the offer, but rather bent forward to take a bite. She watched him savor the mouthful before he continued his story.

"The instructor told the class about a summer internship at the State Department. At the time I was seeing this girl from Howard. I wanted to get away for a while. I needed a summer job; I liked the idea of being in Washington. I applied and got accepted.

"So, off I go thinking how cool it was that I'm getting paid to be near my girl."

"What happened?"

Hayden grinned at the memory. "They worked my ass off and my girl threw me over for a guy who was pre-med."

"Could she have simply fallen in love with someone else?"

"Maybe. But people have been known to fall in love, break up, and/or marry for all the wrong reasons."

"It's too bad she didn't hang around long enough to see how great your life turned out."

"You think so? My mother used to tell me she'd be happy if I didn't end up working for minimum wage at a fast-food joint."

"I don't believe you. Did she really say that to you?"

"Something pretty close. Unlike my brother. She was grooming him to be another Robert Johnson, the guy who founded Black Entertainment Television. Johnson's a billionaire," he said dryly.

She hadn't known that Hayden had a brother. And although he sounded flippant about his mother's devotion to his brother, April thought she could detect a hint of resentment.

"I take it that your brother didn't become president of his own corporation. What happened to him?" she asked.

Hayden sighed and sat back in his seat. "That's another story."

His response was firm. End of story. Or at least, that part of it. "What about you?"

"My girl broke my heart, but I had a great summer. I worked with the cultural exchange officers. I remember asking why they weren't making any effort to send more black performers overseas. Jazz has always been big in Europe, but I knew that other black music like rap and hip-hop and R&B were also popular over here. They said, 'So put something together.' And I did. I arranged for a reggae troupe to travel to Sweden."

"Did you get to go along?"

"No, but that was okay. At the time I still had a homeboy

mentality. I wasn't sure I was ready to go someplace where I didn't speak the language. I had to finish my degree."

"But you did join the service. What changed your mind?"

"My brother," he said shortly.

Despite his reticence, April couldn't help herself from asking, "What's his name?"

Hayden's gaze briefly met hers then dropped away. "Reese."

"Reese," April repeated quietly to herself, testing the name.

"When I finished interning that summer, I was invited to apply for the Foreign Service when I got my degree. Instead, I joined the Air Force. I spent a year in Germany."

"You went into the military?" April asked, stunned.

"What's wrong with that?"

"Nothing. I just never thought of you as the kind of person who liked to be told what to do."

"You'd be surprised what you're willing to do when you have to."

"I agree," April said, finishing her cappuccino. "What happened next?"

"I met a woman during my tour. Joyce was from San Diego. Father was a lawyer, mother a teacher, brother in high school. She worked for a senator on the Armed Services Committee. One thing led to another, fast forward . . . I asked her to marry me."

Here it is, April thought. "Did you marry her?"

A slow hard smile tightened the line of his mouth. "Almost. I got the 'Dear John' call. She was in love with someone else."

"Oh no. Someone in the service?"

"With my brother."

She stared. She found it odd. Two women, at least, hadn't found him worthy of their love and devotion. What were they thinking? "What did you do?" Then, *What a stupid question,* she thought, too late.

"I finished my tour, left the military, and took the offer to apply to the State Department." He spread his arms wide to encompass his present universe. "End of 'This Is Your Life, Hayden Calloway.' "

"I think you get the prize for the student with the most interesting life," April said carefully.

"That's one way to put it. Are you ready?"

They left the bar and remounted their bicycles. Hayden led the way again, peddling away from the waterfront. Riding single file made it difficult to hold a conversation, so April spent the time honing her riding skills, watching out for pedestrians, and enjoying the beauty of the *Lido*. She also spent a fair amount of time staring at Hayden's back and watching the play of muscles beneath his shirt. He was in great physical shape; added to that was his worldliness, adaptability, and humor. April saw him as someone who'd navigated the pitfalls of his life pretty well.

"Let's parallel the beach for a few miles," Hayden directed over his shoulder as he turned to the left along a different street.

"Are you prepared to carry me back when my legs give out?" April complained, eliciting a laugh.

"Think of the calories you're burning from that biscuit you just ate."

Biking turned out to be a cool and easy way to see the island. Despite the summer influx of European vacationers, the *Lido* was a lovely, serene village. Hayden eventually turned them back to the piazza that marked the main public entrance to the beach, where he secured the bikes at a rack. They walked through the piazza past concession stands selling drinks, gelato, and other snacks, and reached the beach.

As Hayden maneuvered a path through the sprawl of sun worshippers, April removed her sandals. She was surprised at how firm the sand was under her bare feet. Not particularly soft or deep. Not at all hot. She followed him until he found an empty spot between an older couple who were sitting in beach chairs, reading, and a trio of young women who were sunbathing. He spread a lightweight blanket on the sand, and then grabbed the hem of his shirt and peeled it over his head. Next he removed his white slacks. She blushed, realizing that she was waiting to see if he wore a Speedo or Jammers. Hayden's swim trunks were somewhere in between, like boxer shorts. Much to her relief he had firm thigh and calf muscles, not what her girlfriends used to call "chicken legs," common among black boys even if they were into sports.

April set down her tote bag. Turning her back to him, she unbuttoned and wiggled out of her skirt.

"I don't mind the sun, but maybe you'd like an umbrella?" Hayden asked.

"Please."

Taking his wallet, he walked to the piazza to rent one. April used his absence to quickly remove her yellow top and replace it with a gauzy white cover-up. Through it, her navy-blue tank suit was discernible, but April felt sufficiently protected. The beach was crowded with sunbathers, children, towels, cabanas, and umbrellas. European women seemed to favor bikinis, regardless of the amount of flesh that actually fit into them. April looked around, realizing that she was the oddity, wearing more than needed for the setting. Hayden returned and set up the umbrella with their things beneath it.

"It's hot." He pointed to her outfit. "Why don't you take that top thing off?"

"I'm fine." April explained in a light tone. "See how it matches the trim on my suit?"

Hayden shook his head as if her logic made no sense to him. She covertly checked to make sure that her breasts were sufficiently covered and that no scarred flesh was visible. She then carefully dropped down to sit by him on the blanket. She drew her legs up to her chest and wrapped her arms around them.

"Now it's my turn," he suddenly said, sitting in pretty much the same position.

"Your turn for what?"

"Twenty Questions. There are a few things I'd like cleared up about you."

She shook her head vigorously. "No. Five questions. That's it."

"Only five? That's not fair. I answered all of yours."

"Thank you very much," she said, unapologetic.

Hayden chuckled. "That's all right. I'll get even." He gave her a careful, considering look. "One. How long have you been divorced? What happened?"

"I've been divorced about six years. Sinclair found out I wasn't perfect. *I* found out I wasn't perfect," April added flippantly.

"I don't understand."

"What I mean is, I stopped being the woman he married. He stopped being the husband I wanted."

"You just grew apart?"

"You could say that," April agreed softly.

"So, it wasn't like he had another woman on the side or anything? And this *doesn't* count as one of my questions," he clarified quickly.

"No, nothing like that," April said slowly. "It was a bad time in my life . . . our life. We just couldn't adjust, and he needed and wanted something I could no longer give him. And vice versa. Don't misunderstand me. We don't dislike each other, but there was a lot of . . . disappointment."

She could see him silently processing her response, and wondered what he was thinking.

"Okay, number two. Why did you do dreads? Why blond?"

"That's question three and four, Hayden. I'm paying

attention," April said smoothly. A faint smile played around his lips at her perception. "I wanted something different. I was reinventing myself at the time. I got divorced, quit teaching, started a business."

"And the blond part?"

"I heard blonds have more fun."

He gave his trademark laugh, and she was glad.

"One more," she said, making sure he kept to the letter of their agreement.

His gaze swept slowly over her face. "Do you ever want to get married again?"

April's mind went blank. She hadn't seen that one coming.

"I don't think about it," she said honestly. "But I don't think I've completely ruled it out, either. I guess it depends."

"I'd be surprised if you didn't remarry," Hayden said thoughtfully.

"What makes you say that?"

"I bet you were probably good at being married."

He stretched out on his back, his upper body supported on his elbows, gazing at all the activity around them. She did the same, thinking about the questions he'd asked. Why those questions? What was it he was trying to find out?

She glanced at him, shamelessly studying him. She was fascinated with the tight little curls of hair on his chest, the subtle development of his chest muscles . . . his dark, male nipples. She looked away, feeling an odd lethargy and embarrassment as an image, unbidden, crossed her mind. She closed her eyes, giving in to it in the privacy of her own head.

"I hope you're thinking what I'm thinking."

She started at Hayden's voice and quickly vanquished her wayward thoughts as sophomoric and inappropriate. Was it possible that he was actually reading her mind?

"What?" she croaked, a jolt of nervousness making her mouth dry.

"That it's time for lunch."

"Not even close," she grinned, relieved, "but I can take a hint."

She didn't mind when he lay there, watching, as she did the female thing and prepared to serve the food. She pulled out two paper-wrapped sandwiches and napkins from the plastic shopping bag. There was another tightly sealed plastic bag inside with the two bottles of orange drink.

"Marcello packed these in ice." She handed him one dripping-wet bottle.

"It's cold enough."

He didn't bother to sit up but rolled to his side, balancing on one elbow as he twisted the cap off first one then, switching with her, the other bottle. He unwrapped his sandwich carefully and began eating. The domesticity of the moment was not lost on April, who smiled at the irony. It had been years since she'd waited on a man. It wasn't the "waited on" part that felt pleasant. It was the sense of companionship.

Thoughtfully, she ate her lunch, reflecting on the last seven years and how she'd gone from being "there" to here. It still felt strange that her whole life had been turned upside down, that a force beyond her control had changed its direction, shuffled her priorities, had even threatened her with its loss, and given her a second chance. And it did seem to her rather fortuitous that she and Hayden had wandered into one another's paths while she was exploring hers.

"So, what's the verdict? Is Venice everything you wanted it to be?"

She considered his question while she began to bag the debris from their lunch. She slowly smiled. "It's even better."

"You can say that even after what happened when you arrived?"

"I don't want to sound too mystical or religious, but I believe things happen for a reason. My passport may have been lost, but look at all the things that happened because of it. I met Marina and her family. I've done things that weren't even on my must do list. I've been introduced to so many possibilities for my work back home with teens."

"And we met up again. Don't forget that."

"I haven't."

He had taken off his sunglasses, and he stared at her now as if looking for something in her face, her eyes. "And you're telling me you really believe that was supposed to happen?"

Was he asking a serious question, or just humoring her? "Of course. Who else would have spent so much time with me, getting me out of trouble?"

He continued to stare, then slowly shook his head. "I have to tell you—it wasn't all work. It's not the consulate's responsibility to make sure American visitors have a good time on their vacation."

"Then you've gone above and beyond the call of duty. Thank you."

"My pleasure." He came agilely to his feet. He held out his hand. "Come on, let's get into the water. You can't come all this way and not go into the Adriatic Sea."

"I don't think so," April said, drawing up her knees again and hugging them to her chest. "I don't swim, and—"

"You don't want to get your hair wet, right?"

That was the last thing on her mind. "I just ate. I might get a cramp . . ."

"That's an old wives tale."

". . . and one of us should stay here with our things."

"Okay, I buy that," he conceded. "I'll take a quick dip and be right back."

April watched Hayden walk to the water's edge. He let the gentle surf lap at his ankles, then, slowly, he entered until the water was up to his thighs. He made no preparatory action, like splashing water on his arms or ducking beneath the surface to get over the chill. He simply curved his body forward and slipped under the water. April stood in order to see him better. It seemed like it took a long time for his head to pop above the surface, some distance from the shore. He hung there treading water, occasionally breaking into the American crawl or breast-stroke, before finally heading back in.

April quickly sat down again, pulling out her guidebook and finding something to focus on besides him. She didn't want him to know that she'd been watching his every move. When he reached the blanket, she glanced up as if surprised to see him. She took her towel from her tote and held it out to him.

"That felt good. You don't know what you're missing," he said, scrubbing the towel up and down his chest and arms, then his face and head.

"I'll take your word for it."

He settled down on the blanket, folded the towel to use as a pillow, and lay down with a deep, contented sigh. At least, April thought it sounded like contentment. She went back to looking at her guidebook, although every nerve was aware of the man beside her, sensitive to his body and his mind. It was not a sexual intimacy, but a sensual one, as though she and Hayden were sharing the same space.

Unable to concentrate on her reading, April put the book down. Hayden appeared to be sleeping. She watched the steady rhythmic rise and fall of his chest, his hands clasped together and resting on his belly. His long legs were crossed at the ankles, his feet encrusted with sand. April sighed, and turned to look out to the water and the horizon and the sky. She was going to remember this day for the rest of her life.

It was the next best thing to having it all.

Chapter 8

When Hayden woke, it was to the sound of voices carried on the air. The heat of the sun spread across the lower half of his body. His back was damp with perspiration. He slowly turned his head. April sat next to him, quietly and attentively looking at the water. She seemed at peace, and in no hurry to move. He would have enjoyed the sight of her in just her swimsuit. He would have liked to have seen the fit of the suit against her slender frame . . . and to imagine the rest.

But she still wore her cover-up. It made him feel wet and sticky just to see her in it. He wasn't clear what purpose it served. He hadn't thought of her as being so modest that she needed to hide.

He sat up. "How long was I sleeping?"

"About twenty minutes."

"Sorry about that."

"Why? I didn't mind." She grinned impishly. "Maybe I'm wearing you out."

"You think so, eh?"

"I'm not the one who felt the need for an afternoon nap," she reminded him.

Hayden yawned behind a hand and rotated his shoulders to stretch the muscles.

"It's hard keeping up with you," he said easily. "I hope you're not on speed or something like that." He adroitly caught the towel she threw at him. "Ready to go?"

"Yes, I think so."

They gathered their few things. Hayden reached for his slacks, shirt and shoes. "I think it'll be easier to dress up on the piazza," he suggested. April helped fold the blanket. He stuffed it into his bag and then guided her around the beach-goers, climbing the stairs to the piazza level. April indicated the ladies' room and went inside, returning a short time later fully dressed. They headed to the bicycle rack.

"We'll drop the bikes off across from the motor landing," Hayden told her. April gingerly climbed onto her bike; Hayden held the handlebars while she positioned herself. "Are you sore?"

"It's not too bad," she said, gamely following him as he rode back toward the waterfront.

The main street of the *Lido* was now congested with people who crisscrossed in front of their bikes, forcing them several times to stop and start. He glanced once over his shoulder and found that she was keeping up despite her obviously tender muscles.

Hayden was glad to see that a vaporetto was approaching the landing stage. They had just enough time to return the bikes and hurry to join the growing crowd of people waiting to return to the city.

He took her hand as they boarded so they wouldn't get separated, and resourcefully found two seats under cover of the canopy. Only when April glanced up at him and said "thank you" did he realize she was more tired than she'd let on. He expected her to pull her hand free now that they were seated, but she didn't. Her hand was narrow and delicate; her fingers curled trustingly around his. He was aware of the warmth of her smooth soft skin. He liked the way it felt.

Once they were under way, Hayden squeezed her hand and she looked at him quizzically.

"You done good today," he complimented her. "I mean about riding the bike."

"Do I get a reward?" she asked.

"I assume you can be bribed with gelato."

"I guess I'm becoming pretty predictable."

He chortled quietly. "Actually, you're not predictable at all. Although I do believe that one of the ways to your heart is through ice cream."

She made a face and appeared to think about it. "I'm not *that* easy. And you forgot the diamonds part. You know . . . a girl's best friend and all that?"

Hayden laughed and settled back to watch her as she gazed at the shoreline. He was okay with the silence, satisfied to hold her hand and let a peaceful lethargy lighten his body. He had a tremendous sense of freedom, an uncharacteristic sense of well-being.

He saw that April sat with her eyes closed, asleep, her face completely relaxed and unguarded. She seemed so young. Her mouth was soft, and there was a look of tranquility on her features. Carefully he released her hand and placed his arm around her, gently encouraging her to rest her head against him. She did so without ever opening her eyes, snuggling into the firm support of his body.

Her hair tickled his chin and jaw, and he felt a peculiar satisfaction. He recalled her telling him that she believed in fate. Hayden knew with a certainty that *this* was one of those fated moments. And yet when all was said and done, this moment was only temporary.

The boat reached the landing stage for San Marco. April continued to sleep so peacefully that he was sorry he had to wake her. He gently stroked her arm. She dragged her eyes open, looking around in a daze to see that they were almost the last ones on board. She sat up and stifled a yawn.

"I didn't mean to fall asleep."

"Don't worry about it. You've been on the go since you got here. It was bound to catch up with you."

"You don't have to take me all the way back," April said. "You must be tired, too."

"I'm fine. Come on. I'll walk you back to your hotel." He was suddenly very aware that their time together . . . his time with her . . . was running out.

"Thanks," April consented. She glanced at him and smiled. "And thank you for the beach outing."

"I know you weren't all that excited about going, so I hope you enjoyed yourself."

"Oh, I did, Hayden. To be honest, it was much more fun than I thought it would be."

"Does that mean you forgive me for dragging you all over the island on a bicycle?"

"If it wasn't for you, I wouldn't have seen it at all. So you're off the hook."

They left the waterfront and started down the interior alley leading to the hotel. There were very few people about, and it was quiet. Hayden looked at April as she walked next to him. He knew he was staring, and he made no attempt to avert his gaze when she caught him.

"What are you thinking?" she asked.

"You know how, when you were younger, hanging out with a bunch of your friends, it seemed like you always had a great time?" he began quietly. "Maybe you weren't even doing anything special, but you were with people you liked and it made you feel really good inside. It made you feel that no matter what else happened, you had these great friends and they'd always be there for you. You got a high from that kind of feeling. Remember that?"

"I think I know what you mean. It was a little pocket of time and everything felt perfect."

"Exactly."

She frowned at him. "What made you think about that?"

He slowly stopped walking and turned to face her. "That's the kind of feeling I got today, hanging out with you. Maybe I'm not explaining it very well but . . ." he squeezed her hand again, holding it tight. "I can't tell you how long it's been since I've enjoyed myself like this. I wanted you to know. And I wanted to thank you."

Hayden watched as the quizzical expression in her eyes changed, first with surprise and then self-consciousness. He took that as an opening, whether April intended it or not. Bending, he kissed her.

He felt her surprise, felt the automatic defensive stiffness of her upper body. But she also puckered her lips against his, responding. Then her mouth softened, and he took advantage. He drew her carefully toward him; his mouth slowly opened and settled over hers. This time she was prepared, willingly meeting him, her mouth fitting perfectly to his.

He kissed her slowly and tenderly, with all the depth of a long-postponed wish. He knew by the way her hands moved restlessly against his chest that April's reaction to him, at least in that instant, was mutual. Her mouth was sweet and caressing.

Hayden heard whistling, and when he broke the embrace, he realized they had an audience of four or five young men who were openly and avidly watching them. They began shouting something at him, all of them talking at once. It was a few seconds before his mind cleared enough to understand.

"*Grazie*," he said, waving briefly as they walked away. He turned back to April. Her eyes were bright but slightly dazed.

"What were they saying?"

He grinned, repeating, in Italian, "They said I was a lucky man."

Then he reacted to her bewilderment, her silent question, picking up where he'd left off, kissing her again. To make their kiss more intimate, Hayden took an infinitesimal step forward. So did April, closing the space between them and what remained of distance, time, and the past.

"You're right about Marina and her family," Stephanie said, craning her neck, as she'd done since arriving, to look into every corner of the large airy rooms adorned with paintings, sculptures, and *objects d'art*. "They seem to be lovely people. I like them."

"Ummmm," April responded absently. She led the way out to the courtyard of the Cesso home, Marina having suggested that they relax in the warm summer evening now that dinner was over.

"Andrea is cute. Doesn't she remind you a little of Anesa? I think they'd like each other."

"Probably."

"In all my trips to Italy I've never been to a private home, let alone a palazzo. I can't believe this place," Stephanie whispered in awe.

"Yes, it's fabulous," April absently agreed. She stopped, deep in thought, before aimlessly finding her way to a wrought-iron settee and sitting down.

"I'm going to invite you to travel with me more often," Stephanie said with a wry chuckle, exploring the beautifully appointed garden. "I've been hanging with the wrong crowd."

"I can't take any credit," April said. "I'd say I've been blessed to be having such a wonderful adventure."

Stephanie sat next to her. "Me too."

"I'm glad. It seemed like all you've done is go to meetings and sample showrooms."

"Usually I don't mind. I'm not big on visiting museums and churches, and I know you like that stuff."

"I felt so guilty about leaving you to go to the beach. When I left this morning you were still sleeping. What did you do all day?"

"Oh . . . not much. I finally got up around ten. By the time I dressed and left the hotel I was starving. I went over to Marcello's."

April sat straighter. "Did you? Was he there?"

"He's always there. I asked him if he ever did anything else but work."

"And?" April prompted when Stephanie didn't seem inclined to add more.

"He said he didn't mind. He likes meeting people. He . . . he said he was glad I came back."

April stared closely at her. "To eat? Or to see him?"

Stephanie appeared slightly offended. "To eat, of course."

"Well, that didn't take all day. What else did you do?"

Stephanie said nothing right away. It seemed to April that she was taking far too long to answer a simple question. Beyond that, April also thought that, uncharacteristically, Stephanie seemed shy about responding.

"Spent more money than you should? You said you never shop because . . ."

Stephanie turned to her. "I spent the day with Marcello." There was no mistaking the bemusement and uncertainty on her face. "As usual he was very polite and attentive. I told him I would never eat at his place again if he didn't let me pay. He laughed, took my money, and asked me out."

April felt an odd kinship. "I hope you had a good time."

"I did."

"What did you do?"

"He took me to his house. He wanted me to see where he lived. After all the warnings I've been giving you, I just up and go off with a man I don't know anything about."

"That's not exactly true. You said yourself you eat at his restaurant whenever you're in Venice. So . . . you go to his house . . ."

Stephanie laughed. "April, I'm telling you, nothing happened. His home is lovely, small, and neat. We sat on a kind of rooftop deck that Marcello said he constructed with the help of his brother. I could see part of the Grand Canal from there. He lives in a pretty little neighborhood. He walks to work every day.

"He served me *limoncello*. He showed me pictures of his grown children, two girls and a boy. He wanted to know if I was married, if I had children. I told him about Chazz, of course. He said . . ." Stephanie's voice dropped. "He said my son was fortunate to have such a beautiful mother."

"Oh, Stephanie," April whispered, moved by the surprise in her friend's voice.

"I said to him, 'Marcello, why me? Why are you interested in me?' And he said . . . 'Don't you know?'"

"Do you?" April asked, the suspense killing her.

Stephanie sighed and got up from the settee. She began to walk slowly around the courtyard.

"Stephanie?" April joined her.

"The first time I wandered into Marcello's restaurant, all I wanted was a cannoli and espresso. Yet from the first, something clicked. It sounds sophomoric and dumb, but it was one of those moments when you look at another person and you know. It scared the hell out of me."

April put her arm through Stephanie's and hugged it against her side. "Why?"

"I don't believe in stuff like that. I'm not romantic. Men are dogs . . ." April burst out laughing. "I can count on one hand the ones I've known since my divorce that I could trust, and that I might be interested in."

"Then maybe it's time you got over it."

"I could say the same to you, you know."

April stopped walking. She stood in the middle of the courtyard facing off with Stephanie, unwilling to go there. Her stomach roiled at the truth and dare reflected in Stephanie's knowing gaze.

"My situation is entirely different," she murmured.

Stephanie's grin was warm with understanding. "I don't think so."

"April. *Scuzi.*"

April turned to Andrea, who came rushing into the courtyard. In her hand the young teen carried the fanciful tiara with gauzy attachments she was to wear to the ball.

"What is it?" April asked her, as she accepted the headpiece held out to her.

"You tell me you will fix my hair so this will stay."

"*Prego*, Andrea. Do not trouble our guests because of a hair ornament," Marina fussed as she joined them.

"I did promise, Marina. It's no trouble at all and will only take a few minutes," April assured her.

Marina threw up her hands in surrender and turned to Stephanie. "So, your costumes will be delivered to your hotel tomorrow in time for the evening."

"It's incredibly generous of you to invite April and me to your ball. I'm looking forward to it . . ."

The two women engaged in friendly conversation, their voices fading as they walked to a far corner of the courtyard. Andrea sat down in a garden chair, shook out her hair and held up a comb. Taking it from her, April began to gently comb Andrea's hair, parting the long, soft strands in places before she began to braid several rows away from Andrea's forehead.

She found it a soothing chore, a quiet distraction from the

turmoil created by Stephanie's revelation, and by her own secret. It was still disturbing to April that she had allowed Hayden to kiss her the way he had. It had felt like she was never going to be able to breathe properly again. She had no warning, no way to prepare, no defense for herself . . . except to kiss him back. Had he picked up on some signal that she hadn't known she'd sent? Or had she left herself too open and exposed, providing him a chance for a full frontal attack?

The questions only increased her anxiety. She was sure, now, that it had been a huge mistake to let Hayden kiss her.

"It is finished?" Andrea asked.

"Almost," April said. Holding the tiny combs attached to the headpiece, she fastened it to Andrea's braided hair so the headpiece was secured and anchored in place.

"It will be easy for you to put this on tomorrow evening," April said to the girl. "You can unbraid your hair after the ball is over."

"No, I leave it like this," Andrea declared, shaking her head back and forth to test the attachments. "Like girls in the magazines."

"Well, maybe for a day or two. You can still wash your hair."

Marina said she liked the effect. April announced that it was time she and Stephanie left to return to their hotel.

"I need to begin packing," April said. "I fly home day after tomorrow."

"Agh! So soon." Marina seemed genuinely sorry. "But you are fortunate to be here a week. Most people, they come and go in one day. You cannot really see and experience Venice in one day."

"I completely agree with you, Marina," April said.

Leaving the palazzo, April and Stephanie began walking, rather than heading to the nearest *vaporetti* landing. The silence between them was introspective in nature. They both needed fresh air, needed to think.

"Are you going to see Marcello again?"

"I don't know. He asked me to join him for dinner tomorrow night before the ball. He wants me to meet his daughter, Patrizia, I think. Her husband is a photographer, and she works at the Peggy Guggenheim Museum. He says his children want to know about this woman he's been talking about for more than a year."

"Wow. That sounds serious," April murmured.

"It sure does," Stephanie sighed.

"What are you going to do?"

"I don't know."

"Do you care about him?"

"I was really hoping not to, but I think I do. But there are so many complications. Marcello lives here. I live in the States. I don't speak his language well enough. I don't know if I could or want to live in Italy. I don't think he'd be happy in Philly. Maybe we should just have a torrid affair and get it out of our systems."

"What if that doesn't work? What if it's not enough?"

"Then I'm in trouble," Stephanie lamented. "What do you think?"

"Stop looking for excuses. Life already comes with obstacles we're constantly dodging. Don't put up more roadblocks. The idea is to find and embrace love, not reject it. Maybe this isn't the real thing. But what if it is? Go for it. One of my mottos is . . ."

"I know, I know. Something about loving like there's no tomorrow," Stephanie recited.

"'Love like your heart has never been broken.'"

"Easy and clever to say. Not so easy to do. What about you and your friend Hayden?"

Stephanie had begun walking up the incline of a footbridge. She stopped when she realized that April hung back.

"Why do you ask?" April inquired cautiously.

"Is Hayden just another unexpected but nice part of your trip, or is he more than that?"

"It's irrelevant."

"No it's not."

"Yes it is."

"You're getting upset with me," Stephanie said calmly.

April stared at Stephanie. "I don't want you making up something in your head that's not really happening."

"Maybe that's what you're trying to tell yourself, but I don't buy it," Stephanie said, not relenting. "I know what you've been through, how you've changed, and I know what you want."

"*I* don't even know that."

"You want to read every book on the best-seller list. You want to travel the world, except for places where there are snakes and bugs, and you'd like to learn how to knit. You want to live to see your daughter grow up, finish school, and maybe someday get married. April, you don't want to miss a thing."

"And what has all of that got to do with me running into Hayden Calloway?"

"Maybe he reminds you of what else you're missing."

"I have everything I want," April said.

"Which is not the same as *getting* everything you want. Why stop with the glass half full?"

"Don't forget I almost didn't have that."

April caught up to Stephanie and they continued over the bridge in silence. They approached the next landing stage and decided to catch the waterbus for the rest of the return trip. Once on the boat, they stood silently near the bow, squinting against the breeze at the skyline of the city, each consumed with the sudden digressions their planned vacation had taken. In almost five days their worlds had changed, their lives had taken a detour. The effect was disorienting, to say the least.

April realized that this was one of the last times she would be taking this ride. That feeling of suspension she'd had a while ago was disappearing. She had to start thinking in terms of resuming her real life. She had to start sorting through her experiences in Venice and putting them into her memory banks.

She had to remember that Hayden Calloway would always be the dream of an adolescent girl, a dream that had come close enough to almost being true.

Chapter 9

April knew it was going to be awkward getting from the hotel to the Ca'Rezzonico, where Marina Cesso's ball was to be held, dressed in full masquerade regalia. She and Stephanie had discussed several options, keeping in mind that an element of surprise was key to the purpose and fun of coming incognito. They decided to carry their masks and long robes and put them on once they'd arrived. Designed to completely cover their clothing, the decorative garments were too heavy to be worn in the heat of the summer evening.

Her concerns, however, were for the moment overshadowed by the discussion she'd had earlier with Stephanie as they'd dressed for the evening.

"Are you okay? You seem awfully quiet," April had said to her.

Stephanie stood in front of the mirror styling her hair, her features stern, almost scowling. "I guess I'm a little preoccupied."

April sat on the side of the bed. "Is this about Marcello? You look so . . . so down."

Stephanie turned, leaning back against the edge of the bureau. Her eyes were troubled, her expression deeply pensive.

"He wants me to stay. What I mean is Marcello would like it if I didn't go home right away."

April couldn't think of anything smart or wise to say. "I guess that's the acid test, isn't it? Are you prepared to do that?"

Stephanie, looking very unlike the normally strong and self-possessed black businesswoman she was, sat down heavily next to April.

"April, I don't know what I'm doing, what I want . . ."

April put her arm around Stephanie's shoulder, hugging her gently. "Maybe you shouldn't do anything, Steph. Maybe this is happening too fast. I mean, I like Marcello a lot. But maybe you need to take a step back. Go home; get back to work and your life. See how things look from there. You can always come back. There are flights every day between Philadelphia and Venice."

"I keep telling myself that, but I'm still so confused."

April kissed her cheek affectionately. "Just don't do anything until you're sure."

And then it was time to leave. What should have been an exciting and glamorous culmination to her visit to Venice was instead a dreaded ordeal. How would she face Hayden for the last time? What would they say to each other? How would they say good-bye? What would she have said if he, like Marcello, asked *her* to stay?

She couldn't, of course, no matter what her feelings. There was Anesa to consider, and her work, her health. She had been blessed the last several years; she was doing better than anyone could have predicted. But she wasn't out of the woods yet.

They crossed the Canal, arriving by *vaporetti*. April could see dozens of boats heading to the pier in front of the Ca'Rezzonico. Guests were already in costume, their heads and faces covered by elaborately painted masks adorned with feathers. April and Stephanie were helped ashore and greeted by an attendant dressed as a seventeenth-century noble. At their query, he directed April and Stephanie to the ladies' changing room.

"At least I'll know you when I see you," Stephanie said. "Your mask is so unique and beautiful."

"I'm glad I could pick the one I wanted to wear. I love the shiny black feathers."

They adjusted their outfits, set the masks in place, and went out to join the other guests.

Crossing the marble floor, April caught a glimpse of Marina at the entrance to the ballroom. Although she was fully dressed, she was not yet wearing a mask. There was no sign of Antonio, Santiago or even Andrea, who April would recognize in her distinctive, ethereal garment. April took one more look, hoping to recognize Hayden among the guests who'd already arrived in their colorful ensembles, but did not see anyone she believed could be him.

The ballroom was crowded with nearly three hundred guests wearing the stunning displays of feathered and beaded garments. The music of the Rolling Stones echoed through the hall, mixing with laughter, a polyglot of foreign languages, and the pop of champagne corks.

They moved along the outskirts of the crowd, watching rather than participating, feeling a bit out of place because they didn't know anyone. April laughed at the incongruity of dancing to rock music in seventeenth-century dress when Stephanie grabbed her arm and shouted something at her.

"I can't hear you," April shouted back.

Stephanie pointed to a table set up as an open bar between two pillars and pantomimed drinking. April mimed back that she would wait. Stephanie started off and was soon lost to April's view in the crowd.

The ballroom was filled beyond capacity and April was jostled and pushed as people moved, or tried to, squeezing their way to the dance floor in their wide-layered skirts, robes, and

capes. Tall hats swayed, gloved hands waved and all in all, it
was a kaleidoscope of colors, movement, music, and laughter.

Someone touched her arm. She glanced hopefully around,
expecting to see Hayden, but the white-masked guest standing before her was shorter and much wider. He made a
courtly bow, and she realized he was asking her to dance.
April looked for Stephanie in the crowd. Not seeing her, she
decided to accept the invitation and allowed herself to be led
onto the packed dance floor.

As they danced to the contemporary beat, her partner
began to talk. She could barely hear him, but knew he was not
speaking English.

"Sorry," April tried to say, pointing to her ear and shaking
her head as she moved to the music.

He shrugged and continued to lead her through the dance
until the music ended. He politely escorted her off the dance
floor and left her with another bow. April looked around again
for Stephanie. Not seeing her, she decided to make her way
to the bar.

"Signorina . . ." a voice said close to her.

April turned to decline another offer to dance when she
saw the spectacles visible through the eyeholes of the mask.
She chuckled in relief. "Santiago."

"Agh. You guess too soon."

"I'm sorry if I spoiled the surprise, but you have no idea
how glad I am to find someone I know."

"Yes, it is very crowded. You have seen my mother? She
looks for you."

"When I arrived, she was busy. I haven't seen her since."

The band was starting a new number, and Santiago began
talking louder.

"She worry that you get here okay with your friend. She
send me and Hayden to look for you."

"Hayden? I haven't seen him, I don't think. It's so hard to tell with everyone wearing masks."

Santiago laughed. "But I find you. Come. I show you."

"I can't. I'm waiting for Stephanie. She went to get a drink."

Santiago made another suggestion, but the words were lost in the booming music. He leaned close and spoke into her ear.

"Hayden say he will find you. The music will stop for a moment, and my mother will begin to speak to the guests. Andrea will come out, representing all the children. Then everybody eat and dance again."

April nodded. "I understand."

Santiago indicated five minutes with his hands, and disappeared.

April sighed in frustration. She knew she'd be lucky if she saw him again for the rest of the night. Someone grabbed her hand, and before she could protest, April found herself dancing again. This partner spoke English, although with an accent the origins of which she couldn't determine.

"You are American?" he asked.

"Yes."

"You are a black American?"

April grinned, cautious. "How can you tell?"

"You must hide your hair. Pull your gloves higher over your arms. This is wonderful. I enjoy meeting new people. Dr. Cesso's wife is very good at this finding people. What is your connection to the hospital, if I may ask?"

"I don't have any. I'm only visiting Venice. I met Signora Cesso, and she was kind enough to invite me to her charity ball."

"Splendid! Isn't it a wonderful event? A bit of a crush, but everyone looks forward to it. So, how do you like Venice?"

"I love it," April said, as he energetically swung her around. She laughed at the unexpected move. He caught her hand and pulled her back.

"And what do you do?"

"I operate an organization for training and mentoring young adults who are leaving high school and just starting college. I try to find work opportunities and mentors that will introduce them to the workplace. I'd love to try and set something up that will allow my students to come to Europe. I want them to think globally."

"This is an excellent idea. Perhaps I am able to help you?"

"Excuse me?" April wasn't sure she'd heard him correctly, or that he fully understood her.

"I would like to know more about your program and students. When I was a young man, I went to study at a newspaper in Chicago. Wonderful experience."

The gentleman opened the front of his fitted cape, stuck his hand inside and began searching. "If you give me a minute . . . ah, here's my card. Please get in touch with me."

"I'm sorry I don't have one of mine to give you."

"Send me e-mail . . ."

April laughed at his offhand suggestion. E-mail was nearly universal.

"I know someone else you should meet before you leave. He will be a perfect contact for you."

"I'm going to have to pay you a referral fee," April laughed again.

"No need. I think your idea is excellent. And I know your students must have support," he said significantly. "You must meet Hayden Calloway. He will also know how to help you. Very smart gentleman from your country. I'm sure he is here, somewhere."

Hayden had decided that it was pointless to try and wander around the great hall and rooms of the Ca'Rezzonico in search of April. He'd arrived early enough that he should have been able to see her among the arriving guests. Marina had inadvertently squelched that idea with her request that he make sure an elderly guest was comfortably settled where she and her husband could see all the activities of the evening, and be seen. By the time he'd returned to the receiving line, he knew he'd missed his chance.

There was also the added problem of not knowing what April would be wearing. Marina had not been able to help, not knowing herself what costume April had chosen the day before at the rental shop. But Hayden was not without a backup plan.

The band had begun to play as soon as the guests began filling the room. Waiters circulated with wine, champagne and delicate finger foods. There were also several food stations for more substantial fare. Hayden took a slow walk around the outside of the room that allowed him his best chance to scan the crowds. He'd come full circle, but had had no luck in identifying April.

"You have seen her?" Marina asked

"I'm afraid not. Too many people."

"Santiago tells me he found her. Near the dance floor."

"Then let me go and . . ."

"Not now. It is time to welcome everyone. Andrea is anxious to do her part so she can relax."

On cue the band made a grand musical introduction and slowly the crowd quieted down. Hayden continued to peruse the guests as Marina, looking magnificent in her courtly dress and intricate mask and headdress, entered a spotlight at the front of the assembly and spoke through a microphone. Her welcome and introductions were first in Italian, and then in English. She talked about the work being done at the children's hospital, drawing laughter when she said firmly the ball had nothing to do with her husband, who did not even like to dance. She emphasized the importance of monetary contributions and pleaded with her guests to be generous, for the sake of the children.

Marina then introduced her daughter, dressed to represent innocence, youth, and the future. The crowd became absolutely silent as the lights dimmed and the spotlight fell on an elaborately decorated float upon which were seated a dozen or so children of varying ages. They were all dressed as angels and nymphs and fairies positioned around a throne-like chair in which Andrea sat. Everyone applauded as the wagon came to the center of the room and stopped.

Slowly Andrea stood. Hayden smiled to himself at the incredible picture she presented. He was particularly caught by Andrea's headpiece and the way it sat upon her head. He narrowed his gaze and realized that her hair appeared to be braided in wide cornrows above her forehead.

April, Hayden mused. The effect on Andrea was exotic and stunning, and he knew the style was drawing attention.

When the speeches were done, and the wagon rolled out of sight, the music started playing once more. The festivities continued in loud, boisterous abandon.

"Congratulations," Hayden whispered to Marina, squeezing her hand as she returned to the entrance. "Everyone seems to be having a good time. Your ball is a success."

"Only if everyone gives money," she said succinctly, making him laugh. "Come. You dance with me, and then I go back to work."

Hayden gladly complied through two dances before leaving Marina to circulate again around the room. He hadn't gotten very far before he was waylaid by Santiago and Julianna.

"Have you found April?"

"No, not yet," Hayden said. "Can you give me a hint? What is she wearing?"

"But that would spoil the fun." Santiago grinned. "I tell you, you will know when you see her. She is wearing a beautiful mask. It is not traditional like many here. Please. You will dance with Julianna."

Hayden willingly took Santiago's fiancée onto the dance floor. But after a few minutes his attention was drawn to a woman standing near the open bar, sipping thoughtfully from a glass of wine. He knew enough about Marina's circle of friends to know she had no quiet ones. This woman's mask exposed the lower part of her face, her mouth and chin. He didn't know who she was, but recognized that she was a little overwhelmed by the activity around her, and she seemed to be all alone.

When his dance with Julianna ended, curiosity and instinct drew him to the woman. Her gaze glanced off him as he approached, and only targeted him again when she realized he meant to speak with her.

"Are you by yourself?" Hayden asked.

"I came with a friend. Why?"

"You're American."

"So are you," she observed, trying to see past his disguise.

"Are you Stephanie?" Hayden asked. She registered surprise and gave him her full attention.

"How did you know that?" She leaned toward him, looking closer. "Who are you?"

"I'm Hayden Calloway. April mentioned you." He could see the relief and surprise relax her body.

"Oh, I'm so glad to meet you. I don't know a soul here and I seem to have lost April. Have you seen her?"

"Not yet. I thought you would know where she is."

Stephanie chortled and shook her head. "Somewhere out there having a good time," she said, waving her glass toward the crush of people. "I left her to get us something to drink. You know how you have to have something in your hand, like a cigarette, so you look like you belong?" Hayden grinned.

"But then I couldn't get back to her. I figure if I stay in one place, sooner or later she'll find me."

"Good plan, but it doesn't look like it's working," Hayden said.

"Not hardly," Stephanie lamented, with a shake of her head. She used a cocktail napkin to dab at the perspiration beading on her chin and forehead. "I know this is a masquerade, but it's hot under this thing."

"The idea is to meet new people."

"Well, I've done my part. I met you, right?"

Hayden looked around and spotted a bench against a wall. "Would you like to sit while you're waiting?"

"Thanks," Stephanie answered gratefully. "I was getting a little tired of standing."

Hayden quickly grabbed a glass from the bar before joining her.

"April told me about meeting you. You guys go back a long ways," Stephanie commented, studying him more closely.

"You could say that. But we didn't run with the same crowd back then."

"I can believe it. According to April she was something of a bookworm and social outcast."

"It wasn't that bad. I was known as the guy who'd never amount to anything."

"Yeah, April told me that, too. Well they were wrong. She said you're with the State Department. Not too shabby, if you ask me."

He glanced down at her with a smile. Stephanie was probably a few inches taller and fifteen pounds heavier than April, with a pretty smile and engaging personality, as far as he could tell. She sported a short, feathery haircut above her mask that made her look youthful.

Stephanie looked out to where people were still crushed together. "The girl has forgotten all about both of us."

"She'll turn up."

"Soon, I hope. I worry about her."

Hayden found the comment odd, but didn't question it as Stephanie continued. "Was it fun catching up on old times?" She looked at him with a coy expression. "Did April tell you she used to have a crush on you? According to her, you were something of a hottie back then."

Hayden grinned broadly. "I don't know about all that."

"To hear her say it, she was a pariah in high school. If that's true then she sure changed over the years."

"She's too hard on herself. You know the kind of cliques that form in school."

"Yeah, I know. All things considered, the girl turned out okay."

"I agree with that," Hayden nodded. "She hasn't really said much about her divorce, but she speaks with mommy-pride about her daughter."

"Anesa. That child is her whole life. And her students. April works real hard at helping them succeed."

"It sounds pretty cool. I like what she wants to do, and I offered to help if I can."

"Good. It's ambitious and she'll need all the help she can get. I love her to death, but sometimes I think she takes on too much, you know?"

"She sounds like a workaholic. Or like she's using work to distract her from things."

"She's had a few hard times in the last few years, but you'll *never* hear her complain. After she was diagnosed and had the mastectomy—well, at least it was modified—she went through two reconstructive surgeries—you'd think she'd pull back and want to slow down for a while. Not April. She makes a list of one thousand and one things she has to do before she dies. Her humor, not mine," Stephanie added.

He felt as if every drop of blood had drained from his body.

He worked hard to keep his expression neutral and tried not to show Stephanie that her news had, quite literally, taken his breath away.

Stephanie's voice began to sound far away until he realized he was no longer listening to what she was saying, but was, instead, recalling every single moment he'd spent in April's company since she'd arrived in Venice. He tried to remember if she had ever said *anything* that would have alerted him to her medical problem. Nothing. He could only remember that, as Stephanie had confirmed, April was not a complainer. If anything, he remembered all the times she had made him laugh, had shown spunk and a rich sense of humor. She had been the butt of some of her own jokes, demonstrating an ability not to take herself too seriously. From the first he'd found that astonishing and refreshing.

"The good news is, April seems okay. She'll be fine, right?" he asked, hoping his inquiry did not betray a sudden urgency.

"Well . . ." Stephanie drew out. She lifted her hand and let it drop helplessly. "Her breast cancer was something called in situ. I think that means it didn't spread. But the doctors are monitoring her closely. She'd been in remission for more than three years. But, you never know."

You never know, Hayden repeated to himself.

But now that he *did* know, the revelation from Stephanie suddenly crystallized a few uncertainties he'd been experiencing and shifted them into the definitive.

Hayden felt restless. He was anxious to go and find April. Time suddenly seemed imperative. He knew he would lose something vital when April left the next day. He glanced at Stephanie, but didn't want to be rude. Another time, place, and circumstance, he'd want to know more about her.

"You know," he said suddenly, "you're probably right. She's out there dancing the night away while we wait. Will you dance with me? We might see her."

Stephanie showed her surprise and gratitude. She reached out and briefly squeezed his arm. "Thanks for asking, but I'm not in the mood. April arranged for me to be included in her invitation but . . . my mind's been somewhere else all evening."

"Nothing serious, I hope."

"In a way, but not life and death," she said evasively. "Look, you go find her and when you do, please tell her I'm okay but I wanted to go back to the hotel. She'll understand."

"I'll make sure she gets back later."

Stephanie put down her glass and took a deep breath. "Well then, I'm off. I hope you two enjoy the rest of the ball. I'm so glad we met."

Hayden smiled with genuine warmth. "Me too."

April was sure that Stephanie must have had a major hissy fit by now because they'd gotten separated so early on in the evening. While she'd enjoyed the chance to dance and to cut loose, her mind had not been on Stephanie, but on Hayden. The masks covering everyone's face notwithstanding, April was sure she would recognize him.

She managed to inch her way toward a table where refreshments were laid out, and was able to intercept a waiter who carefully balanced a tray of wine glasses as he expertly wove his way through the guests. Sipping, April used her other hand to fan herself. Despite the cool interior of the museum she was warm under the long gown and mask.

Determined that she had to find Stephanie or risk her friend's wrath, April turned down two requests to dance and tried to maneuver her way to the edge of the crowd. Someone suddenly grabbed her hand. She turned to face her captor, ready to reject yet another dance offer.

"No, thank you. I have to . . ."

"Signorina, *prego*."

The man, dressed in a royal purple robe and full mask painted gold, silently held up his gloved hand and one finger.

April hesitated, ambivalent. "*Grazie, no*. I can't. I really need . . ."

Slowly, gently, inexorably, he was moving backward to the dance floor, pulling her with him.

"*Prego, signorina molta bella*," he whispered.

April laughed lightly. "All right, all right. *Uno*." She, too, held up one finger.

The music was lively, but without the frantic beat that would have required clever rhythmic movements. April was happy to just move her shoulders and hips in time to the rhythm, savoring a partner who danced well and whom she could follow. They'd begun dancing in the middle of a song which segued after a few minutes into the next. Her partner held her hand captive, indicating his desire to continue to dance. The music slowed, one of only a few all evening that required being held in a stranger's arms.

"You're cheating," April said with mock indignation when the one dance became another, but she willingly let him put his arm around her waist and hold her close.

Behind her mask she smiled while she examined his. It was a beautiful creation with purple and red plumes and beads. Like many around them, his had no open mouth area, and she could only discern that his eyes were brown, and bright. He seemed to be staring hard at her and she quickly averted her gaze to glance beyond her partner to the other dancers. She spotted Marina approaching the band leader. The music ended and the band finished in the flourish of a drum roll.

A spotlight again caught Marina on the raised platform. She stood before a microphone and as silence fell, began to speak. April used the time to scan the guests, hoping to see Stephanie, but when her eyes connected with her most recent dance partner, she realized that he was still studying her.

Suddenly, everyone around her began applauding. She automatically joined in, expecting that someone else was about to speak. Instead, the lights dimmed until the room was dark. A small murmur of anticipation rolled through the gathering . . . and a countdown began.

"Five . . ."

April waited, wondering what was coming.

"Two . . ."

She felt her mask being lifted off her face. She grabbed her dance partner's wrists, but he'd already succeeded in taking the black-feathered creation away. She gasped, both at his audacity and at the sudden impact of cool air on her face.

"One . . ." Applause rang out and the lights turned on. Indignant, April turned, but before she could say a word, her dance partner removed his own mask.

Hayden stood gazing down on her. April smiled in relief and surprise. Later she would remember whispering his name and that, although all the other guests were laughing and exclaiming in surprise at the revealed identities of those around them, Hayden chose to draw her back into his arms again, and kiss her.

Before she could gather her wits and respond, he stepped back. His gaze was filled with satisfaction and only mildly apologetic.

"I figured that was a surefire way to get your attention."

April didn't believe him for a minute. He'd taken advantage but . . . who was she to complain? His kiss, though furtive, was long enough for her to feel a definite erotic charge, to feel his provocative invasion of her mouth. Something fundamental ignited within April, shaking her to the core. It was a sensation she hadn't experienced with a man in years.

Flustered, she said, "I . . . wondered if I'd see you."

"And I was afraid you'd give up and leave before you did."

"No. I'm staying until the last drop of champagne is served . . ." she laughed quietly. "Even if it's not in my glass."

"Would you like some more?"

"I better not. I should keep my wits about me. I don't want to miss anything tonight. And I want to remember it all after I've left Venice."

"I want you to remember, too."

April found herself almost blushing at the subtle innuendo. She pretended to ignore it, observing instead, "You look very royal."

He gazed down. "Do I? I'm not really into velvet. I feel like Darth Vader in drag. Anyway, this is short-lived. I turn back into a frog at midnight."

April laughed merrily at his self-deprecating humor. She suddenly felt refreshed and light-hearted, and glad to be with him. "I suppose you'll expect me to kiss you so you'll stay a prince." She held her breath, shocked at her own suggestion.

His eyes sparkled. "That's a great idea, and I'm glad you thought of it. Just don't throw water all over me to see if I'll croak like a frog."

"In another hour it will be midnight. I've somehow managed to lose Stephanie."

Hayden stuck his mask under his arm and began steering her out of the hall. "I saw her."

"Did you?"

"We introduced ourselves and talked for a while."

"Where is she? Is she upset with me?"

"She said not to worry about her, she's fine. But she decided to leave."

"Oh. Okay," she acknowledged, knowing the reason why. She turned to Hayden. "Maybe I should leave, too."

"I don't think she expected you to. I said I'd keep an eye on you."

"Did you? But it's our last night together in Venice."

Hayden's gaze studied her closely. "It's *our* last night, too."

"I know." Her voice, she knew, was laced with an unavoidable sadness.

So much time had been lost while they'd played hide-and-seek all evening among the other guests. It was no one's fault, of course, but the end of the ball loomed close, as well as the time to have to say good-bye.

"Hear that?" he asked.

"No, what?"

"The music's still playing." She didn't resist when he gently pulled her toward a deserted corridor as the melodic sound of a popular love song echoed. "It's another slow number."

He took both their masks and sat them on the floor near a pillar. They faced each other and came smoothly together to dance.

It wasn't the music that affected her, or the words lamenting an ill-used love, and begging for a chance to start over again. It was the firm band of Hayden's arm around her waist, holding her very close. It was their hands not positioned out, but pressed together to his chest. It was feeling his chin against her temple, and smelling the sultry heat of his body, the hint of perspiration and fabric, and that something about him that she'd grown accustomed to in such a short time.

She filled her senses with everything about him, feeling in that moment feminine and sexual, like a whole woman. He slowly released her hand, and she found herself swaying from side to side against him within the circle of his embrace. He moved his head. She felt his lips press to her forehead. Unconsciously she moved closer, then realizing what she was doing, what she was suggesting, she quickly stepped away.

He didn't question. He seemed to know.

"Sorry," April laughed feebly. "It's so hot. I was feeling a little faint."

"Me too."

"That's not what I meant," she quickly tried to amend.

"April." He curved his hand to her waist and drew her back toward him. "It's what I meant." He kissed her cheek and tried to work his way to her mouth.

"We can't. This is crazy. You don't know that . . ." she stopped abruptly on the verge of a confession she wasn't ready to make. "Hayden, I go home tomorrow."

"And right now we're both thinking the same thing. We don't want the night to end. Maybe you're afraid of staying. I'm afraid of you going. Maybe five days isn't enough time to be sure, but if this is your last night, then I want you to stay with me. I'm very sure about that."

April looked at him in fascination. He meant it. She could see it in the dark probing of his gaze, in the strength of his hand, in his reluctance to let her go. He was waiting on her, and she had to ask herself what, exactly, was *she* waiting for? The perfect moment? The perfect man? A sign from the gods?

There were no such things. She knew that. She only had what she was willing to fight for, to risk, or accept without question and without fear. She'd be lying to herself if she didn't know she wanted to be with Hayden. She wanted that glorious feeling of breathlessness, passion and lust, wanton abandon to satisfy her body and her senses. He had hinted at it each time he'd kissed her; every time she'd stood in his embrace. She had no idea if she could still feel love, but *that* was what she wanted, at this moment, in this place . . . with this man.

He must have seen the conflicting emotions of fear and desire in her eyes. She offered no resistance when he put his arms around her. She needed him to make her feel safe. Then he kissed her, assuring her that everything was going to be okay, saying, through the tenderness of his lips, *You won't be sorry*.

She kissed him back, trusting that he'd keep his word.

Chapter 10

The party was over.

The last of the guests were finally leaving the Ca'Rezzonico, perhaps a little too merry and a little too drunk for the late hour. Marina and her family had long since departed, but not before April had had a chance to thank them profusely, tearfully, for making her stay in Venice so memorable. The band had packed up and gone, but the caterers were still collecting the glasses and plates strewn around the complex of niches and alcoves on the main floor of the converted Baroque palace.

She didn't know where Hayden was leading her and didn't really care. April only knew she was completely wrapped up in the romantic notion that for this moment, she was his girl. They strolled hand-in-hand through mostly deserted streets, drawing curious looks, smiles and comments on their costumes, their masks in their hands. Hayden led her through a passage that opened into a small *campo*. There was a building on each of the four sides. He proceeded to one and began climbing an outside stone staircase.

"Where are we going?" April finally asked.

Instead of getting any answer, she was simply warned by

Hayden to watch her step and be careful. When they reached the top level, about three stories above the ground, he led her to the edge of what seemed like a parapet. He didn't have to explain why he'd brought her there. Out in front of her lay Venice in all its nighttime splendor. From this perspective she could identify many of the major buildings, but she'd not seen them like this before, lit up and detailed with shadows and light.

"I wanted this to be your last image of the city before you left in the morning," Hayden said, standing right behind her.

"This is beautiful."

April felt his hands lightly on her waist. Her back was against his chest. She felt an eerie giddiness, a sense of magic that made her heart thud against her chest. Lethargy attacked her limbs, and it was backed with a dreamy state of anticipation. She felt his chin resting against her temple.

"I wanted you to remember you saw Venice this way with me, April," he whispered.

Her eyes drifted close.

"I don't think I can explain what it's meant to me to be with you. It was like meeting and getting to know you for the first time. I've never looked at this city or anywhere else in Italy the way I have with you. There are things I never would have done or cared about, if you hadn't shown me. And the way you made me laugh . . ." he shook his head as if in amazement. "It felt so good to laugh."

His voice was barely a whisper, but the words were like a caress. His confession was not only poignant, but kind of sweet and candid. Unexpectedly, she felt overwhelmed as tears welled up within her.

"Hayden . . ." her voice broke.

"I have a feeling that if you leave right now, we're going to lose something we've been building all week."

He turned her around to face him and gently drew her into his arms, holding her. "Do you feel safe with me?"

"Yes," she slowly nodded. "But I . . . I think I'm nervous."

"Trust me on this."

April listened to the calming, quiet cadence of his voice. Maybe it was the lack of urgency, the sureness of his words, the gentle way one of his hands rubbed her back. She had learned firsthand that life offered no guarantees, that it was pointless to suffer regrets. April hoped that if there was one thing she wanted as her mantra, it was to live her life fully, in the moment. "I do trust you. But I think you should know . . ."

"I do, April."

She let Hayden lead her back to the staircase. He descended one flight, then used a key to unlock and open what seemed like a magic opening in the wall. He went in first through a heavy wooden door. She followed. Several lights had been left on in the interior of an apartment.

"The government owns several properties around the country besides their consulate and embassy buildings. Some of them are used as meeting spaces and, like this place, temporary residences for visiting VIPs from the States, and their families. I always stay here when I'm in Venice."

April stood silently looking around. It was a good-sized room divided by furniture to create a living room and dining room area. There were bookcases and tables and chairs, a white-fabric-covered sofa, and a plasma-screen TV with components for music and DVDs.

He had already removed and set aside his costume and mask when he turned to her. April was only vaguely aware when Hayden relieved her of the mask, and helped her out of her robe. Underneath she wore a lightweight white blouse and cotton skirt.

"Want the grand tour?" he asked heading toward another room.

Besides the main space, there was a smaller room that seemed to serve as a den/guest room, a huge bathroom that had been modernized, and a bedroom. A large neatly made-up bed dominated the room. There was a small round table and chair placed near a window and two end tables with reading lamps on either side of the bed. One small bureau and an ornate armoire for clothing occupied another wall.

April thoroughly scanned the room while Hayden stood back quietly watching. The table near the window was topped by copies of *Ebony* and *Black Enterprise,* and an open box of cookies. On the chair next to it was a cat, its charcoal-gray fur so dark April hadn't noticed it sleeping. Even now that she and Hayden had entered the room, the cat's only acknowledgment of their presence was a swish of its tail and a pert rotation of its ears.

April made cooing sounds in her throat and bent to scratch the cat's back. She could feel the slight arch of its spine against her hand. "He's beautiful."

"That's Cat," Hayden said, standing next to her. "It's a she, and she's not mine. Whenever I stay here, she appears out of nowhere and makes herself at home. I think everyone in the building takes turns feeding and caring for her." He ruffled the top of the cat's head, and she meowed faintly in delight.

"Are you saying she can vouch for you?" How could she not trust a man who liked animals?

Hayden looked at her. "Would Cat and my word be enough?"

"Maybe. Hayden, I want to be honest. I think I should . . ."

Catching her in mid-sentence, Hayden stepped forward and kissed her until she relaxed and softened within his arms. The sure, firm movement of his mouth on hers, his tongue stroking against hers, was electrifying. April was getting dizzy and disoriented. The tantalizing warmth of desire filled up her groin and stomach, moving up toward her breasts and nipples. The sensation there was totally unexpected and she moaned in surprise.

Hayden broke the kiss, hugging her and breathing softly near her ear. "I'll turn out all the lights, okay?"

He didn't wait for a response, but returned to the front room to turn out all but one light. In the bedroom, what little light there was came solely through the window. April watched his tall, dark shadow move across the room to her. She froze, instinctively crossing her arms protectively over her chest. Rather than touch her, he began to undress, removing shirt, slacks and underwear in short order.

She didn't seem able to move. He stood before her, naked. He reached out and placed his hands on either side of her face. His gaze mesmerizing, he bent to kiss her mouth, his touch light and gentle. It was the reassurance and encouragement she needed to unlock her arms, to remove her clothing. She did so automatically, not seductively, her mind forging ahead, instructing her body on how to feel and act under a man's touch. Blouse, skirt, underwear, and she too was naked. She clenched her fists, forcing herself to not cover her breasts again, assured that the dark hid her secrets.

Hayden turned away to peel back the bed linens. Cat, apparently used to sleeping on the bed with him, jumped right up and began prowling around for a comfortable spot on which to lie. Hayden scooped her up and put her out into the hall before closing the door.

April took advantage of the distraction to quickly get into the bed. Hayden joined her, and when he reached to touch her it was to lie on his side and gather her with her back against his chest. She hadn't expected to cuddle, but felt relief that this was part of Hayden's foreplay. She sighed as he, unhurried, nuzzled the back of her neck, her shoulders. His hands began a slow exploration of her thighs, slid across her tummy, moving toward her breast. She grabbed his wrist.

"Are you ticklish?" he asked, his tone slightly teasing.

"No, but . . . I . . ."

"I get it. You've been divorced a long time. It's been a while and that's okay. Personally, I'm glad to hear it."

"It's not that. It's something else."

"There are certain places you don't want me to touch you?"

April sighed. "Yes."

He gently pulled his hand free, changing tactics and moving down her torso toward her groin. Her skin rippled with swirls of pleasure. His exploration was bold and knowing and excruciatingly tender. Heat rushed to all parts of her. She undulated against him, feeling his arousal against her buttocks.

His hand moved slowly upward again. This time he foiled her attempt to stop him and gently cupped his hand around a breast.

"Oh my God . . ." April moaned.

"Don't think. I won't hurt you."

He was massaging the flesh, his thumb rolling back and forth over the nipple. There was an immediate response, delighting even April as the sensation made them erect. She felt as if all the nerve ends in her body were going to explode.

The hard contact of his body only fueled the fire that burned under her skin. She heard her own voice, moaning in agitation, torment . . . longing. April's mind resisted, but her body was responding of its own accord. She was grateful, and she was scared.

Hayden was shifting, moving so that she could settle onto her back. And he was whispering to her again, but she couldn't get her mind around a single word. He took control and manipulated her body, and it betrayed her by bending to his will. And by doing so she started to fill up with heat and a need to release it.

He murmured her name against her mouth as he absorbed her moan with a kiss. His weight was both reassuring and seductive. Her breathing was labored and her hands became restless. They glided over his skin, seeking his sensitive zones. She knew a fierce satisfaction and relief that she could give him pleasure as well. Carefully he brought them together, settling between her legs. She wrapped her arms, her legs around him, aware of the protection he wore and gasped at the invasion, at the intimate locking of their bodies. She held him tightly, afraid that if she let go, she'd fly off into space.

Her body rode with his. She couldn't recall just then the number of years since a man had made love to her; her body had not forgotten how.

Emotions overwhelmed her. She realized that he was waiting for her, holding back and catering to her needs. The sheer magnitude of his selflessness caused her to gasp, sending her tightly wound body into spasms of release, knowing the instant he, too, let go. Together, at the very end, as they went limp and were replete, Hayden moaned deep within his chest . . . and she started to cry.

She thought for sure he would turn away in impatience. But he kept whispering, "It's all right, it's all right," as he changed positions to lie next to her. He held her and gently stroked her back. She was embarrassed and annoyed with herself for losing control, but the crying jag was swift, intense, and then over.

"*Please* tell me those are tears of joy."

Even in the moment she was tempted to giggle at the uncertainty in his voice. She silently nodded, afraid to try and talk.

"Good. For a minute, my whole life was about to flash before my eyes."

April tilted her head back to look at him, but the room was too dark to detect anything. She would have to trust in the sound and cadence of his voice, in the touch of his hands. It was just as well. She didn't want him to see the watery smile of satisfaction on her face.

She loved that he knew exactly when enough time had past and she'd recovered, that there was no need for small talk. She loved that he seemed to know what was going through her mind as they lay entwined. Her hand began to roam with bold curiosity. She sighed with pleasure and anticipation when it was clear that Hayden hadn't considered them done; that he began to explore the contours, nooks, and crannies of her body. And she let him, knowing they would only get better with practice.

April hurried down the corridor to her hotel room. All the excuses she had mentally composed on her way back to the hotel about why she had not called once during the night, why she had not even thought to call Stephanie, boiled down to one truth. She had needed to find out if she was still desirable to a man. She knew it was unconscionable for her not to consider the impact her unexplained absence might have on her friend; yet, in hindsight, it seemed incredible that she'd allowed Hayden to sweep her past her own fears and insecurities, past common sense so that she gave no thought to anything but their making love.

She inserted her key into the lock and quietly opened the door. Stephanie was asleep. Her bedside lamp was still on, the illumination lost in the early-morning sunlight that filled the room.

April quietly approached the bed and switched off the lamp. Stephanie sighed deeply, turned over, and dragged her eyes open.

She squinted up at April. "Hi. You're back."

"Steph, I'm so sorry. I should have called you."

Stephanie yawned. "What time is it?"

April fumbled to read her watch. "It's almost seven."

"Oh God . . ." Stephanie moaned as if in agony.

April sat stiffly on the edge of the other bed, facing her.

"Hayden wanted to go for a walk after the ball, and I didn't think how late it was, and . . ." Stephanie only stared at her. "I'm sorry if I made you worry. I don't know what I was thinking. I didn't even call to say . . ."

"Did you have a good time?"

"Yes."

"I couldn't stay," Stephanie said absently. "I hope Hayden told you."

"Yes. Are you okay?" Her hair was sticking out in all directions, surprising April. Usually Stephanie set her hair before she went to bed.

Stephanie struggled to sit up, propping herself against the pillows. "Yeah, I'm fine. There's something I have to tell you . . ."

"I know. You're furious with me."

"I'm not flying home with you."

April, about to plead her case, sat with her mouth open. "What?"

"I'm staying in Venice. Just a few extra days."

April tried to read her friend's expression, interpret her demeanor and the soft look in her eyes. "Okay," she finally responded foolishly. "Are you sure?"

"Not yet. That's why I'm staying. I went to Marcello when I left the ball last night. You can guess what happened next. I need more time to find out how I feel about him, April. I'm attracted to him. He's a good man. And he *is* kind of cute. He's confident and not pushy. I like that."

"When did you change your mind?"

"Last night, after I got lost at the ball and couldn't find you." She reached out and took hold of April's hand. "This has nothing to do with you. Except you made me realize that I might be passing up something important. To be honest, it's been a long time since I've met a man I couldn't get out of my mind. *And* he's Italian. Go figure." Stephanie shook her head ruefully.

April pressed Stephanie's hand. "Then I hope it works out for you."

"I'll let you know." She focused on April. "So, I met Hayden. I can see why he was so popular and why you had a crush on him. He seems like a nice man."

"I think he is."

"Tell me about last night."

April pulled off her sandals and curled up on her side. "The ball was a lot of fun. Noisy and crowded, and it's been a long time since I attended such a big party. I met some lovely people. Everyone was friendly and patient when they saw I didn't speak Italian."

Stephanie chuckled. "I meant, tell me about last night *after* the ball."

April was relieved that Stephanie didn't seem upset at her thoughtlessness. "Hayden and I sat in front of the museum for a long time. Just talking."

"Yeah," Stephanie coaxed.

"Then we went for a walk. Talked some more about my trip and returning home."

"Yeah."

"Hayden wanted to show me what the Venice skyline looked like from the top of this building."

"What building?"

"Where he lives when he stays in Venice," April explained nonchalantly.

"And?" Stephanie persisted, raising her eyebrows.

April shifted, shrugging her shoulders. "We went to his place for a while. He has this beautiful cat. Actually, it's not really his, but . . ."

"It was longer than 'a while,' April. It was the whole night. I bet it didn't take that long for Hayden to show you the apartment, the cat, his etchings . . ." April giggled, "or his belly-button lint."

April slowly began to smile. "I don't think he had any."

Stephanie squealed and bounced around her bed. Then she composed herself and sat up, tangled in her nightgown and the bed linens. "Girrrrrrrl! It's about time."

"You don't have to remind me. I never thought I'd find myself with a man again in this lifetime."

"I'm glad you were wrong."

"I was feeling, 'Who'd want a thirty-seven-year-old divorcée who hadn't slept with a man in six years?' My life has been so damaged, patched up, and glued together," April said pensively.

"You've still survived better than a lot of women I know. I say, God bless Hayden for getting you into bed, girl."

"It took a little while for me to get into the swing of things. You know what I mean. I wasn't sure I'd be able to . . ."

"Did the man know what he was doing?"

"Very well, thank you. It was lovely."

Even hours later she was still reliving those vibrant moments, still experiencing the thrill of his touch and the solid security of his body pressed against hers. The memory alone made her feel light-headed again. They'd fallen asleep wrapped in each other's arms. She'd liked that part, too. He kissed her awake just as the sky was showing a hint of royal blue. She knew she had to leave, but she didn't object when the languid drowsiness of sleep turned into a hasty and heated reawakening of desire that was all the more wonderful because they had so little time.

"Too bad you're leaving today. Just when you're starting to get the hang of it," Stephanie said in sympathy.

April had considered that very same thing. But she'd had enough time with Hayden to know that she was glad she'd waited, for the right time and the right person.

In just a few hours she would be in the air flying back home. She had refused to let Hayden bring her back to the hotel; she hadn't wanted to drag out their farewell. She'd been afraid of each of them saying things in the finality of the moment that would soon be forgotten when they returned to their separate lives. He'd compromised, putting her on the *vaporetto* going across the canal. April watched him, a tall, brown, solitary being on the pier until her boat motored away and he was lost to view. The last she'd seen was his wave just before the distance made it impossible to see him at all . . .

"April? April, wake up."

She opened her eyes and found Stephanie leaning over her. "Did I fall asleep?"

"Me, too. I got in this morning only an hour ahead of you."

April reluctantly got out of the bed and began pulling herself together. She showered and put on fresh clothes for traveling, and packed the rest of her things. She checked her documents, astonished to think that a mere six days earlier she had just arrived and all of what she now held in her hand had been lost. If not for that incident she would never have met Hayden again.

They had almost overslept, so instead of going out, they went to the hotel dining room for a continental breakfast. They chatted easily about when Stephanie might return home, when they'd next talk to one another; they listed all the things they hadn't done together that they'd planned. After, Stephanie accompanied April to the pier where the *Alilaguna* launch would pick her up for the transfer to the airport. They hugged and kissed good-bye; April warned Stephanie to be careful. Stephanie sent a message for Anesa that she had a fabulous present for her that she'd get when Stephanie got back home.

April felt precariously close to tears as she boarded the launch, although she couldn't put her finger on exactly why. Was it because her fondest wish—to visit Venice—had come true? Was it leaving her new friend, Marina Cesso, and her incredible kindness and the generosity of her family? Or was it meeting Hayden and finding that he gave her a reason to feel like a woman again?

There was no time or opportunity for April to indulge in reflection or theory. The airport was a madhouse of people checking in, passing through customs and immigration, lining up for security, wandering around aimlessly in that pretrip state that all travelers seem to suffer.

Before passing through security, April was randomly selected to have her suitcase checked. She was asked the usual questions: Had she accepted any packages from strangers; had she been asked to carry anything on board the plane? Her clothes and other personal items were rifled through, repositioned, carelessly put back. At last cleared by the inspector, April headed for the final hurdle—security—before continuing on to her boarding gate.

She had just placed her jacket, purse and documents into the plastic tub that would pass through the X-ray machine when she felt someone coming up behind her.

"Miss. You come, please."

"What? But I've already had my things . . ."

"Signorina, a moment."

A middle-aged man in a uniform that identified him as airport security spoke rapidly to the agent who was about to pass her into the gate area. She watched, confused, as the plastic bin with her things was removed from the conveyor belt of the X-ray machine and handed back to her. The middle-aged man indicated that she was to follow him.

"Excuse me, what is the problem? I have a ticket. I have a plane to catch."

"*Si, si* signorina," he acknowledged, and kept walking.

April was led to a counter where four other security officers waited. It took a moment before she realized that Hayden waited there as well.

Her escort seemed to be apologizing, but April wasn't paying much attention. She was much more interested in Hayden. What she saw in his eyes made her breath catch in her throat. She knew her own gaze was bright with the surprise of seeing him.

Another officer spoke to Hayden, who nodded, and then they all discreetly stepped aside. Hayden came toward her.

"What are you doing here?" She was unable to keep the smile from her eyes or her mouth.

"You forgot something. I had to use my diplomatic ID before they'd help me."

"What did I forget?"

"Your costume. You left it at my place this morning."

"Oh, no. What am I going to do? It has to be returned to the rental shop."

His smile was slow and seductive. "You had something else on your mind at the time."

"It was all your fault," she said with mock indignation.

"I hope so. Don't worry. I'll see that it's returned."

"Hayden, you didn't come all the way out to the airport to tell me about the costume."

"No. I came to give you something. Two things, actually. I'm still willing to bet you never got yourself anything that would be a reminder of this trip. So I did it for you."

Hayden reached behind him for a tissue-wrapped package he'd left leaning against the counter. It was irregularly shaped. When April silently accepted it from him, she realized that despite the shape and size, it was very light.

"Should I open it now?" she asked.

"Wait until you get home. I know you like surprises. I've already cleared it with security for you, since you didn't arrive with it."

She fingered the tissue paper, unable to even guess what it was he was giving her. "You didn't have to get me anything. I don't know what to say."

"Say, 'Thank you, Hayden.'"

She laughed. "Thank you, Hayden."

"There's one more thing." He put his arms loosely around her, packages and all, and kissed her. It was not a kiss of passion like the ones they'd shared in the darkness of his room, but a kiss that tasted of promises and good-bye.

"You're a lot of fun, April Stockwood," he said softly into her ear before he released her. "I'm glad I waited for you to grow up."

His voice and words send a coil of desire through her, but already Hayden was stepping back. He looked at her one long moment, then simply turned and walked away.

April, unable to gather her wits, said nothing as she watched him vanish into the crowd. She was sitting in the boarding area waiting for her flight when it hit her. Hayden Calloway was exactly the kind of man she'd always dreamed he would become.

Chapter 11

As she passed the open den window, April could hear giddy voices. She stopped to gaze out at the backyard through the sheer curtain panels, craning her neck to see what the five young girls were up to. She was only minutely bothered by the possibility that she could be accused of eavesdropping on Anesa and her friends, but instantly forgave herself by order of parental privilege.

She stopped short of listening to their actual conversation, although she did catch one remark. Anesa's best friend, Gillian, was complaining that she didn't find so-and-so's brother all that cute. He was bowlegged. That sent the girls into peels of laughing agreement. The girls had suddenly become boy-conscious. April was relieved that Anesa was still somewhat leery of them.

April still couldn't believe how much Anesa had changed since the start of the summer. She'd grown two inches and had begun to develop defining curves. By her birthday that coming November, her baby was going to look more like a teenager and much less like a little girl.

The girls were sprawled on lawn chairs and loungers, or

sitting cross-legged on the grass. They were protected from the high-noon sun by the shade of an ancient dogwood tree.

April continued through the house until she reached the kitchen. She'd promised the girls a platter of treats, and she got busy putting it together. For a minute, she stood in the middle of her spacious kitchen trying to recall where she'd last seen the serving platter or, for that matter, the pitcher she normally used for lemonade. Then in a flash she remembered and headed for the pantry.

She was annoyed and impatient. Ever since she'd returned home from Italy she seemed to be functioning in a daze, easily distracted and forgetful. She had been home more than three weeks, and yet she couldn't seem to get her act together.

She'd never experienced anything like it. She'd picked up her car at the airport, and driving through Philadelphia to the outlying community of Maple Shade had been a letdown. She had been overwhelmed with cars and traffic lights and trucks and noise, arriving at her house after only a week away and finding that everything was alien.

As she walked into the kitchen with the tray and pitcher, she felt enormous guilt that she wasn't absolutely thrilled to be back home.

Where was the Grand Canal?

"Mom, can I stay over at Tisha's house tonight?"

Forced out of her introspection, April turned to Anesa. "Not tonight. You were over there last weekend. I'm starting to think you don't want to live here anymore." She began cleaning and culling strawberries and arranging them attractively on the platter.

"That's not it. We want to talk about what we're wearing to Eric Harris's birthday party." Anesa slouched against the kitchen counter, watching her mother work and helping herself to a strawberry.

April focused on her daughter and felt a surge of pride. She was so beautiful. April knew she couldn't accept all the credit for that. She could easily find the ways in which Sinclair had contributed his fair share of "good" genes. Anesa's long hair, until recently braided for ease of care while she visited her father, hung thick and loose around her shoulders, framing a face that was sloe-eyed, had a pointed chin, and dimples in her cheeks.

April was pleased to note that Anesa was wearing the huggy earrings she'd purchased for her in San Marco Square. She hadn't been as enthusiastic about the lace skirt and top from Burano.

"Why don't you wear that outfit I brought you from Italy?" Anesa made a face. "Don't you like it?"

"It's not that," she said carefully, "but it's not like things I buy when I go shopping with my friends."

"I hate to clue you in, but you and your friends don't always have the best of taste," April said wryly. "You all want to look exactly alike. Don't you know that you'd get more attention if you looked different?"

"Yeah, but not *that* different. It looks old-fashioned."

"Have you shown it to Tisha?"

"No," Anesa reluctantly admitted.

"Okay, I tell you what. I bet that when they all see it, they're going to love it."

"No, they won't," Anesa countered, doubt tingeing her words.

"If I'm right, you wear it to the party and I'll let you borrow my gold necklace with the diamond stud in the middle."

"Really? Okay, I want to make a bet, too."

April smiled at her daughter lovingly. "What have you got to bet that you think I want?"

"No, not like that. If I'm right and nobody likes that lace thing, you'll let me have the mask you got in Italy."

"No."

"Mommmmmm. That's not fair."

"The mask isn't yours to barter. It's a very special gift and I will break your arm if you go anywhere near it."

Anesa giggled. "No you won't. It's just hanging on the wall in your bedroom."

"Where it's going to stay."

"I could wear it at Halloween . . ."

"No."

"But . . ."

April put her paring knife down and faced Anesa. "You know how, when Daddy buys you something that I hate, I don't always say anything about it. I let you have it because I understand it has special meaning since he gave it to you. Right?"

"Yeah?" Anesa said, trying to follow her mother's logic.

"Well, that's the way I feel about the mask. It represents something and someone that means a lot to me. It's the only thing I brought back from my trip just for myself, okay? End of discussion. Now, do we have a bet or not?"

Anesa came to life. "Okay, I'm going to put it on right now and you'll see that nobody likes it."

While Anesa disappeared upstairs, April took the plate of fruit and pitcher of lemonade out to her daughter's friends. They attacked the food in typical kid fashion. She'd hung around long enough to chat with them about how their summer was going and to hear some of the amusing travails of being adolescent. She was glad when the telephone rang, giving her an excuse to return to the house. She grabbed the cordless and headed for the air-conditioned comfort of her bedroom, curling up in the Queen Anne chair near her window.

"How's the backyard gathering of the young and the restless?" Stephanie asked.

April laughed. "Fine, fine. You know how it is. I can't believe the things that are important to these girls. Do you remember being like that?"

"Probably. Thank God we grew up."

It was an innocent enough remark, but April zeroed in on Stephanie's words, recalling Hayden saying how glad he was that he'd waited until she'd grown up. It had only been later that she'd questioned his meaning. Was he glad that she was old enough to pursue? Was he glad that she'd changed and was now worth pursuing? Or was he glad that he'd waited because he'd grown up, too?

She had no idea.

April wanted to believe that it was a combination of the three. She had been living on the afterglow of her trip and especially time spent with him since returning home, but the farther away she got from the actual trip, the more she was coming to think that perhaps that magical night hadn't meant as much to him as it had to her. She'd wanted to have the adventure of a lifetime. She'd gotten more than that.

"I've only seen you once since you got back. What's going on?" April voiced.

"I know. I'm calling to see if you want to get together for dinner next week."

"That sounds good. I have a doctor's appointment and Anesa's spending the following weekend with my sister and her family in New Jersey. I should spend some time working on what I want to do with my students in the fall. Before you know it, the summer is going to be over."

"I've been busy as well. It almost seems like we never had a vacation, doesn't it?"

"Unfortunately, you're right," April sighed. "Then sometimes I think about it and feel like I was just there yesterday."

"Exactly which parts are you talking about?" Stephanie asked.

"All of it."

"I'm talking about Hayden Calloway."

"I know you are. I'm not going there."

"Haven't heard from him?"

"Nope," April said, lightly covering. But the admission cost her. She missed him. More specifically, she missed the two of them together. Being with Hayden had been sweet and romantic. It had breathed life into her as a woman.

"Well, I wouldn't worry about it too much. August is vacation hell in Europe, and he's probably overwhelmed. He might have been sent somewhere to handle a crisis. You never know."

"If you say so. Have you heard from Marcello?"

"I have."

Stephanie said it with such a degree of satisfaction that April knew it had to be more than that. She was relieved and pleased that all of her friend's doubts had, so far, proven groundless.

"Are you calling to tell me you're going back to Venice?" April guessed.

"You got it. At the end of the month."

"I hate you," April grinned.

Stephanie chuckled. "I'd ask you to come with me again . . ."

"I can't. I don't know what I'd do with Anesa, even if I could afford to go."

"I could loan you the money."

"Stephanie, if this is your attempt to play matchmaker between me and Hayden, forget it. I admit I like him, I loved being with him, but if I meant anything to him he would have contacted me, no matter how busy he was. E-mail, phone call, smoke signals—"

"You're right."

"But thanks for the thought. It was sweet of you."

"What's this doctor's appointment next week?"

"My oncologist. She wants to see if I'm going to need another round of maintenance treatments."

"I'll come with you."

"Thanks, but it's not necessary."

"How are you feeling?"

"Great. As a matter of fact, I gained five pounds in Italy. I need to do something about that."

"Mommmmmmm! Where are you?"

April sat forward on the edge of her chair. "Anesa's bellowing. I'd better go see what's going on."

"Give her a hug and kiss for me."

"I will. We'll talk later about getting together?"

"Yes, I'll call. And stop being so prissy, April. Remember what you told me about regrets. I think you should get in touch with Hayden. Do it on the pretense of thanking him for taking care of getting you a new passport."

"He'll see right through that. I don't want him to think I'm chasing him. Gotta run."

After putting the receiver down, April discovered that the call had the unfortunate effect of churning up not so much memories as feelings: sensations that swept through her body, the ghost of touches and kisses and deep laughter at unexpected moments. She couldn't decide if she would have been better off never to have felt any of those things again. In the middle of the night, alone in her room, they were all she wanted.

"Mom, come here. Come here!"

"Coming," April shouted as she headed for the backyard.

She opened the door and found Anesa surrounded by her girlfriends. Her daughter had put on the two-piece lace outfit, and the girls were exclaiming over it. "This is really nice," one girl said.

"Look, you can see through the skirt," another commented.

"No, you can't," Anesa corrected. "It's lined with silk."

"If you wear this to Eric's party I bet he's going to ask you out."

The girls giggled at the thought.

"I wish I had a dress like this," Tisha lamented. "Where'd you buy it?"

April was pleased and relieved when Anesa smiled at her, eyes bright with the knowledge that she'd scored with her friends.

"My mom bought it for me in Italy," she boasted.

"I'm finished packing," Anesa said, sliding into a dining room chair adjacent to her mother.

"Good. Your uncle Max said he'd pick you up in the morning around nine," April murmured, distracted as she read a letter she'd just received.

"Can I see the pictures?" Anesa reached for the envelope the letter had arrived in, where a handful of photographs were visible under the flap.

"I haven't seen them yet," April said, but Anesa had already appropriated them.

"Oh. I saw these. They're from Italy."

Sighing, April put her half-read letter down and joined her daughter in examining the photographs. "No you haven't seen these. I just got them in the mail from Marina Cesso. Oh, these are nice."

"Where is this?" Anesa asked, pointing to the image.

"That's me at the Cesso house. I think Andrea took that picture. And this one is when we all went to rent costumes for the masquerade ball."

She took the picture from her daughter and studied it. There she was with Marina and Stephanie, posing for the shop owner who'd taken the picture as they'd tried on masks. A faint smile played around her lips at the memory of that day.

"Who's this?"

April looked down at the picture Anesa held. Hayden's face stared back at her. The photograph had been taken at the ball after the unmasking. She and Hayden were saying good-night to Andrea, who was leaving to return home with her father.

Staring closely, she wondered if her eyes looked a little too bright. Were she and Hayden standing a little too close? They were holding hands. April hoped that Anesa hadn't noticed.

"That's a friend of mine," April explained casually.

"Who is he?"

"His name is Hayden Calloway. I know him from high school. I ran into him in Venice. I told you about the Cessos. Well, Hayden is a friend of theirs, too."

"His name is Hayden? That sounds cool. What happened to him?"

April put the photograph down and picked up another. "I don't know. Still there, I guess. Listen, I just got this letter from signora Cesso. Her daughter, Andrea, would like to come to visit. Isn't that great? How would you feel if she came and stayed with us for a week?"

Anesa shrugged. "I don't know. How old is she?"

"Fifteen. Only a year and a half older than you."

"Does she speak English?"

"Very well. She's a lovely girl. Friendly and very pretty."

"She's not stuck-up or anything?"

"Not at all. I think it would be a good experience for you to spend time with someone about your own age who's from another country."

"Mom, you make her sound like a homework assignment."

April laughed. "Sorry. That's not the impression I want you to have. Are you interested?"

"Hmmmmmm. I'll think about it."

"You have twenty-four hours, Anesa. You can call me from your Aunt June's. I have to let Andrea's mother know so she can make arrangements."

"Okay."

"I think you'll like Andrea. She's never been to America."

"Really? I guess I could show her around Philadelphia." Anesa was already planning. "Do you think she'll want to hang out with my friends? Maybe we can go down to Washington, too."

"Good idea, sweetie. I think that would be fun. I could take you . . ."

"Maybe Daddy can take us. If she comes."

"If you want," April said calmly. Sinclair was a much better father than he'd been a husband, especially during her illness. And she would never say anything to discourage Anesa's relationship with him.

She hadn't finished reading the letter from Marina, but decided to wait until she was alone. April couldn't deny that she hoped that there would be some mention of Hayden.

"Mommy, look at this one."

"What, sweetie?"

April took the photograph, and stared at it. Andrea or Marina or Santiago or *someone* had snapped a picture of her and Hayden dancing together at the ball during the last song they'd danced to, the slow one. When he held her and she had been aware of his arms and thighs and the subtle heat from his body. In the picture they seemed to have eyes only for each other, which would certainly explain how she could have missed knowing their photograph was being taken.

"Wow, Mom. Your costume was so pretty."

"Thank you. How about taking a drive to the Riverdale Mall and getting some ice cream?"

"Ooooh, yeaaahhhhh," Anesa said, running to put her sandals on.

April discreetly pulled the photo from the pile. She was going to add it to the ones she'd already put aside of Hayden.

"I understand that you're upset, Mr. Powers, but we can't take a stand against local customs. The most that the consulate can do is offer to have someone talk with the manager of the restaurant. We can't demand a refund because you were dissatisfied with the food and the service. That's part of the risk you accept when you travel anywhere." Hayden listened patiently as the distraught and angry American caller aired his grievance.

He'd been surprised when he'd first begun his tour of duty in Milan, not by the numbers of incidents reported by U.S. citizens traveling abroad, but by the triviality of them. At least, in his mind, they were not terribly significant. He found out firsthand that most people expected to have the exact same protection and privileges abroad as their government provided them back home. His job was to comfort and appease them when they found out that wasn't the way international relationships worked.

"Yes, sir. I understand how you feel. As I said, I'll be glad to make the call on your behalf . . . certainly sir, my name is Hayden Calloway."

He began taking information and filling out the perfunctory forms for reporting an incident. He offered the standard words of sympathy, but no guarantees. It was only the second call he'd had of this nature, but increasingly he found himself impatient with the attitude of entitlement that accompanied the calls.

When he was finished, he sat back heavily in his chair. Ever since returning to his consulate office nearly a month earlier, he'd found it difficult to resume his duties with an impartial mindset. For one thing, Hayden had quickly realized that he'd begun comparing every caller with April, but only because he'd never known her to complain about anything. God knows, she would have had just cause.

In hindsight he'd come to fully appreciate and admire her equanimity. On a day-to-day basis, he hadn't met anyone who came close to her self-possession. At any given time he found himself conjuring up her laugh, her wide bright smile, and the mischief and inquisitiveness in her eyes. He was grateful that his memory served him so well.

He couldn't believe how much he missed her.

With that mental confession Hayden bounced forward in his chair in hopes of dispelling the thought, but he only succeeded in feeling a terrible restlessness and a regret that he'd made no attempt to contact April since she'd flown back to the States. In the meantime, he'd had to endure cheerful reports from Marina about the letters she'd received from April. This only made Hayden feel more isolated and further away from her with each passing day.

Of course, she'd made no attempt to contact him, either.

He spotted the printed copy of an e-mail he'd received several days ago. Reluctantly, he read it through. Each time he did so, he felt himself pulled back inexorably to a past he'd tried for years to get away from. Reese wrote that he was needed at home. A family issue had arisen, his brother claimed, that couldn't wait until he returned on his next leave or whenever it suited him.

Whenever it suited him.

He hadn't written back, yet. It made him angry just to think about going back to where he'd always been made to feel like an intruder. Bracing himself, Hayden opened his e-mail window and began composing a response. It would help if he knew more about the nature of the family matter and why it was believed he had to come home. He had the most trouble with that part. *Home.*

"Hayden, it is late. We go now."

Hayden ignored Santiago's suggestion and frowned over his screen as he carefully chose his words. "In a minute. I want to finish this first."

Santiago made himself comfortable in the visitor's chair in front of Hayden's desk. He grinned at Hayden.

"A phone call would be nicer."

Hayden frowned but continued typing. "What?"

"Call her. It is more romantic. E-mail is . . ." Santiago made an inarticulate gesture with his hand, as if to describe "horrible."

"Call who?" He continued to write.

"I don't think you should send an e-mail to April. Very impersonal, no?"

Hayden stopped mid-sentence. He had to shift mental and emotional gears as he was again reminded of her. "I'm not writing to April."

"Why not? Aren't you interested in how she is doing? We know how she is doing."

Hayden went back to his letter, forcing himself to concentrate. He wanted to get the e-mail done before he changed his mind about answering at all. "How is she?"

"Good, my mother says. But you should find out for yourself. You are writing to Simone? Ah, this is too bad," Santiago lamented with a sad shake of his head.

"I got an e-mail from my brother, Reese."

Santiago nodded silently in understanding. He dropped his teasing demeanor.

"We will be late for the concert. The *duomo* will get full very quickly."

"I know. I'm almost done." He continued for another line or two, typed his name, and hit the "send" button.

Hayden gathered his things and left his office with Santiago. He was not into the kind of classical music that was often performed inside or out of the major cathedral in the center of downtown Milan, but he'd grown to like the opportunity to people-watch. It was the kind of music that Hayden knew would allow him to slip into his own deep thoughts and consider what, if anything, he should, could, or would do about April.

"Tonight we hear *Tosca*."

Hayden groaned. "Opera."

"It is very famous."

"It is very weird. All those singers screaming at the top of their lungs at each other . . ."

Santiago laughed and slapped him on the shoulder as they walked the several blocks from the consulate toward the *duomo*. Hayden had quickly readjusted to a city of cars and motorbikes, horns and ringing bells of street cars and trolleys. But he missed the *vaporetti* and the Grand Canal. He might never have paid attention to the difference if not for April.

When they reached the front of the cathedral, it was indeed crowded. Despite Hayden's attempt to bow out of the evening, Santiago was determined to make him stay.

"You know, if Julianna were here you wouldn't care if I stayed or not."

"This is true," Santiago conceded. "I think the same is true if April were here. You are a terrible date, but better than nothing."

Hayden laughed sadly at the truth of what Santiago was saying. While they searched for seats, his attention was caught by a vendor who was selling newspapers and postcards.

"I'll be right back," Hayden said, moving toward the display. He carefully looked through the rack of cards, finding one of the *Pieta*, another of a fashionable street in the design district, and a third of a park. He purchased all three and rejoined Santiago.

The music began and the crowd quieted down. As the drama of love and betrayal began, Hayden's attention—as he'd known it would—began to wander. To his surprise, the opera became a soothing background to the turmoil which had raged within him for weeks. He closed his eyes, and instead of trying to fight the inevitable, tried to figure out how to deal with it. His life, his family. April.

The first act ended.

"I must ask you something important," Santiago said.

"Okay," Hayden reluctantly agreed, hoping it was nothing personal.

"I would like you to be the best man."

"The best man?" he asked. "So you've finally set the date."

"Of course. Julianna said, enough waiting."

Hayden put out his hand and, as he'd taught him, Santiago skillfully executed a soul handshake. "Way to go, my man. I'm happy for you."

"You are happy, I am happy. My mother is relieved."

Hayden laughed. "I bet. When?"

"In the spring of next year. It will not be very big. But I want my good friend to be there."

"Thank you, Santiago. I'm honored you asked. I'll be happy to serve as your best man."

"This is good. I have asked Andrea to tell April."

"Tell April? Why Andrea?"

"My mother has not spoken to you," Santiago concluded. "Andrea is to visit America. She will stay with April."

Hayden was surprised by the news. In an odd way he also felt that Andrea's going to the U.S. made him feel like *he* was getting closer to April. It would have made much more sense, he couldn't deny, if he'd just gone himself. But distance and time had skewered things in his head. What if she didn't feel any of the things he had?

Santiago gently slapped his shoulder again, shaking it to get his attention.

"Do not worry. I will do the same for you another day."

"What?"

"Be your best man."

Hayden chortled quietly. "Not in this lifetime."

Chapter 12

April could tell by the way Anesa held onto her arm and pressed it against her side that she was nervous. She had been uncharacteristically quiet since they'd arrived at the airport to meet Andrea Cesso's flight from Venice.

April squeezed her daughter's arm reassuringly. Anesa only had two weeks left of summer vacation before school began. April wondered, not for the first time, if it was bad timing to have Andrea as a guest.

"What if I don't like her?" Anesa asked in a small voice.

"I'd be really surprised if that happens, sweetie. One of the things I thought when I first met Andrea was how much she reminded me of you. Don't forget, Andrea is coming to a country where she's never been before. English is not her first language. Think how nervous she must be."

"That's true," Anesa agreed.

"Think of yourself as a junior diplomat. You want Andrea to have a good experience and to get a good impression of African-American teenagers."

"You mean like Hayden?"

"Excuse me? Why did you say that?"

"Didn't you say that he's like a diplomat? He works for the embassy in Venice, right?"

"No. He's with the American consulate in Milan."

April was surprised that Anesa remembered what she had told her about Hayden's job. She'd wanted to make Anesa feel more comfortable about the fact that her mother had spent time with another man.

"Well, it sounds pretty important. What does he do there?"

"He helps American travelers if they have problems."

"What if Andrea doesn't like American food?"

"Honey, you like Italian food. And I'm not talking about pizza." April pulled her arm free and turned to rub her shoulders. "Don't worry. It's going to be okay."

The first of the passengers began filing out from customs and immigration. Not wanting to miss Andrea in the growing crowd, April gave all her attention to the arrivals.

"Oh, there she is. Andrea!" April called out, waving her arm.

Hearing her name, Andrea scanned the gathering. Spotting April, she broke into a smile. Her streaked blond hair had been pulled back into a loose ponytail for the flight; a heavy tote bag hung from her shoulder. April began moving through the bottleneck of people to reach her when she noticed a black man right behind Andrea. He stood out, the only black man arriving on the Italian flight. April did a double take when she realized it was Hayden.

She was so stunned that she thought he had to be an apparition. Had she been thinking of him *that* much? He was staring at her, smiling slowly at her bewilderment. It *was* Hayden, April realized. Her mouth seemed suddenly dry. She had no time to give him her full attention; Andrea was hurrying toward her with a big smile.

"Hello April. I am here." She threw her arms wide and gave April a tight hug.

April welcomed Andrea's exuberant greeting while also aware that Hayden had stopped close by, watching.

April pulled back and examined the teenager. "It's so good to see you again."

"It has not been so long since the last time," Andrea laughed.

"I know. You'd think we hadn't seen one another in years." April reached for her daughter and drew her forward. "Andrea, this is my daughter, Anesa."

"That is a pretty name. Aneesa," she repeated, with her own slight accent added. "I am happy to meet you and happy to be here."

"Hi." Anesa held out her hand, and then froze at the unexpected kiss Andrea lightly planted on both cheeks.

"This is how we say hello in Italy," Andrea explained.

In those few seconds, April finally turned to Hayden. He was focused entirely on her. April caught her breath and smiled. She felt somewhat fluttery inside.

"What a surprise to see you."

"I hoped it would be," Hayden confessed. "I'm here on personal leave," he explained further, in answer to her unspoken questions. "I'm going to see my family."

"Oh," April said, still struggling with the fact that he was actually standing in front of her.

"I offered to escort Andrea on her flight. I knew you'd be my first stop."

"Oh," she repeated warmly. She stared foolishly at him.

Hayden chuckled quietly. Stepping forward, he kissed her lightly on her cheek and spoke into her ear. "It's good to see you again."

April swallowed. Her feelings exactly, even though she seemed to have trouble saying anything intelligent. Anesa grabbed her arm.

"Mom, we have to get Andrea's luggage. Come on."

"Wait, Anesa." April reached for her daughter's hand. "I want you to meet someone. Remember the man in the photographs? The one who works in Milan? This is Hayden Calloway." April looked squarely at him. "My daughter, Anesa."

She watched as he turned to Anesa. His gaze was filled with warmth and good humor.

"It's a great pleasure to meet you. Your mother said you were beautiful, and she's right."

"Thank you," Anesa said shyly. She turned to April. "Mom, is he staying with us too?"

April saw the way Hayden grinned broadly as he overheard the softly asked question. "No. I believe Hayden is here to take care of some personal business." April glanced at him briefly for confirmation.

"That's right. But I am looking forward to seeing you both while I'm here. Did your mother tell you that we went to the same high school?" Hayden addressed Anesa.

"I think she did."

"Man, could I tell you stories about what she was like back then."

Anesa immediately perked up with interest. "Yeah? Like what?"

"Not now," April dismissed. "We have to get Andrea's things and get out of here. And we don't want to hold Hayden up. Unless . . ." she tried to read his expression but gave up, saying instead what she was really thinking. "Would you like to have dinner with us?"

"If I'm not intruding, I'd like that," Hayden said.

"No, not at all. We . . . I'd love to have you join us."

"Thank you."

"Mom, the luggage . . ."

Both girls were already halfway to the moving luggage carousel. Alone with Hayden, April felt awkward and strange being right next to him. He was as handsome and appealing as she remembered. He was dressed for traveling, casual and comfortable. Suddenly, memories sprang to her mind of them making love as the sun was rising the morning she flew back home. It was a titillating thought to have after not seeing him for more than a month.

Yet without the backdrop of Venice, Hayden seemed, in a way, a stranger. It was hard to tell what he might be thinking. Given the incredibly dark and personal way in which he was looking at her, April wondered if he, too, was remembering their last morning together. In any case, the arrivals terminal of the airport did not lend itself to personal conversation or a more intimate hello. However, when Hayden suddenly grabbed her hand and squeezed it tightly, chills rolled through her from head to toe.

Forcing herself to stop acting like a giddy schoolgirl, April caught up to Anesa and Andrea as the two girls were pulling Andrea's suitcase from the conveyor belt. Hayden walked a little ways ahead and lifted a leather duffel belonging to him. When April discovered that he'd made arrangements for a rental car, it was decided that Hayden would follow her.

"We can go to Red Lobster, Mom. They don't have Red Lobster where Andrea comes from. She said so."

Andrea nodded. "We do not have what you call chain food. There are no MacDonald's in Venice."

"Thank goodness," April muttered caustically. "Do you mind?" she asked Hayden. "It's not my first choice, but . . ."

"That's fine with me."

"I'm sorry. I think it would have been nicer to—"

"Don't worry about it," Hayden interrupted her apology. "Maybe there'll be time for dinner together again before I leave the city."

Encouraged by this, April, with Hayden beside her, headed out of the terminal, trailing behind the two girls.

Once she was on the expressway, she kept staring back at

Hayden in her rearview mirror. She was grateful for his willingness to put up with the poor dietary decisions of her daughter. She was convinced that Anesa was taking advantage of the situation to have the kinds of meals Sinclair would allow her when she stayed with him.

Still, April was thrilled to see that the two young girls seemed to be hitting it off just fine. No sooner had they gotten into the back seat of her car than they began sharing information about what they liked and didn't like, and the differences in their cultures. April, acting as chauffeur in the front seat, found it interesting that girls in Italy did not have sleepovers with their girlfriends. And they were still likely to be chaperoned when in the company of boys who were not family.

The restaurant was busy, with the unfortunate thumping of noisy music blaring through the sound system. Neither Andrea nor Anesa seemed to care. Hayden, April was glad to see, had no trouble adapting to the girls' conversation and their interests, although she was aware that Anesa watched and listened to him with cautious interest. Hayden did seem to win points, however, when he offered an opinion that impressed her daughter about the music of the likes of Usher, Nelly, and Beyoncé.

April wasn't inclined to add much to the discussion, but took the opportunity to watch Hayden. She liked the way he dealt with Anesa and Andrea. He wasn't condescending because of their youth; he listened attentively and even made observations that made them laugh. April wondered if seeing him in her world was what was making her feel odd. It was not that either she or Hayden was behaving differently so much as the sense that they couldn't behave the way they might want to.

It was only as they were getting ready to leave the restaurant that April realized that she and Hayden had not been able to have a single private moment or word together. She was grateful when the girls went to use the facilities; she and Hayden waited outside. All around them were the bright neon signs and markings of the local strip mall.

"Not like Venice, is it?" Hayden murmured, looking down at her.

She met his gaze. "No, it's not."

"Surprised to see me?"

"You have no idea."

"Tell me."

She averted her gaze. "I can't. Not here."

"Maybe another time."

"Maybe. You said you came on family business. I got the impression you aren't that close to your family."

"I'm not, but they're still family. I got an e-mail from my brother. It said, in essence, that I was needed at home. I didn't think I could ignore that."

"I'm glad to hear you say that."

He frowned at her. "Why?"

"Because I think forgiveness is very important. Life is too short to carry around grudges."

"Whom did you have a grudge against?" he asked astutely.

April realized she hadn't meant for the conversation to go in this direction but said honestly, "Anesa's father."

"Anesa's father. Not your ex-husband?"

"That's right. That's how I was able to forgive him. The why is not important anymore."

He nodded thoughtfully. "I'll try to remember that when I visit my mother."

The girls joined them, still talking and pretty much wrapped up in one another.

"Okay, we're ready," Anesa announced, as she and Andrea strolled to the parked car.

April hung back. She knew she was reluctant to leave. It was enormously frustrating not to be able to really talk with him. There was no time to reconnect, and their conversation thus far was totally hampered by the presence of the two young girls. As slowly as was reasonable, April headed to her car. Hayden kept pace with her.

He seemed to be waiting on her. What was he expecting from her? What could she say?

"When we get home, I think I should call Andrea's parents and let them know she arrived safely."

"Done. The minute we landed and deplaned."

"Thanks. I got your postcards." She smiled. "All three of them."

"Glad to hear it. I hope you enjoyed them."

"Oh, I did."

"I want you to know, it was a first," he said sheepishly.

"It was such a wonderful surprise to hear from you. I liked seeing those tiny little slivers of Milan."

He laughed. "The city is much bigger, of course. Maybe one of these days you'll get to see it for yourself."

April felt her heart lurch. Was that an invitation? Or was he being officious and polite?

"That's a thought. But I have to warn you, I don't think I'll like any other city as much as Venice."

"I know," he said quietly. "When I sent the cards, it was because I wanted you to know . . ." he stopped.

She waited.

"You wanted me to know what?"

"How much I've been thinking about you."

"About how much trouble I was to you?"

They stopped in the middle of the parking lot and faced one another. She wanted to believe that he was being sincere. She had convinced herself that maybe their night together had been part of the package, part of the itinerary of "What to do while in Venice." Yet there was so much about that night that had kept him constantly in her thoughts.

"Wrong. It was more how much I like you, April."

"It feels so strange hearing you say that and being back here," she confessed.

"I know. That's how I felt after you left. What do you think we should do about it?"

"I don't know. What do you think?"

Hayden glanced toward her parked car where Anesa and Andrea stood chatting, waiting for April to drive them home. He looked back at her again. "I'll call you in a few days. We need to talk."

"Hayden, maybe we should—"

He bent forward suddenly and kissed her. It was soft and quick and instantly reminded her of one of the many reasons she couldn't get him out of her mind.

"I totally agree. I'll call you."

Hayden caught up with the two girls. He kissed and hugged Andrea, telling her briefly in Italian to enjoy her visit.

"I hope I see you again soon," he said to Anesa.

April kept her eyes on Hayden until he'd unlocked his rental car and pulled open its door. As he was about to climb in, he gave her one more long, searching look. In another moment he had started the engine and was driving away.

"Let's go home," she said as she reached the girls. "Andrea must be exhausted."

She fastened her seat belt and turned over the ignition. Anesa leaned forward between the front seats.

"Mom, I saw him. He kissed you."

April's immediate instinct was to deny it. Her body and mind, however, signaled something different. She felt curiously light. She felt the return of some of the abandon she'd experienced in Italy.

"Yes, honey. I know."

***

There was a time, Hayden recalled, when he could not make a visit to his mother's house without a multitude of emotions going to war within him. Most, especially when he was growing up, had kept him in a perpetual state of anxiety, rage, and desperate longing. Like a ritual of punishment, these feelings had lived for years in his gut and in his mind, oftentimes nearly strangling him with their intensity. So it was with acute relief that Hayden recognized a shift in his feelings as he pulled his rental car into his mother's driveway. He was able to keep his primal responses under control for one simple reason: He seemed to have outgrown them.

Another car, with New York tags, was already parked in the driveway; the car at the curb was his brother's. The out-of-state car only mildly raised his curiosity. Nor was he concerned about why he was suddenly needed at home. According to his brother's e-mail, his mother was in good health. He couldn't imagine what the crisis might be, but it didn't sound life-threatening. He turned off the engine but continued to sit in the car, considering.

Unlike the welcome he'd experienced seeing April the day before, he felt out of place here. The house, indeed the entire neighborhood, seemed tiny and provincial. Even before he'd been exposed to the openheartedness of Marina and her family, and certainly years earlier than he'd been witness to the warmth and trust between April and her daughter, he'd stopped considering this place his home. It was pathetic that through other people's families, he was learning about the kind of love he himself wanted. He knew he had no reason to delay the inevitable, so he got out of the car and approached the front door. Almost immediately after he'd rung the bell, Reese opened the door. They greeted each other civilly with a handshake.

"You're looking good, man," Reese said with approval, clapping him on the shoulder and urging him inside.

"Thanks," Hayden said, looking at his brother, who was an

inch taller and three years older. "I wish I could say the same about you."

Reese grinned good-naturedly. "Yeah, I know. The hairline is creeping back a bit."

"I'm talking about your gut, man," Hayden said, tapping his brother on the stomach with the back of his hand. "What's your wife been feeding you?"

"It's not too much food. It's not enough exercise."

Hayden critically examined the changes he saw in Reese in the time it took to walk from the front doorway, through a small and tidy living room, and into the brightly lit dining room. His brother hadn't changed, only grown older. There was still nothing between them, even after three years of separation, except superficial small talk.

He was fully prepared to find his mother at the table. He was surprised, however, to find a stranger keeping his mother company. There was something familiar in the man, although Hayden couldn't quite place him.

He walked around the table. Rather than standing, his mother swiveled in her chair and held her arms open. He still considered his mother attractive at sixty-seven. Helaine's almond-toned skin was virtually without wrinkles, and although she'd gained some middle-age weight, it was not enough to make her look her age. She'd let her hair go gray naturally and the affect was stunning, reminding him of the jazz singer Nancy Wilson, who was exactly his mother's age. He kissed her offered cheek. Her embrace was loose and impersonal.

"How've you been, Mom?"

"Can't complain. My blood pressure's a little high and my left knee bothers me. The doctor says it's probably bursitis."

"You look great," he said honestly, ignoring the irony of her response.

"Thank you. Reese and I are trying to lose a few pounds. Joyce has us on one of those new diets. I forget which one."

"Joyce didn't come, but she sends her regards. She's taking the kids shopping for school," Reese explained, sitting down at the table.

Hayden listened unemotionally, unable to relate to his sister-in-law *cum* former fiancée and the saga of the joint family efforts to lose weight. It wasn't lost on him that neither his brother nor mother had inquired into how he was doing, given the amount of time since they'd last been together; nor had they introduced the stranger.

He was a sturdy, athletically built man close to Hayden's age. He wore glasses and sported a mustache. Again his facial features seemed familiar, though Hayden couldn't recall whether they'd ever met.

Hayden held out his hand. "I'm Hayden. And you're . . ."

The man rose and shook it. "Brett Jameson." He looked from Hayden to his mother.

"Brett's your half-brother," she announced casually.

As if she was giving the time of day, Hayden would later think, except for the fact that he felt as if the wind had been knocked out of him. A brother? His chest tightened, and he lost the ability to clearly think. In a flash everything that he knew about himself, had believed or assumed had just become null and void. He was so disoriented that the room seemed to tilt.

His gaze, focused on his mother, turned to Reese, who sat passive and mildly interested. Why not? The information had little to do with him. He'd always known that the two of them had had different fathers. The only difference had been that Reese's father married their mother. In contrast, his own paternity had been a mystery. He looked to Brett Jameson, one minute a perfect stranger, in the next . . . a brother.

Jameson was speaking but, to Hayden, whose mind was a whirl of impressions and emotions, it might has well have been in Swahili.

". . . know about each other. I was as blown away as you are, when I found out. My mother never knew, none of us knew, all these years. My father was in the military, and our family moved every three years or so. Naturally, my mother was upset when we found out but it happened before my parents got married. Even so . . ." Brett looked at Hayden's mother.

Clearly she'd already heard much of the story. Hayden noted that she sat still, her face completely expressionless.

"What was his name?" Hayden asked Brett.

"Hayden Mark Jameson. Hayden is his mother's family name. We think at one point he only used Hayden Mark," Brett said.

"That's what he said his name was," his mother murmured.

"I'm really sorry," Brett said to her.

"You should write a book about this, Hay," Reese said, shaking his head. "Love, secrets, betrayal."

"My father was not a bad person," Brett continued. "I'd say he was young, wasn't sure what he was going to do with himself, and when the opportunity to have a military career presented itself, he took it."

Hayden realized he was clenching his fists tightly where they rested on his thighs. He forced himself to release and relax the fingers. "So you're here to . . . what?" he couldn't help asking.

"I came to meet the brother or sister I never knew. When the family went through my dad's papers after he died, we found the three letters your mother wrote when she discovered she was pregnant. I think she was expecting he'd come back and do the right thing."

"I sure did," Helaine nodded. "I'd lost my first husband and was trying to raise one child. Another baby was too much."

Too much, Hayden repeated to himself. He was too numb to even be angry.

"I thought Hayden was a real gentleman, and very caring.

He said he had to go home to New York for a while, but he did ask me to marry him. A month after he was gone I found out I was going to have a baby. I wrote. I tried to find a phone number. After a few months, my letters started coming back. I never heard from him again."

Hayden felt Reese's hand on his shoulder and turned to his brother.

"Mom thought it was best that you be here to hear all of this," he said.

Hayden wasn't so sure. Although he'd always wanted to know about the father his mother would never talk about, hearing it like this made him feel naked, exposed. Years ago he'd stopped letting that missing part of his life have major significance. He wondered if it would have been better not to know. Knowing made him feel like an afterthought, an accident.

Brett didn't know why his father chose not to contact Hayden's mother or acknowledge the birth of a son. He had no apologies, nor, Hayden acknowledged, was it Brett's responsibility to make any. But he suggested the one thing that did appeal to Hayden.

"I have two sisters," Brett said. "And we all would really like to get to know you, despite the way this all happened. Man, I look at you and I see we have the same nose and mouth. I'm almost as tall as you are. And I always wished I had a brother. But we need to know how you feel about it."

"How do I feel about it?" Hayden repeated, a touch of irony, bewilderment and tension in his voice. "I suddenly discover that I'm the missing link between two families. In half an hour, by two degrees of separation, I discover I have three new relatives." He looked steadily at his mother. He could see that the news had been much harder on her than on him. For the first time, he could appreciate what she might have gone through, abandoned by the man she might have loved and pregnant with his child, then abandoned a second time. "To tell the truth, I'm going to need some time to process all of this. I mean, I just got hit upside the head," he said dryly.

Reese and Brett chuckled appreciatively. His mother only looked sad.

"I was able to track down your mother. When I called her, she wasn't sure she wanted you to know the truth," Brett said.

"I didn't want to go messing with the past," Helaine interrupted, irritated.

Reese spoke up. "Maybe you were scared, or still mad with the man. The point is, Hayden, I told Mom you had to know. It wasn't right to keep this sort of thing from you."

"You're right," Hayden said. He put his hand on his mother's arm and stroked it. "I'm sorry things didn't work out the way you thought they would. I always knew you were unhappy about something. I always believed it was because of me, that somehow, I was to blame."

Helaine didn't respond beyond nodding her head, accepting his sympathy. He wasn't surprised that she made no attempt to dissuade him of the notion that she'd suffered because of him. She'd always blamed him for being born rather than accepting her own mistake. The child in him was less sanguine, only wanting his mother's love.

The adult felt a rush of relief that swept through his body. He knew that he was going to feel overwhelmed by Brett's life-altering visit for a while, not because of how his father had behaved, but because he had found the missing piece of the puzzle.

He'd also found a new family. Brett didn't seem to be judgmental about either the circumstances of Hayden's birth or their father's duplicity. Instead he seemed eager to embrace him as a brother, far more readily than his mother had ever embraced him as her son. That was sad, but he knew it was her loss more than his.

"Reese said something about you working for the State

Department. That sounds interesting," Brett said, genuinely enthused.

Hayden had to admit he derived a lot of satisfaction out of boasting about his career. It didn't have the educational heft of Reese's degree in law, but he was dealing with the world on a global scale as opposed to litigating civil suits and car accidents.

"How long are you here for?" Brett later asked, as the decision was made that they would all go out for dinner.

"No more than a week. I have to be back in four or five days. I have someone else that it's important for me to see before I leave the Philly area."

"If it's all right, I'd planned on hanging around for a few days until we have a chance to talk, maybe get acquainted. Are you free tomorrow? I brought along some pictures of Dad taken over the years. You might want to see them."

Hayden hesitated. *Dad*, he thought to himself. He was never going to be able to use that term, but at least now he had a reference point. "Yeah, that sounds good. I'm staying at . . ."

Plans were made: a time set, a place to meet. As an afterthought, although he knew they would most likely not be interested, Hayden invited both Reese and his mother to join them.

"No, I don't think so," Helaine said firmly. "You go on without me. I'm sure you don't need me there."

For once, she was absolutely right.

Chapter 13

"Mom, can we go over to Tisha's for a while?"

"Anesa, you girls have not sat still for more than ten minutes. You spent the entire day doing the historic sights downtown. You just finished dinner," April recited, looking over her shoulder at her daughter as she loaded the dishwasher. "Aren't you two tired? I'm exhausted."

"We're not tired, and Tisha wants to take a lot of pictures of us 'cause Andrea has to leave as soon as we get back from Washington, and we're going tomorrow. There's no other time."

April sighed. "I know. 'My, how time flies . . .'"

"Please?"

"Okay, but only for a few hours. That means two, Anesa. Not two and a half. Do you hear me?"

"Yeah," Anesa yelled, already streaking down the hall in her bare feet to tell Andrea the news.

The phone rang. April dried her hands on a dish towel and reached for the cordless. Tired, she sat at the kitchen table. While Anesa and Andrea had certainly kept her on the go, she couldn't ignore the possibility that her depleted strength might be for another reason. She had neglected her usual routine recently.

"Hello?"

"Hi. Did I catch you at a bad time?"

"Hayden," she responded, a bit breathless. She cleared her throat. "Hi. How are you doing?"

"I'll live."

"Excuse me?"

"Sorry. I didn't mean to be flippant. I'm good."

"Is everything okay with your family?" she asked, remembering that was the primary reason for his trip.

"Yeah, everything is fine. It was family business that only I could take care of."

"Oh."

"I'll explain sometime. How about yourself? The girls driving you crazy yet?"

"Pretty close," she grinned, leaning on her elbow with her head propped up by her hand. "They're having a great time, and that's the most important thing."

"And the age difference isn't a problem?"

"Not much. I think Anesa realizes that Andrea's not as silly as some of her friends. I think Andrea is amazed at how much freedom teens in the States have."

"Need a break yet?"

"I'd love a break." She sat up straight. "What do you have in mind?"

"Any chance of just you and me having dinner together?"

"I think that can be arranged. Anesa and Andrea are going down to D.C. in the morning. Sinclair is going to show them around for two days and then send them back. Andrea flies home the day after they return."

"Me, too. I arranged my time so that I could escort her. Then, I take it, you're free tomorrow evening?"

"Tomorrow . . . and tomorrow," she said provocatively.

He laughed. "Good. Put me down for all available openings. I'll make a reservation for someplace in Philly. Is that okay, or is there someplace special you would prefer?"

"Just surprise me."

"Believe me, I plan to."

The time with Hayden in Venice notwithstanding, April couldn't remember the last time she'd had an actual date. The kind you dressed up for, the kind where you wore perfume and makeup and high heels. The kind that let a woman know that a man she looked forward to being with was paying attention to her. That said April was very nervous when Hayden picked her up.

Her jitters were waylaid when she realized that nothing had changed between them. Nor, if rapid heartbeat, damp hands, dry mouth, and erotic dreams had anything to do with it, about the way she was starting to feel.

He was dressed in black slacks and a Hawaiian shirt with a bold leafy print on a black background that was eye-catching and attractive. As they drove into Philadelphia from her home, the dark glasses seemed to give him an aura of mystery and excitement that enhanced his appeal even more. And yet Hayden seemed unaware that he drew the attention of other women, black and white, as they walked to the restaurant from where he'd parked the car. As they leisurely strolled, he held her hand, and April couldn't keep the smile from her lips.

He'd made reservations for Devon, a popular, upscale seafood restaurant on Rittenhouse Square. April was glad that she'd decided on a simple Ralph Lauren black tank dress that swished and floated against her thighs and knees in a flattering way. She'd accessorized simply with dangly freshwater pearl earrings and a single-strand pearl necklace that lay just above her breastbone. She'd added a pearl-beaded hair comb to hold a few twists of her locked hair from her face. And, although there was no need for it outdoors, April carried a bright orange silk wrap folded over her arm.

They opted to sit inside where there was less distraction from people walking by, sheltered from the fumes of passing cars, so different from Venice. Most of their conversation since he'd arrived to pick her up had centered on Anesa and Andrea's escapades. April loved hearing his throaty laugh. She loved that his total concentration was on her.

"You look beautiful," Hayden said after the waiter left with the drink orders.

"So do you."

He laughed; she grinned impishly.

"I've been wearing jeans and shorts the whole week. I should thank you for rescuing me," April said.

"You can thank me later, if you like."

His suggestion sounded provocative to April. She watched his face to see if Hayden was trying to be calculating, but his expression was not the least disingenuous. Still, "later" suddenly took on a meaning that April had more than passingly considered since agreeing to go out with him. Was she fooling herself to think that the evening would end any other way but with the two of them in bed? Did she want it any other way?

She gave him her attention and tried to look earnest, not wanting to display any of her doubts or anxiety. "If you don't mind me asking, how's your family?" She noted his gaze was warm, but slightly distant.

"Complicated. And getting more so by the minute. I've told you very little about my family."

"Except that your relationships appear to be strained," April said.

"That's true. I was called home to be told that my father had died."

"Oh, Hayden. I'm so sorry." April reached to touch his hand.

Hayden smiled affectionately at her. "Thank you. But he apparently died a number of months ago. I never knew my father, April. In fact, I never met the man in my life, and I knew nothing about him."

April was riveted to the abridged story of his family dynamics, and the sudden appearance of siblings he'd never met. His *was* a complicated history, but she was pleased to see that although meeting an unknown brother had come as a shock, Hayden seemed at peace with the news and the truth.

Their drinks arrived, and they paused in their conversation to make a toast.

"Me first," April said. "To a delightful evening, to remembering a wonderful time."

"To you, the evening, and the future."

April tried not to show how much his comment had caught her off guard as she watched him over the rim of her glass as she sipped. Apparently she wasn't successful.

"Are you okay?" he asked, holding her hand across the table.

"I was just thinking that this summer has been the most magical I've ever had. I can't help but think about all the wonderful things I've done, all the lovely people I've met."

"Including me?" he asked boldly.

She smiled. "Of course, including you."

He squeezed her hand. "Then why do you sound like it's all going to end?"

"It could," she murmured, staring at their entwined fingers. "Things do, you know. I want to remember moments like this. I want to be grateful that . . ."

Hayden lifted their joined hands and kissed the back of

hers. She held her breath. His lips were warm and firm, and fervent against her skin. His teeth gently nipped at her knuckle.

"I don't want you to be grateful. I want you to be happy that we're together right now. When you left Venice my only thought was when I would see you each again. Not *if*, April. *When*."

"Was it?" Her voice was almost inaudible.

"Are you telling me you didn't feel the same way?"

"I . . . I didn't think I should. It seemed like too much to ask. That there could be more than Venice."

"Oh, yes," he drawled, a smile playing around his mouth. "There can be something . . . much more."

She stared at him, afraid to speak. He rubbed his fingers against her palm.

"I'm warning you. If you keep looking at me that way, I'm going to lean over and kiss you."

She blushed. "I didn't mean to stare."

Much to April's relief, the waiter appeared to take their order. By the time he left, she managed to direct talk to other subjects. She mentioned having to get on the ball and start planning for her school groups and graduating seniors for the coming school year. That reminded Hayden that he wanted to talk about her proposal for international internships for her students. He was looking into programs sponsored specifically by the State Department for educational exchanges for which her organization might qualify. He had a short list of three Italian and Italian-based American companies who were interested in working with her.

April was thrilled with Hayden's intervention and talked excitedly about her vision. He suggested that perhaps she might include Anesa, but April felt that she was still too young. "Perhaps when she's in high school, in another year," April said.

"How's Stephanie?"

"I think she's in love," April said. "His name is Marcello, and he owns a restaurant in Venice, near the hotel where we stayed."

"That was fast."

"Not really. She knows him from earlier business trips. This is something that's been happening slowly."

"Is it serious?" Hayden asked.

"I would say so. She's over there right now. I'm waiting for a full report when she gets back."

She realized that Hayden became thoughtful and quiet after that, and the conversation once again became neutral. Dinner was served, and after a while April felt him regain his comfortable good humor and affectionate teasing and banter with her.

They decided against dessert. After leaving the restaurant they took a slow walk the long way around the square until they finally stopped where they'd started outside the restaurant and headed for the car. She didn't need to be told that he was delaying the inevitable of taking her back home. She too wasn't ready to go because it signaled the end of what was, for her, a perfect romantic evening. To say good-night meant that Hayden was that much closer to having to return to Italy. It meant she would once again have to consider the possibility of never seeing him again.

He took a different route out of the city, driving through South Philly along Broad Street, which separated the black and Italian communities. Although curious, April didn't question this decision or Hayden's explanation that he had to make a stop. He parked in front of a hydrant with the hazard lights blinking, leaving her in the car for ten minutes. When he returned he held a plastic cup of gelato, and he handed it to her through the car window.

"Where'd you find this?" she asked, spooning some of the

ice cream into her mouth and savoring it. "Mmmmmm, it's delicious."

"Is it as good as the real thing in Venice?" he asked, once he was again behind the wheel.

"Here, have some. You tell me." She scooped up a generous glob of the gelato and spoon-fed it to him.

"Not bad," Hayden declared, getting back into traffic.

"But not quite the same. I think what this needs is the Rialto Bridge in the background. Or the Academia across the canal," she added. "But since we don't have those, there's no point in letting almost the same gelato go to waste."

Having said that, April alternated feeding each of them until the gelato was gone.

By the time they reached her house, conversation had ceased between them. She mutilated the empty ice-cream cup by folding and crushing it between her fingers. The moment seemed anticlimactic, and in her mind the whole evening boiled down to only this moment. Wanting to postpone having to say good-bye, she quickly got out of the car and headed to unlock her door. Hayden followed behind her.

When she turned to face him, April saw that he'd stopped at the top of the path to the house. She looked into his face, and although she could clearly discern his features and expression, she also saw the man who'd occupied her imagination most of the summer and who, miraculously, had found a way to see her again. She couldn't deny how happy she was to see him, but neither could she pretend that there was any serious possibility of a relationship.

She stepped inside the entrance of her house and stood watching him on the outside. "Would you like to come in?"

"Yes," he said simply.

The phone was ringing when she closed the door. She left Hayden and headed for the kitchen to answer. It was Anesa.

"Hi, sweetie. Is everything all right? Are you and Andrea

having a good time? . . . Good, I'm glad to hear that . . .
Daddy took you where? . . . Well, I guess it's okay. I wish I'd
known first . . . you tried calling earlier? . . . I was out . . . with
Hayden. We went to dinner . . . of course I like him. Don't you
remember we went to high school together? . . . it was lovely.
We had seafood . . ." She suddenly chuckled. "No, it wasn't
Red Lobster. We went to an adult restaurant . . . I don't have
any plans for tomorrow. I have to meet your train from D.C.
in the afternoon. Andrea has to pack for her flight home the
day after . . . Honey, we'll see. You can't show her everything
in a week . . . Daddy says hi? Oh. Well, tell him I said hi back.
Good-night, sweetie. I'll see you and Andrea tomorrow . . .
love you, too."

April smiled to herself as she replaced the cordless in its
cradle. She returned to the living room. Hayden was standing
in the middle of the room, his hands in the pockets of his
slacks, his feet slightly akimbo. He was staring at her with a
solemn expression that made her hesitate as she entered.

"That was my daughter."

"I heard. She still seems curious about you and me."

"You can't blame her. She's used to thinking of me as
Mommy. For me to go out with a man might mean something
else."

"What?"

"I don't know," she said softly, slightly agitated. "Is this
Twenty Questions again?"

"You didn't allow me twenty questions the first time. I
think you owe me." He walked slowly toward her until there
was less than a foot of space between them. "Do you like
me?"

She met his gaze squarely. "Yes."

"Then you must understand what her concerns mean.
Anesa is smart enough to know you could feel something
more for me. Do you?"

She lowered he gaze, her heart pounding. "I think so."

He put his arms gently around her and held her. "I'll take that for now. But I'll be perfectly honest with you. I want more. And unless I'm really off the mark, I think you feel the same way."

She didn't bother to deny it. If anything, April was thrilled, astonished, and petrified that he had ferreted out her feelings. Or had she been showing her desire all along? Her body felt like jelly when his lips touched hers. And when he kissed her, she felt as if she'd been holding her breath, waiting only for this since the moment she'd seen him step off the plane. Realizing, she simply gave in to the inevitable.

His kiss was like a slow-acting drug and she felt herself succumbing to the effects. His hand at the back of her head held her steady as his kiss deepened, sending her senses reeling. April held onto him, her restless fingers kneading through the fabric of his shirt to memorize the muscles in his back and shoulders.

Their kiss was leading to only one possibility, and she needed to speak before their passion could move them out of this embrace and into her bed without parameters and rules. Reluctantly she pulled away from him when they reached her bedroom. Hayden stood still, listening to her move about the darkened room. He reached for the lamp beside her bed.

"Don't. Please leave it off."

He hesitated, but obeyed. Silently, he started to undress. He finished before she did. He walked to her and helped remove the dress. Before he could touch her intimate garments, April had slipped into bed with them on. He made sure to slip on a condom. By the time he joined her under the cover, she had covertly removed her bra and panties.

"I want to see you," he whispered, already stroking her body, and kissing her neck and throat. His hand curved to her bottom and pressed her to him.

"No, not yet."

By then it didn't matter to either of them whether he saw her or not. They moved naturally together, their bodies fitting and melding in rhythm and heat. The only sounds were their hushed breathing and moans. There were whispered words of encouragement and pleasure. The most important thing became giving themselves to each other with a need that was sweet, urgent, and unstoppable, and which went beyond the physical release that was inevitable to an emotional conjunction, like the perfect alignment of stars.

She knew Hayden was surprised but relieved when she gave him free reign to touch her wherever he wished. Her reward for such openness was more sensation and pleasure than she could have imagined. She arched her back upon his entry. He thrust forward against her undulating pelvis. They held tightly to one another, free-falling as their hearts and bodies lost control.

It was soothingly erotic to lay connected afterward, unable to move, not wanting to. Holding her, he turned so that she lay half across his body, her head resting on his chest. Silently they curled and cuddled. April let out a long, soft, satisfied sigh. Slowly, her body went completely limp.

"I don't want to leave," Hayden murmured.

She heard the quiet admission, knowing it was more an admission to himself than to her. But it made her think about the future and the possibilities. She didn't come to any conclusion before she'd fallen asleep.

What woke her later was the sound of gentle snoring. It had an odd comforting rhythm, but rather than lying listening to Hayden sleep, his arm pillowing her head, April knew she had to rise. It was later than she expected, and she could see early-morning light beneath her window shade. April allowed herself a few more minutes of the warm hard contact with his body before she lightly slid her hand across his stomach, feeling the rise and fall of it with his even breathing. She began to ease away, trying to get out of the bed without disturbing him. He rolled toward her, effortlessly pulling her back into his arms.

"Not yet," he slurred.

"It's getting late."

"The sun is barely a dot on the horizon."

"I know, but . . . I need to get up." She tried to pull away. He held her. "Why?"

"You must have things to do. You leave tomorrow."

"That's precisely why I don't want to rush now. Tomorrow will be here soon enough."

"Hayden . . ."

"Stay with me a little longer." His hands began to roam. He leaned forward to nuzzle the side of her neck.

April let his fingers massage under her breast. They crept up to the nipple, and she drew in her breath sharply. She twisted away from him. "We can't . . ."

His arms tightened gently but inexorably until her back was against his chest, one of his thighs on top of her slender legs. "April, listen to me. You're okay, and you can trust me. Why don't you want me to see your body?"

She went still, but started to breathe hard. "I don't know what you mean."

"Yes, you do. I know you had cancer. I know you had to have reconstruction surgery. Do you hear me? I know all about it."

She twisted free, struggling to sit up and pulling the linens around her for protection.

"How do you know that? How do you know that?" she repeated.

Hayden lay looking up at her. Although he appeared relaxed and at ease, his eyes were dark and his gaze direct and probing. He reached out and rested his hand near her thigh.

"Stephanie told me when I met her at the ball. She thought I already knew. I didn't let on that you hadn't told me yet."

"Why should I have?" April said, her voice defensive and hard. "We were nothing to each other. Just former school-mates. I'm sorry but that wasn't enough reason to tell you my personal business."

He watched her closely. "What about now?"

April tried to get out of bed, rather than answer. Hayden sat up quickly and grabbed her hands. The cover started to slip down her breasts. She squirmed.

"Hayden, no! Let me go." He wouldn't, trying to force her to look at him, but April felt too overwhelmed and exposed.

"Are you ashamed or too scared to let me see you? You trust me enough to let me make love to you, but not enough to realize making love has nothing to do with your breasts or your cancer."

"Stop saying that. If I wanted you to know I would have said something."

"No you wouldn't. You think I'm going to reject you. I thought you knew me well enough to know better, and to think better of me. I thought that by now, you'd realize that I love you, and that there is nothing, *nothing* that could change that. It's too late. I'm already hooked. I want you."

She hated that she was going to cry. When she pulled again, Hayden let her go. She was surprised that he did, but then she got out of the bed and stood near the bureau looking at him suspiciously. "It's not that easy. How do you know you really love me? You haven't seen me sick. You haven't seen me without my hair and eyebrows, and . . . and without half a breast."

"I don't need to. I can see what's inside." He jabbed a finger into his chest, then got out of the bed and stood naked before her. "I'm not a goddamn kid, and I'm not shallow, and I'm not afraid of your cancer."

"I don't believe you. You should be afraid. How could you be in love with someone who could die at any time?"

"How could I not be? I don't know what your prognosis is. I don't know how much time you're talking about. However much it is, it doesn't matter. I want to be with you because I love you."

She turned away from him, crying in earnest. Hayden came closer, but didn't touch her. She wasn't sure what she would do if he did. "I can't. I shouldn't have let you . . . I shouldn't have . . ." She couldn't get the words out or make sense.

"What? Let yourself feel something for me? Maybe you don't love me the same way I love you, but maybe you do and just won't admit it. The woman I've been with is incredibly warm and giving and damned beautiful. She's cheerful and full of life. I was more than half in love with her while we were in Venice. The woman I held last night and the one who won't let me near her now is the same woman. Put them all together and they're you, April. It's you I want, breasts or no breasts. Cancer or no cancer. I think what we have, what we *can* have is worth everything."

She wiped her face with the back of her hand, and then a corner of the sheet she'd yanked from the bed. "I can't do that to you, me, or my daughter. It's not over, Hayden. It's never going to be over for me until I can't fight anymore. I have to be here and stay strong for Anesa. I have to do the best I can."

He crept behind her and put his arm around her. April cried even harder, but let him hold her, not fighting anymore. "Why can't we fight this together? Who said that just because you have a disease you're not entitled to be happy, to love, to make plans? I don't need you to protect my feelings. I need you to trust me. And to let me love you."

April cried until there were no more tears. All the while Hayden held her, rocking her gently. Having him love her and knowing she loved him was almost more than she could have

hoped for, more than she could bear. For a moment she was
tempted to give in to him, but she knew the risk was too great.
If her cancer didn't kill her, losing him surely would.

"I'll always remember that you told me you love me, Hayden. I'll always remember what you gave to me this summer.
Don't ask for more. I can't."

"Don't do this. Don't I deserve a chance?"

She turned to face him, her eyes bright and watery, slightly
red. But she smiled at him, with more love than she realized.
"Oh, yes you do. But it can't be with me."

Hayden watched their progress through the check-in
process from a distance. He'd left a message on April's answering machine that he would see her, Anesa, and Andrea at
the airport before the flight back to Venice. He'd arrived early
enough to see the three of them enter the terminal, check Andrea's bag and get her boarding pass.

The two young girls were still enjoying each other's company, oblivious to April, who was mostly quiet, pensive, and
looked drawn and tired. He could see her raw emotions in
moments when she couldn't control them, turning away so
that her daughter and Andrea would not know. He could not
give her any more assurances than what he'd attempted the
day before. And at that he'd failed.

Keeping his gaze on their amble toward security, Hayden
made a wide circuitous path in their direction, taking what
time was left to him to watch April. He wished there was
something he could have done, could have said, *should* have
done or said to convince her of his sincerity, but he had realized late last night, in the quiet of his hotel room, that the call
was hers, and she'd already made it. She wasn't going to let
him into her life to either share it, or watch it end.

The girls were looking around, trying to find him. It was

time to pass through security, and to say good-bye. Clenching his jaw so as not to let his expression betray his true feelings, Hayden waved and shouted out, "Made it. Bet you thought I was late."

He knew April was staring, trying to see his eyes beneath his dark glasses. He wouldn't let her, yet. He hugged Andrea, and briefly touched Anesa's shoulder. He asked about their visit, the trip to D.C., and if they would stay in touch. April said nothing, letting him orchestrate the good-byes. He wanted to touch her in some way, wanted to let her know he had not changed his mind, and never would. But he didn't. He knew it would do no good to push her. She was scared enough as it was.

So was he.

Anesa and Andrea hugged tightly. Hayden had to smile as they said good-bye in Italian, Anesa giggling at her newly learned language skills. Andrea wrapped herself around April, who hugged her back fervently.

"Anesa and I loved having you here. Come back soon," she said. Her voice warbled, although neither girl seemed to notice. He did.

"Thank you for everything. I had such a good time," Andrea said, putting her things into the gray plastic tubs on the security conveyor.

April put her arm around her daughter's shoulder and said, "Tell your family hello for me," turning her gaze away from him.

"Come, Hayden," Andrea beckoned as he hung back. "We must go now."

Anesa politely held out her hand. "It was nice to meet you, Hayden."

He grinned and pulled her forward a little so he could kiss her forehead. "And I enjoyed meeting you. You should come to Italy."

Anesa looked at her mother. "Mom said maybe next year. Andrea invited me to come."

"Good." Hayden removed his sunglasses and turned to April.

"'Bye Hayden. Safe back," she said softly.

He could see the effort she was making to face him, and he had to admire her strength and resolve. Despite the outcome, he knew that it was one of the things he loved about her. She wasn't going to make the first move, and he didn't expect her to. He took her by the shoulders and held her as he planted a light kiss on her cheek. When he pulled back he saw the tears welling up in her eyes.

"Be well," he said with a small smile. Then he proceeded through security, collecting his personal things on the other side.

"'Bye, Hayden."

He recognized Anesa's voice. But he never looked back.

Chapter 14

April dreaded the visits to her doctor. Because no matter how often she was reassured that she was doing great and the blood tests were excellent, her anticipation of the worst prevailed until it was over.

She stared at the wall of the tiny examination room as she put back on her bra and top. She was just stepping into her shoes when the assistant stuck her head in the door.

"The blood tests look good. The doctor will see you in her office."

April silently nodded. It was now a familiar routine, and to be honest she had to admit that it hadn't changed in more than three years. She had reached the stage during her scheduled visit when she could start to relax. She'd made it another three months.

The oncologist, a middle-aged woman from Israel, was on the phone with another patient. April sat in one of the chairs opposite her desk and waited until the doctor was free. On the bookcase behind the doctor's desk was a haphazard collection of framed photographs. April knew the names of her three children, her husband, and her first grandchild. That she knew so much intimate detail used to disturb her. It meant she was spending far too much time with Dr. Gellen, and their lives had meld in a way beyond the professional.

"Everything is fine," the doctor announced, once finished with her call and with April's record folder, opened in front of her.

"Are you sure?"

The doctor looked at her and smiled. "You ask me the same question every time. And I say the same thing to you. Why don't you believe me, Ms. Stockwood? You are doing very well."

"That doesn't mean I can relax."

"I understand that. But you must trust me when I say right now there is absolutely no cause for you to be alarmed. Believe me, I will tell you when there is."

"I know. But I can't help but feel that in the three months between my visits with you, something is going to sneak up on me, and there won't be anything we can do about it."

"It doesn't happen that way. And as long as you're self-examining the way you were taught, and not experiencing any of the other symptoms, there really isn't any reason to be concerned."

April sighed. "I know I've been lucky."

"Very lucky. You are my star patient, you know. I love telling my students about your case because your diagnosis, treatment, surgery and recovery, your remission and maintenance couldn't have gone more perfectly. Yes, you'd rather not be here at all . . . but at least you have options.

"How was your summer? The last time we met, you were very excited about an upcoming trip to Italy. Did you go?"

"Yes," April said simply.

She hoped the inquiry would end there. She still had a tendency to get teary and blue at the mention of anything regarding Hayden. Anesa and Andrea had been e-mailing since their visit, and although April knew that at this point Hayden was back at the consulate in Milan, the memory of his visit was still strong enough to create an acute pain in the middle of her chest.

"I think Venice is the most beautiful city," the doctor reminisced.

"I thought so."

"Well, we're done. I'll have the secretary schedule for . . . let's see . . . early December. Do you have any questions?"

April half stood up, and then sat down again. "I would like to ask you something. It's kind of personal."

The doctor smiled kindly. "Of course it is. We're discussing your life and future."

"That's the thing. I met this man. Actually, I've known him for a long time, but we ran into each other again after many years. Well, anyway. We sort of . . . got together this summer."

"I see," the doctor said sagely, playing with her pen and staring at it thoughtfully. "Is it serious?"

April opened her mouth to speak, felt her lips quiver, and clamped her lips closed. She swallowed as the doctor watched and waited for her response. "Not anymore. I ended it."

"Why would you do that?"

"Why? Because I have cancer."

"Yes, you have cancer, April, but that is not cause for you to put your life on hold. If you have fallen in love, this is very good. And sex is always a good thing. It gets the blood flowing and rushing through your body," the doctor gently teased.

April gnawed her lip, trying not to embarrass herself and cry. She visibly jumped when the doctor's intercom buzzed.

The doctor immediately answered. "I can't take any calls right now. Take a message and I'll call back." She released the button. "Listen to me. I have a lot of patients, far too many actually, who know they cannot make plans for more than three to five years into the future. That is their prognosis. Fortunately, that is *not* the case with you. I predict you could do fine on maintenance for fifteen, even twenty years, probably more. You know you will have to be watched as you get older. But there is *very* little I need to warn you against. Falling in love is not one of them. Even possibly having another child is not forbidden. You can have a long, good life, April. You simply have to want to."

"But, don't you think it's unfair to the other person? I'd be making a promise I can't keep."

"Then you're not only denying yourself happiness, but the other person as well. That's not noble at all, you know."

"I don't want to tie him down."

"Have you asked him what he wants? I can see by your guilty expression that you ignored it. You know, you must really care about this man."

"Why do you say that?"

"You've been through a lot, April. But I've never seen you afraid like you are now."

"I wish I'd been here. I never would have let you get away with that. Why, in God's name, did you let him go? What were you thinking?"

April's mind went blank. She didn't know how to answer Stephanie. Instead she sat staring at her Oriental chicken salad. She hadn't touched it, and the thought of eating at the moment was not very appealing. She should. She'd lost the five pounds she'd gained in Venice, and another two since. She knew that the loss had nothing to do with her condition.

She had expected more sympathy from Stephanie, or at least some insight. But so far, Stephanie's response to what had happened with Hayden had left her speechless. It was no different from what Dr. Gellen, her sister, or even her mother—who, unbelievably, remembered Hayden from her high school—had said.

"I had no choice. I know what's ahead of me."

"So now you're clairvoyant?" Stephanie said sarcastically.

"Steph, stop yelling at me. I didn't say it was easy. I didn't even say it was what I wanted to do. But I know I did the right thing."

"You don't believe that for a minute. If you did you wouldn't start crying every time I get on the phone with you. Look, I know you think you had good reasons for sending Hayden away, but did you forget your resolve to not miss a moment of life. You know, like giving yourself a chance to love as if there's no tomorrow."

April laughed, despite herself. "You always get it wrong. It's, 'love like your heart has never been broken.'"

"That's it. You forgot to put your money where your mouth is. Something like that."

"I'll get over it. I'm sure Hayden will. He's smart and good-looking, and he'll find someone else. He'll have his own children, and . . ."

"Go on," Stephanie said patiently, watching her.

April covered her mouth and took a deep breath. "What is *wrong* with me?" Her voice was high and squeaky.

"For God's sake. Why don't you just admit that you're in love? It's breaking my heart to see you so unhappy. Why now? You're the original Ms. Sunshine. You're my role model. I could not have handled Marcello if it hadn't been for you telling me 'Go for it.' Why can't you do the same for yourself?"

"Are you happy?"

"Girl, I'm stupid happy."

"Good for you. But my case is different."

April watched as Stephanie finished the last of her own lunch, a Rueben sandwich with a side of salad. They were at the mall, waiting on Anesa and several of her friends who were at the cineplex. Listlessly, April picked up her fork and poked around her plate, separating the crispy noodles that topped her salad into two neat piles. She put her fork down.

"I can't eat. I'm not really hungry."

"Tell them to bag it. You can eat it later at home. Don't make me have to come over and force-feed you, April." She glanced at her watch. "The movie should be over soon. Let's start walking over."

They left the food court and walked through the busy Saturday-afternoon crowds at the mall, headed in the direction of the movie theater.

"Have you heard from him at all?" Stephanie suddenly asked.

"No."

"Does Sinclair know about Hayden?"

"I don't think so. Not unless Anesa said something."

They stepped on the escalator going down, standing side by side.

"Do you love him?"

"If you mean Sinclair, not any more." Stephanie sucked her teeth in exasperation. "If you're talking about Hayden . . . yes."

"Are you going to do anything about it?"

"No."

They stepped off the escalator and Stephanie grabbed her arm.

"I just want to say one more thing and then I'll shut up and mind my own business. I never would have given Marcello a chance if it hadn't been for you. I never would have taken the risk and shown my interest in him if you hadn't encouraged me. One day I realized that I could go the rest of my life traveling the world, having an affair now and then, but not having one person love just me. I don't know what's going to happen tomorrow. Marcello could change his mind. I could go down in a plane crash. The world could end.

"I think you need to give yourself a break, and Hayden a chance. Maybe it will be just for a month or more. Maybe a year. Take it, April. Grab all the happiness you can."

April listened to Stephanie, hearing some of her own words and advice given back to her. Why hadn't she been able to apply her own beliefs to her own life? She felt suddenly fearful. Panic set in as a truth dawned on her. Her life would run its course, with or without love, or Hayden. What, exactly, would she gain by living it alone?

"Oh, my God—"

"What?" Stephanie asked, seeing the stricken look on her face. "Are you all right?"

"Stephanie, do me a favor? Wait until Anesa comes out of the movie. Wait for me there. I'll be right back."

"April, what's wrong? Where are you going?"

"I have to make a phone call."

April was so nervous, so agitated that she could barely punch in the right numbers, and had to do it twice. The phone rang three times before she realized he might not be home. He could be anywhere. It was Saturday, after all. The answering machine came on. April left a message, urgently requesting a return call as soon as possible. She had better luck with the cell-phone number. There was an answer.

"Sinclair, it's me."

"April. Hey."

"If you have a minute, I really need to talk with you."

"This isn't a good time, April. I'm about to sit for a haircut. Is this about Anesa?"

"Kind of. But she's okay."

"Then, can it wait until later?"

"No. No, it can't. Please, Sinclair. I only need three minutes and a yes or no answer."

"All right. What is it?"

April heard the slight impatience but curiosity in his voice. It used to intimidate her when Sinclair made her feel like his time was more important than hers. Not even her diagnosis had proven stronger than his will.

"Something really important has come up and I need your help. I have to fly to Europe and I'd like you to stay with Anesa while I'm away."

"What? Are you serious? That would mean I'd have to take time from work and come up to Philadelphia."

"I know."

"Well . . . can she come down here with me while you're gone? What's this about, anyway?"

"It's about something very important to me. And it's personal. Like life and death."

"Life and death . . ." he repeated. "I thought you said the doctors . . ."

"It's not like that. I'm okay. Sinclair, please. I never ask you for anything for myself. I can't go into it right now, but I need your help. Anesa's just started back to school. I don't think I should pull her out so soon. It makes more sense for you to stay here with her. It will only be a few days. No more than a week."

"What about my life? This sudden emergency of yours will seriously disrupt my schedule."

"I understand that. Yes or no?"

"And you can't tell me what this is about?"

"Can't you just do it because I asked you?" April asked, annoyed. "Why do I have to justify my need? Why do I have to get your approval?"

"This isn't helping your case," he said smoothly.

She started to argue and changed her mind in frustration. "I'm sorry. You're absolutely right."

"When are you planning on leaving?"

She sagged in relief. "As soon as I can get a flight."

"I can't do a whole week, April. Five days at the most."

"That's fine. Thank you," she said, her voice shaky. "Thank you."

"Can you give me a hint?" Sinclair persisted. "Why do you have to go to Europe?"

"It's about my future. I'm going there to take a leap of faith."

"Hayden, I am looking for that itinerary for the dance group coming from California for the festival in Siena. Where did you put it?"

Hayden turned from his computer screen to cast a quick glance around his office. He pointed to a folder on a chair just inside the door. "There. You can take it, but bring it back. I need to add some more information."

No sooner had his co-worker left then someone else replaced her. A low-level office clerk and gofer. "*Scuzi*. There is someone waiting to see you."

"What about?" Hayden asked, never taking his attention from his computer screen. "Can someone else help? I can't stop right now."

"I will find out."

The staffer disappeared and Hayden continued to focus on his work. He kept busy, anesthetized by the minute details of some of his workload that kept him distracted and made for great productivity. His near-nonstop routine had proven to be an ideal way of getting through each day. He was thankful for the never-ending parade of American travelers with their problems and mishaps which provided the fodder for his assignments. But it was nights that were proving to be his undoing. He wasn't getting enough sleep, and he was starting to feel it.

"*Scuzi* again. The lady say there is no rush. She wait."

"Where's Amelia? Can she help this woman?"

"It is her day off. Santiago is back from the Mayor's office. I ask him, yes?"

"Please," Hayden nodded.

As soon as the young man had gone Hayden knew he'd lost his concentration on what he was doing, and an image of April filled his head, stopping him cold. He'd learned over the last several weeks that the only way to get past this mental and emotional interruption was to give in to it. He sat back in his chair and closed his eyes. An agony of longing swept over him. It was always the same image. It was one of April laughing, full of life and energy and curiosity.

After a few moments of reliving time spent with her, the memory would fade and he was able to get back to work. He slid his chair closer to his computer and returned to the business at hand. He'd found a way to make his life work . . . but it was no way to live.

"Hayden."

He swung away from the screen again and faced Santiago. He stood frowning at a document and shaking his head.

"What is it?"

"This is very bad. I don't think I can help this lady. So many things are wrong, so many problems."

"Like?"

"She arrive by plane this morning. But she has no hotel reservation. She has little luggage. She doesn't speak Italian and has never been to Milan before."

"Okay. So why is she here?"

Santiago shrugged. "She say she come because of the postcard."

Hayden frowned. "Postcard? What does that mean?"

"I go find out."

"No, don't bother," Hayden said, weary. "I'll talk with her.

She's not some college kid strung out on something, is she? She's lucky the police haven't picked her up."

Hayden took the document from Santiago and didn't even bother to look at it as he left his office and headed for the front reception area, and security.

"I put her in the conference room. Just in case she is . . ." Santiago rolled his eyes and made the face of someone possibly having a fit.

"Fine. Does she have a valid passport?" Hayden asked, switching directions and heading down another corridor.

"Yes, of course. It is only been used once before."

"All right. I'm going to interview her. In the meantime, check on the day's list of hotel openings. We'll probably have to help her find a place to stay, at least for tonight."

Santiago clapped him on the shoulder as he opened the conference room door. "Maybe she stay longer, eh?"

Hayden, puzzled by the remark, entered the room briefly scanning the document where the woman had printed in preliminary information, like her name and address.

"I'm officer Callo—"

He stopped, read the first line again, looked up swiftly at the woman who stood at the end of the table. April stared back at him. He blinked to make sure she was real, and that he wasn't hallucinating. He swallowed, but it felt like something had lodged in his throat. He couldn't get past the obstruction so that he could talk.

She had lost weight. Not much, but it bothered him. Her eyes seemed overly bright, and he realized that if she did truly just arrive, she may not have gotten any sleep the night before. He hadn't, and that had been going on for weeks.

She tentatively smiled. She even looked fairly calm. But her arms were crossed over her chest and her hands were clenched under each elbow. And he could see the tremors that shook her shoulders.

"Hi."

She spoke first, so softly he almost couldn't hear her. He couldn't seem to respond.

"I guess you want to know what I'm doing here."

Hayden put the sheet of paper on the conference table. He reached behind him and quietly locked the door. He never took his gaze from her. "Where's Anesa?" He began walking toward her.

"With her father. He agreed to stay with her so I could come here."

"Did you tell him why?"

She shook her head; her eyes were trying to read him, trying to assess his mood and mannerisms. "I couldn't. Not before I had a chance to tell you."

"Then tell me. I'm listening."

She stared at the front of his shirt. He was close enough to hear her ragged breathing. She tried to talk, the words caught in her throat.

He held her elbows and carefully pulled them away from her body to release her hands.

"What? I didn't hear you," Hayden said.

"I said, I love you. And if you still . . ."

She said more, but that was all Hayden wanted to hear. He smoothly slipped his arms around April and held her so tightly that whatever she was going to say was abruptly cut off. She clung to him, burying her face against his chest.

"Yes, I still want you." He rubbed his cheek against hers.

"Luther helped me decide," she said.

"Luther?"

"As in Vandross."

"I don't get it."

"He has a song that goes he'd rather live with some person in his life than live without them. Stephanie gave me the

CD. She even called once and when I answered the phone it was playing over the speaker."

"Is that what finally persuaded you?"

"No, but it got me thinking. I love you, Hayden. I realized that I was going to be miserable without you."

"I wasn't sure I'd ever see you again. It's been hell, April."

"I don't want to tie you down."

"I know."

"I can't make any promises," she whispered, unable to talk louder as her voice wavered. "I don't know what's going to happen, or when it will happen."

"Then you're just like me. We'll pay our dues and take our chances, so long as we can be together." He pulled back so he could look into her face. "Does Anesa know about us?"

"I was honest with her. She thought about it and said she worried that I'd be alone when she left for college. But that raises another issue, Hayden."

He kissed her forehead and hugged her again. "I'm taking care of it now. I've put in for a transfer back to the States after I finish my assignment here."

"You didn't even know if we'd ever see each other again."

"I would have put in for reassignment anyway. I think it's time for me to come back and face up to my own life. I've got stuff to deal with, too."

"But do you really want to leave Italy?"

"I've grown to like it here. But a lot of my appreciation is because of you. It doesn't much matter where I am."

She wrapped her arms around him. "You'd really do that for me?"

"I see I haven't convinced you yet that I love you. What I want is for us to build a life together, for however long that is. I want to try and do what's best for you, me, and Anesa. If I'm still with the State Department when she graduates, we'll discuss our options."

She was looking into his face. He laid his hand against her cheek and April pressed her hand on top. "I love you," he whispered.

"Are you sure?"

"You can't back out on me now. Besides, you owe me."

"What?"

"I seem to recall an offer on the table for your firstborn male child. In exchange for my help."

"That was just a figure of speech."

"I believed you."

"You're teasing me. Right?"

"What do I have to do to prove I mean it?"

"Besides treating me to gelato, you mean?"

He laughed. "Man, you're easy to please." He looked around. "Where're your things?"

April held up an oversized tote. "This is it. I didn't bring much, in case I had to turn around and come right back home."

"It doesn't matter. What I have in mind won't require any clothes."

She grinned, beaming at him, and it was all the reassurance he knew he wanted. The light of love sparkled in April's eyes. It was a kick-start to his heart. He took her hand and turned toward the door. When he unlocked and opened it, he found Santiago sitting in a chair just outside the room.

"What are you doing?"

"I say very important meeting in conference room. No one can enter. The supervisor says, what meeting? I say you are conducting an interview."

"Thank you, Santiago. I appreciate your help," Hayden said.

"So, everything is okay now?" he asked, looking between April and Hayden.

"I think so," April smiled at Santiago.

"I'm taking April to my place. If anyone asks for me—"

"Don't worry, I know what to say. You left to take care of a minor international incident. Will you be back today?"

"Probably not. I have to see if both parties are willing to negotiate."

Dear Reader:

I was nineteen years old and a college sophomore when I made my first trip to Europe, to Paris. I went with five friends from college, and we stayed at a student hotel that was cheap but clean. It was Christmas time and one of the coldest winters the City of Lights had experienced in two decades.

This was a long time ago, and as an African American teen traveling abroad I was concerned about how I would be treated. I'd heard how the French didn't like Americans. I needn't have worried on either count. Despite the cold and my lack of French, I had the time of my life and came home with memories that I still recall from time to time with great fondness.

My point is this . . . renew your passport. If you don't have one, get one. And then start traveling and see the world. Dare to be adventurous and seek out new experiences. Meet new people and make new friends. Your life will be so much richer for the chance to realize that the world is much bigger than your neighborhood.

I hope *The Next Best Thing* will get you excited about packing your bags, leaving home, and traveling wherever your curiosity takes you. Have fun!

Sandra Kitt

NEXT BEST THING CONTEST—WIN A GENUINE VENETIAN MASK

In my novel, *The Next Best Thing*, the heroine, April Stockwood, gets invited to a charity ball while on vacation in Venice, Italy. The Venetians take their carnival, not unlike the ones held each year in Brazil and throughout the Caribbean, *very* seriously. Even when it's not carnival season, the citizens don't need much of an excuse to hold masquerades, parties, and balls, with all the guests in capes and masks.

Mask making has a long tradition in Venice, and they are highly prized among tourists who appreciate the elaborate use of gilding and feathers that decorate each creation. In honor of this craft, and to remind my readers of April Stockwood's great adventure, I will be raffling off a genuine Venetian mask *exactly* like the one April wore to the ball.

Visit my website for more details about how you can enter. The contest will begin with the June 2005 release of *The Next Best Thing* and continue until Labor Day. It's easy to win . . . and you could find yourself with a real piece of Venice to hang on your wall.

Visit my website, *www.sandrakitt.com*.

Q & A WITH SANDRA KITT

The June 2005 release of *The Next Best Thing* will mark the twenty-eighth novel from acclaimed author Sandra Kitt. Her stories, known for their emotional depth and strong character development, have been critically praised by *Library Journal*, *Publisher's Weekly*, *Entertainment Weekly*, *USA TODAY*, and *ESSENCE*, to name a few publications. Sandra took the time to answer questions about her long and successful career as one of the foremost African American writers of women's fiction:

Q: You launched the Arabesque Line in 1994 with your book Serenade. *Arabesque celebrated its Tenth Anniversary last year. How does that make you feel?*

A: Very proud to be affiliated with the line. It was very experimental at the time it launched but has proven to be a huge success with readers. It's nice to know I contributed to that success in some way.

Q: What motivates you to write the kind of stories you do that, according to previous interviews, explore social and familial issues as well as romance?

A: I guess I would say my own curiosity about the world I live in and how it's changing right under my nose. I've never been particularly interested in writing about the past. But I am fascinated with how ever-changing social values, demographics, and race play a part in how we connect to one another, become friends, or even fall in love. Whenever I think about the possibilities for the future, my imagination goes into overdrive with ideas for stories.

Q: So you don't fear running out of ideas.

A: I'm more concerned with making sure I don't disappoint my readers. I have an amazingly loyal fan base, and I hear from readers all over the world. They also tend to be very vocal about my work . . . like wanting sequels to their favorite stories or characters or going so far as to suggest casting for my books if they should be made into movies.

Q: Is there interest in your books being made into movies?

A: Yes, there is now and then. But I don't hold my breath! I've had a number of options, but I keep writing my books, and I certainly don't sit around waiting for Hollywood to call. It would be nice, but . . .

Q: What will you be working on next?

A: I'm juggling a number of projects right now, including a novel based on my family. I'm developing a trilogy series as well as a big complicated suspense novel that I've begun.

Q: Any final words for the readers?

A: Yes! Thanks for your great feedback on my books. I love getting your emails.

You can contact Sandra Kitt by emailing her at: *sandikitt@hotmail.com* or *author@sandrakitt.com*. Visit Sandra's website for updates and information about her new projects: *www.sandrakitt.com*.